GRAVITY

by
KATE GRAYSON
A Front Range Mystery

I0564989

Table of Contents

Also by Kate Grayson
FIVE STAR REVIEWS FOR
FRONT RANGE MYSTERIES
MISFORTUNE
HIDE OUT

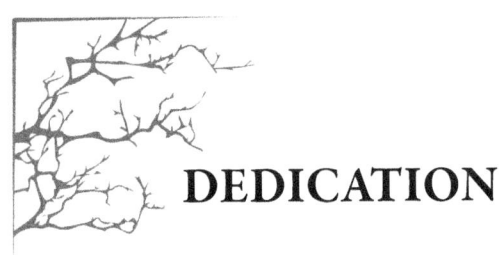

DEDICATION

For Jim and Peggy Cole

Without whose love, support, encouragement, beta reading, copy editing, lunches and a thousand laughs, this book would never have been written.

Gravity: **(1)** the force that attracts a body toward the center of the earth, or toward any other physical body having mass.

(2) extreme or alarming significance or importance

(*Oxford Languages*)

CHAPTER 1

Some nights, like last night, I see and hear the crash in my dreams. A flashbulb memory of three screaming faces, the sound of tires screeching, metal colliding and grinding, sirens wailing. The dream wakes me up, shaken and weeping. It's as if I've lost my family all over again. If I'd been with them, I'd have been lost, too, dead or impossibly damaged. I rarely admitted to myself why I wasn't with them.

The day after the dream is always miserable. Sometimes I look out my fifth story window and consider letting gravity finish the job. A short flight with a sudden stop.

It was just a bad day, I told myself for the umpteenth time, looking out my window. Just another bad day. They came occasionally. Almost always after the dream, or after visiting Joshua — or both. All I had to do was get through them.

The dreams had started after the crash, when I was 14. Between then and 22, I'd self-medicated with whatever came to hand: cigarettes, marijuana, sex, acid, XTC, vodka cocaine — a lot of all of them and sometimes all together. My self-medication had gradually lost me everything — throw-away relationships, money, my parents' house — in roughly that order.

When at 19 I'd ended up on the street, cold, sick and half crazed, someone got me into detox, then rehab where someone else decided that prescription medications might be a better option. They were for a while and allowed me to learn my craft. But besides the side-effects, they were never able to reach the solid core of blackness deep inside me, a core of self-loathing and guilt — I had been selfish and self-centered. I had not been with them, and I was still alive and undamaged. I could see my future of doctors, increasing dosages, more and different drugs.

So now, for the past five years, I'd been going it cold turkey. And that meant that there were going to be bad days. Inevitable.

I'd developed a method for getting through. I didn't stay in bed — well, not very often anyway. I'd get up, crank up the espresso machine, take a shower, force myself to get dressed and focus on one project for the day. Just one. And I'd push through and try not to let anyone know that the black hole of depression was hovering around the corners of my vision, waiting to pull me down into its inescapable gravity. I wouldn't let anyone know either about the pull of high places. Sometimes at night I'd imagine them, though. A short flight with a sudden stop.

So it was just another bad day. I left the window, drank espresso, made the bed, did the dishes, showered, got dressed. I paid special attention to my hair and makeup. *It's better to look good than to feel good,* my mother used to say, quoting Billy Crystal, I think. The sad sack in the mirror had the usual olive skin, brown eyes and un-cooperative mahogany curls. I did the best I could with it all, then embarked on my project for the day.

It was, as so often it was, taking photographs. I photographed almost anything: food, kids, dogs, birds, people, buildings, animals, mountains, forests, skiers, crowds. My photographs were well known among the few people who read the credits, and I made an OK living with them. They appeared in magazines, newspapers, brochures, advertisements, on billboards and greeting cards and websites all over the world. I could have made more money if I'd been willing to photograph people working in offices, or fighting a war, but I drew the line at those even though the demand for emotionally charged war pictures and attractively lit office scenes was high. The one time I'd tried the office stuff, I'd spent the next day in bed staring at the ceiling. It wasn't worth it.

Today's project was to go down to the bike path along the South Platte River in Downtown Denver. I had an assignment from a bike manufacturer, so I figured I'd also get some stock photos of people having fun in the Denver sunshine on this unseasonably warm February day. I photographed lots of bicyclists in brilliant Spandex, tracking them with a slow shutter speed so that the bike name was in perfect focus against the backdrop of blurred high-rise buildings. I also photographed children with brightly colored pails digging and splashing on the river beach, the water droplets sparkling brilliantly. By sheer luck I caught a flight of bright white egrets reflected in almost black water. *A shot for a condolence card*, I thought.

I walked down to Confluence Park where the South Platte meets Cherry Creek in a fairly dramatic clash of blue, brown and white water. Lots of people were sitting on the concrete kayak ramp enjoying the sunshine, the buttery warmth flowing over their faces, legs and arms. I took a few shots, but there really wasn't anything there: no action; no contrasts of light or emotion.

It was about eleven-thirty by that time, and the light had gotten too white, the shadows too sharp. But the black hole of depression had receded, so I thought I'd take the light rail to Technique Camera, my favorite camera shop, just to see what was new, what might be fun. One of the big lens manufacturers had just come out with a super fish-eye that looked interesting. I had no hobbies, so I spent my money on photo equipment. I loved all of it.

I caught the C train at Union Station and took some snaps of people in the carriage. People asleep with their heads against the window. People staring blankly at their phones and wrapped in the privacy of their ear buds, a sharply dressed man reading some papers. A capped and mustached RTD guard in aviator sunglasses checking tickets. A guy standing with his bicycle.

I was scrolling through my photos on my Nikon's back screen when we arrived at the end of the line at Mineral Station, so I was the last to get off the train. Or almost the last. Up near the front of the car, maybe one row of seats back from the bicycle rack, I could see an African American woman was still asleep, her head resting against the window. Her hair was wrapped in a crisp, colorful silk turban, and her shoulders were covered by a red wool coat.

By the time I'd stood to get off, the RTD security guy had entered through the doorway from the carriage in back of ours and was moving officiously toward me, gut first. He had a small mustache and wore aviator sunglasses against the glare of the low winter sun.

"Last stop, Ma'am," he announced to me, his voice deepened by the authority of his uniform. "You need to exit the carriage, now."

"On my way," I mumbled, distracted.

I waited as he swaggered past me to impress his aviators on the sleeping woman.

"Last stop, ma'am," he informed her loudly. I heard him say it again as I reached the doors, but they were closing, so I leaned over to punch the green button to open them again.

"Ma'am?" he said and shook her shoulder.

She pitched forward, her head thumping the steel railing on the back of the seat in front of her.

The guard reeled and sat down gracelessly onto the seat across the aisle.

I went over to him, thinking to be some help.

I was too late. The guard was speaking urgently into his walkie talkie and was using the seat railing to haul himself back onto his feet. He gave me a surprised look that became hostile, but he got hold of himself, remembering his uniform, and said, "Exit the carriage right now, Ma'am."

I looked from him to the sleeping woman. She wasn't sleeping. She was dead.

I snapped a photo. Reflex, I guess you could call it.

"GET OUT OF HERE!" shouted the guard, "NOW!"

I went to the door and stepped out onto the platform. Several RTD security guards were already running toward me, and I could hear sirens in the distance, growing louder.

I pulled my small mirrorless Sony with the wide-angle lens out of my backpack. People were less intimidated by it because it looked like just a point-and-shoot. I was excited. I was going to get some shots of things *happening*. I'd always loved photographing crowds of people all focused on a single thing, whether a car being pulled out of a river or a lion at the zoo. I loved to catch the expressions on their faces, yanked out of themselves and all thinking the same thing. I sold those shots to newspapers and magazines for next to nothing, but I didn't care. They were *fun*.

I checked my big Nikon's review function before stowing it in my backpack. It showed me the woman folded frontwards over a bluish gray nylon sports bag. Her mouth and brown eyes were open. Her bright red lipsticked lips were drawn back revealing good teeth, and gravity had pulled her cheeks and jowls downward, accentuating her high cheekbones. Her left hand — no wedding ring — rested palm up on the seat beside her, the other hung down between her slack thighs. Her ankles were turned outward over stylish but comfortable-looking black leather shoes.

The handle of a slim knife jutted out from under her left breast. I couldn't see any blood, but her red coat may have hidden it. Her bladder had failed.

It was a hell of a photograph in every sense. Unpublishable.

It was going to take a while for the police and EMTs to get to the train. From the police and fire complex in

Littleton, they'd have to fight the traffic and eternal construction on Santa Fe Drive, turn onto Mineral Avenue, park in the Park 'n' Ride lot, then run across the pedestrian bridge spanning Santa Fe Drive. I had a little time.

Thankfully, RTD does a pretty good job of keeping their windows clean, so I set up my little Sony with a high ISO, fast shutter speed and medium aperture, rubbed dust from a window with my sleeve, pressed the Sony's lens snout right against the glass and began snapping. The security guy was squatting next to the dead woman's seat staring vacantly at nothing. Every line of his body showed his distress. He lifted his head and faced the ceiling, eyes closed, mouth open, taking a deep breath. He hauled himself to his feet and stood with his hands on his hips staring unseeing out the window to my left. As pictures of responses to unexpected death, they couldn't have been better.

But pretty soon the platform was crowded with running uniformed figures all jamming themselves into the carriage at once. They were pushed back out by a tall lanky guy with a man-bun and a jacket that said "POLICE PHOTOGRAPHER" on the back.

On the platform, I was on the wrong side of the train to get anything except people's backs, so I trotted down the platform to the last door of the carriage and quietly stepped in. The door hissed shut behind me.

Carefully I edged toward the crowd gathered around the dead woman, snapping photo after photo as quickly as I could. Experience told me that I wouldn't have long before somebody threw me out. The Sony's SD card would hold 749 42-megapixel shots, and I wanted as many as I could get.

Until a security guy caught sight of me. "HEY!" he shouted. "I told you to get outa here!" He turned to another security guy and spat the word "press," through one side of his mouth.

One of the men leaning over the body stood up straight and looked at me. "Press?" he asked. His voice was gravelly and rough, maybe from smoking or maybe from an injury.

"No," I said. "Professional photographer." I pulled a business card out of my pocket and handed it to him.

He was about forty, very tall and lean to the point of boniness, about six-four with medium-length straight brown hair combed back from a high forehead. His nose looked like it had been broken in the distant past, there were acne scars on his cheeks, and he had a scar bisecting his left eyebrow. His gray suit looked expensive, but a size too big, as if he'd lost weight recently. There was a beat-up Rolex on his wrist and polished brown English shoes on his feet. He looked from the card to me. His deep-set hazel cop's eyes showed nothing. "How long have you been here?" he asked.

"All the way from Union Station," I said.

He took my arm and walked me to a seat at the back of the carriage.

"Detective Marshall," he said, showing me a badge in his wallet. "And you are Clare Standish?" I nodded.

Marshall took a small spiral-bound notebook out of his breast pocket, flipped it open to a blank page, and wrote my name, copying it off the card I'd given him. "I need to ask you some questions, Ms. Standish, and I'll be taking notes on your answers. I'll give you a transcript at some point for you to approve and sign." He took a cigar that was nowhere near as large as a baseball bat out of the breast pocket of his coat and lit it with a battered Zippo lighter. At one time, it had had something engraved on it, now almost worn away. *Was that two hearts entwined?* I wondered.

"OK," I said, mystified. Why wouldn't he just record me on his phone?

After a few preliminary questions, he asked, "So what can you tell me about what happened here?" I noticed out the window that uniformed police were rounding up uncooperative passengers on the platform into small groups and taking them to benches to wait for interviews. I lifted the Sony and took a couple of snaps.

Unexpectedly he smiled. There were nice crinkle lines around his eyes. I smiled back. He seemed like a nice enough guy in spite of his cop's eyes. "Have you been taking pictures right along?"

"Yes," I said. "Do you want to see them?" I held up the Sony.

"Not now. But you'll need to hand over the SD card after I've finished talking with you."

I don't hand over the originals of my photos to anyone. Ever. They are my property, with an established value and a copyright. "Afraid not," I said. "But I can download any you want to a thumb drive or your phone once I've had a look at them."

"Nope," he said, and coughed, taking the cigar between his fingers. "I need the card *before* you mess with them in any way. They're evidence in a homicide, and you're at least a witness, if not a suspect. If you don't give me the card, I'll have to confiscate the camera."

I'd paid $2,800 for that camera, and another $800 for the lens, so that was out. I just stared at him, thinking. He held out his hand. "OK, you can have the card, but I need to make a copy of it."

"How?" he asked.

From my backpack, I dug out my iPad Pro and a card reader that plugged into it. He looked interested, I thought. I popped the card out of the camera, inserted it into the card reader now attached to the iPad, waited for the photos to download, and held out the card. He pulled a latex glove and a plastic evidence bag out of his jacket pocket, picked up the card with the glove, dropped the card into the bag, wrote on it, and handed it to a passing uniform.

He went on with the questions and the cigar smoking. I described for him as much as I could about the occupants of the train carriage between Union Station and Mineral. I could remember a lot of it because of all the photos I'd taken in the carriage earlier, with my other camera, the Nikon, but I decided against telling him about those until I'd looked at them myself. Some of those photos, the ones I'd taken downtown of the bicyclists and kids, *were* salable. So I needed to get them all downloaded and removed from the card before I handed over the light rail photos. I knew this plan would be unpopular, possibly illegal, so I didn't mention it.

"Have you got another SD card with you?" Detective Marshall asked me unexpectedly.

"Sure," I said, puzzled. I always carry eight in a little plastic box fitted to hold them.

He sat back on the bench seat and crossed one leg over the other, then twisted the foot around the other ankle, like two entwined saplings. It was a contorted posture I would come to know well. "Would you go out there," he motioned to the platform with his cigar, "and take a bunch of pictures of the crowd? Get as many of the people as you can. Try to get at least one of everyone. *Everyone*, you understand?" I nodded. His look was intense. There was something on his mind, but I didn't know what. I didn't know it then, but that was to be a common experience. "Then give me the card."

"This is getting expensive," I said. "The cards I use aren't cheap."

"I'll give you a receipt," he said, deadpan, knowing that a receipt was worthless.

I sighed. I could afford a couple of SD cards. Civic duty and all that. "OK," I said. "Now?"

He nodded, and I went out on the platform. What he didn't know was that I was trained for this.

People were standing around and sitting on the metal benches looking every kind of way people can. The sharply dressed African American man talked on his phone and consulted a Rolex every five seconds, his mouth turned down impatiently. A kid in a sideways ball cap stared at his phone while pushing a skateboard back and forth. A woman jiggled a crying baby. A priest stood with his hands in his pockets, staring at nothing. Two little boys raced through the crowd bumping into everyone. A person looking like the Unabomber in a black hoodie, jeans and sunglasses sat slouched over his or her hands. An old, bearded man pushed a loaded shopping cart through the crowd, mumbling to himself and asking everyone for spare change. Two slender young men, wearing earrings and very tight jeans with ripped knees, talked intensely to each other. Three uniformed Littleton cops moved purposefully from person to person asking questions and writing down answers. The RTD guard who'd found the dead woman and the train's driver waited their turns, bored and pacing restlessly. The young man who'd stood with his bicycle rode unsteadily in circles looking worried. A guy wearing jogging kit ran under the Mineral Avenue bridge below. I kept snapping as more would-be riders arrived on the platform, milling around and asking each other what was going on.

Finally Marshall stopped me. "You're good, thanks," he said. "Probably don't need any more. I doubt our murderer will arrive to enjoy the show any later than this. You can go." He was holding another lit cigar between the fingers of his left hand. There was a "No Smoking" sign on the platform behind him.

I handed him the Sony's SD card. "I'd rather stay," I said. "I'd like to get some shots for the media."

"So ... you *are* press?" he asked. It wasn't a friendly question.

"Free-lance, yes. This will definitely make the news, and I'd like to be first to file some video and photos. Since I'm here."

"OK." He waved me off, "Do your thing," and turned and walked back into the crowd.

Sheldon Davis, the police photographer, had finished up, and the Medical Examiner was still in the train car, but I could tell he was also just finishing. Ambulance guys were waiting on the platform with a gurney to take the body to the morgue. I dug out my big Nikon and went and did my thing.

CHAPTER 2

The local evening news used my video footage, and the local papers used a still of two orderlies pushing the gurney out the car doors with its burden covered in a blue paper blanket, the ME following, removing his mask and hat, looking relieved. The RTD guard was hovering behind him, slightly out of focus. It must have been a slow news day because both the video and photo were picked up by a couple of nationals. Against all odds, a good day after all.

My condo apartment in the Capitol Hill neighborhood of Denver is the fifth floor of a 19th century red sandstone mansion on Pennsylvania Street, spitting distance from the gold-domed Capitol building on Colfax Avenue and Sherman Street. Beyond the Capitol's gilded dome is the graceful curve of the City and County building, recently lit up in brilliant reds and greens for the holidays and the Western Stock Show in mid-January. Beyond, the snow-capped Rockies shine platinum in winter, and dream in a blue haze in summer. I consider my view the best in Denver. And I've never felt any need for more than its eight hundred square feet of kitchen, sitting room, bedroom and bath.

As usual, there wasn't anybody home except Bradshaw. As usual, he greeted me with dignity and affection and suggested we go for a walk in the evening dusk to get some exercise and work up an appetite for dinner. He was absolutely right, of course, and pretty soon we were stepping out into temperatures plunging toward freezing, despite the fairly warm afternoon. Bradshaw didn't mind. Bradshaw is a Cardigan Welsh Corgi with a fluffy double coat the color of saddle shoes and a brisk manner with strangers.

After our dinner, consisting of one of Bradshaw's favorites, barbecued ribs and mashed potatoes, I took a glass of Chateau de Box over to the shelf-like desk running along the front window wall and fired up my big iMac. I transferred the photos of Confluence Park and the bicycles onto the Mac, leaving them and the rail car photos I took before the body was discovered on the card, and set the card aside. Then I settled in for the long editing process.

I'd taken about five minutes of video and about 250 photos that day, about 75 of them in the train. I'd already sent out the video and the photos of the ME leaving to some media outlets and AP, so I went through the Confluence Park photos, deleting probably half of them for one reason or another. Under-exposed, over-exposed, blurred, unfocused, badly composed, or just ugly, out they went. After the first cut, I gradually pared them down to the most interesting ones, preferably just one or two in each group of shots. I like this process; it's a kind of meditation that I can lose myself in for hours.

At around ten o'clock, Bradshaw politely stepped on my foot and touched my ankle with his wet nose. Bradshaw considers ten o'clock time for another short walk and bed.

I closed down the Mac, put everything away, shrugged into my parka, snapped on Bradshaw's leash, and out we went.

The night was clear and cold with a few stars visible now that Denver had down-lighted the streetlights. We took our usual route around the Capitol, passing the Molly Brown House, the Masonic Temple, the park full of homeless people, and the Basilica of the Immaculate Conception. The route is filled with interesting smells for Bradshaw and interesting sights for me.

As we headed back up Colfax, I became aware of someone behind us. For some reason it made me uneasy. Colfax is nearly always crowded, but I couldn't shake my sense that this wasn't just another nighttime pedestrian. I looked around.

A person wearing sagging slender jeans and a black hoodie pulled low was walking along behind me, head down, talking on a cell phone. I'm rarely nervous on these walks, but he or she seemed just a little too close, so I pretended to look into a window to let them pass. Otherwise, just the usual East Colfax crew — a woman pushing a shopping cart with a sleeping bag and a small dog in it, two giggling underdressed girls talking to an older man outside a strip club, four guys with dreads sharing a joint and a paper-bagged bottle, a man and woman lying on a flattened cardboard box in the doorway of an empty shopfront, and several dog-walkers just like me.

Bradshaw and I continued, but by now my anxiety button had been pushed. And again there was someone behind me. I checked quickly to see a young man with short gelled hair and glasses. But were those the same tight jeans?

And the same black hoodie now pushed back? I couldn't remember, but I thought maybe ...

We reached the corner of Pennsylvania Street and, as I turned right, I was relieved when the young man continued straight up Colfax. But now there was someone standing on the sidewalk across the street from my building. Also talking on a cell phone. Also wearing a black hoodie pulled low. As I let myself into the building's ornate front door, I wondered idly how there were suddenly so many black jeans/black hoodie people walking around. Or was it the same hoodie? Shrugging mentally, I unhooked Bradshaw's leash and started up the stairs.

Bradshaw dashed past me pell-mell on his six-inch legs, barking sharply. And when I got to the fifth floor, I found out why.

My apartment door was open with glacial air spilling out. Inside, my bedroom door was banging softly against the frame. Desk drawers were open; the iMac was on the floor with a foot-sized fracture in its screen. My iPad was missing from its drawer, and both my cameras were gone from the big camera bag in the linen closet. That was all. Everything else, even the box holding my father's cameras, was just as I'd left it, including our dirty supper dishes in the sink. *Bastards could have at least washed up*, I thought.

Quickly I went in the bedroom where a pile of glass on the floor told all too well how the bastards had gotten in. An old-fashioned iron fire escape snaked up the back of the old mansion, and, while it didn't actually give convenient access to my bedroom window, someone with some parkour experience could climb onto the railing, break the glass with something, hop from the railing onto the windowsill and climb in. Which is what I guessed they'd done. The more careful people on the lower floors had bars on their windows, which I'd been meaning to have installed for the last three years. I scolded myself — There was a crucial difference between *meaning* to have bars and *having* bars.

I looked around the bedroom and went back into the sitting room and over to the shelf-desk where the iMac had been. Nothing seemed to have been stolen. So why had they broken in?

I checked around the apartment, but nothing seemed to have been stolen. But to be on the safe side, I tried to think of a place to hide stuff.

Eventually I settled on the "secret" drawer at the bottom of my Victorian mahogany dresser, picking up a few family photos, some pieces of my mother's jewelry and a few other treasured items. As an afterthought, I threw in the little plastic box with the SD cards in it and my back-up drive, so all my photos were safe, too. I hoped that the drawer, disguised by some ornately carved roses, which would have been a dead giveaway to a Victorian burglar, would be invisible to a burglar.

I looked out the window at the street. The person in the black hoodie was gone. I wondered if they'd had anything to do with the break-in. I wondered if they'd been a witness. Now that everything I valued had been hidden, I didn't worry too much about a repeat invasion. I'd lived on the streets. I knew that whoever it was wouldn't break in a second time.

Bradshaw was giving the place a good going over with his nose. He seemed particularly interested in a spot by the dishwasher, but in the end, it turned out to be a molecule of something Corgis like.

I cut up my shower curtain and duct-taped it to the broken window's frame, intending to call somebody in the morning to fix it and install some belated bars. I'd have to call the insurance people and the police, too, I thought, yawning. Bradshaw jumped up on his side of the bed, turned in a circle three times, and settled himself for the night. I stripped and settled down on my side. So, not such a good day after all, I thought as I drifted off.

The phone calls in the morning yielded two Denver cops who didn't hold out much hope, my insurance broker wanting paperwork, and a promise from the window repair company to come fix the window the next day "between noon and five p.m." So ... two days of shooting lost. But then I remembered I had no cameras anyway. The owner of my favorite camera store said, when I called him, that he had a nearly new Nikon D4 and a replacement for my Sony that he would put aside for me.

"What happened?" he asked.

"Break-in," I said succinctly, and said I'd pick up the cameras in a couple of days.

Next I ordered a new iPad from Apple and made an appointment to see if by any chance the Genius Bar at Cherry Creek Mall could fix the iMac. All my photos were backed up on a many-terabyte external drive I'd also hidden in the "secret" drawer, so I could recover them if the iMac was toast, but if it could be fixed, that would be the better option.

I decided I'd better let Detective Marshall know what had happened and arrange to give him the SD card from the Nikon, but when I called the Littleton Police department, frustratingly, he was "unavailable" and couldn't be reached. I left my name and number, but I didn't hear back from him. I dug out an old laptop and sent a few of the bicycle photos off to deadline-jittery editors, but that and a walk and two meals with Bradshaw were about it for the day.

The evening brightened up substantially when I opened my front door to find six feet of extremely handsome man wearing silvery gray slacks and a cream Aran sweater. And carrying flowers and a bottle of Prosecco. As usual when I saw Daniel Coldwell, all my blood rushed north to my face and south to my loins, leaving my heart and lungs wondering what had happened.

I fell for Daniel about five years ago, the first time I saw him at the Blue House. I didn't know at the time that he *owned* the place! I was just there because I was looking it over for my twin brother, Joshua, who'd been badly disabled in the crash that had killed my parents.. It wasn't until about six months later, once Joshua was comfortably settled, that I'd managed to attract his attention. The affair started fast and hot, and it hadn't cooled down much since. Of course, I was also intensely grateful to him for all that he and his staff had done for my brother.

"Hello, my love," he said, as he stepped in and kissed me on the cheek.

I could not suppress my silly grin. "Same to you, Daniel," I gurgled. "How was your conference?"

Daniel put the flowers and Prosecco down on the table by the door and wrapped me in warm wool and his own wonderful fragrance. I have no idea why he smells so good — it's not cologne or deodorant or body wash, it's just *him*. He held me tightly to him, pressing my body against his and kissing me deeply. As an end to a frustrating day, it was very satisfactory indeed.

Pulling a little away, he asked, "It was fine. I'm hungry as a lion. How about dinner? Sushi Den?" I nodded. "Let's save this for afters, shall we?" he tilted his head at the Prosecco.

"Mmmm," I said, not thinking so much about the Prosecco as about the "afters." "Let me just put these in water — they're beautiful!" He followed me into the kitchen while I filled a vase with water, trimmed the flowers' stems and fussed with them.

"Are you OK, my love?" he breathed into my neck. "I wonder if you're really safe here. I could put you up at the Blue House for a few days until the cops sort this out. You *have* told them about the break-in, right? Do they know who it was?" he asked. He leaned elegantly against the kitchen door jamb, and he looked so delicious that I was ready to forego dinner and just jump him. Purely for medicinal purposes, you understand. As a treatment for depression, he was hard to beat.

"Yes, I did tell them, and no, it's too soon. The two cops who came weren't very optimistic. And I haven't been able to get hold of that detective I told you about, so I don't know any more about the murder, either." I patted the flowers into shape. "There! That will do, I think. Do you think I should change?" I examined his casual chic-ness from head to ... ankles. "Why are you wearing running shoes?"

"Yeah, I forgot to change after my run." I admired his great shape. "But you look good enough to eat," he said, his eyes twinkling. "C'mon, let's go before I do."

Sushi Den is a frantically popular restaurant on the Old South Pearl Street, which is glorified by the foodie establishment as the best sushi restaurant in the Rockies, or the West, or even in the U.S. It's also a favorite of mine, though Daniel prefers his fish cooked. We ordered a salmon tartare appetizer, which I ate most of, a platter of assorted Sashimi for me and Alaskan Halibut for Daniel. We each had a pitcher of perfectly warm saki. Daniel had plum wine served in a tiny glass afterwards, but I stuck to green tea, anticipating the Prosecco and "afters" to come.

Daniel is a charming and easy dinner companion. I described to him in some length my adventures on the light rail train and my suspicions about the young people in hoodies I'd seen following me and then across the street from my building's entrance. I was now fairly sure they'd been the same person. Daniel was solicitous and asked a million questions that I didn't want to answer. So he gave up and described to me a funny episode at the Blue House, one of the three five-star nursing homes he owned, where Joshua, was so well taken care of. Daniel was generously supplementing the cost of his care from some kind of endowment. He would never tell me where the money came from. But we could never have afforded it otherwise.

I laughed, and appreciated his dazzling smile, the crinkles around his eyes, his baritone laughter.

His phone buzzed on the table. He looked over at the screen and frowned. "Sorry, Clare, I have to take this. He scribbled on the check while he listened, saying "Uh huh. Yes, that's right. No, don't do anything until I get there. Yup. Half an hour? OK, great." He put the phone down. "I'm sorry, Clare — I'm going to have to rush off after I take you home. There's a situation at the Blue House and I gotta go." He smiled with the corners of his mouth turned down and reached for my hand.

"That's OK," I lied. To say I was disappointed was putting it mildly. "Nothing to do with Joshua, though?" I asked.

"No, no. Your brother's fine. This is ... well, it's something else. I can't talk about it."

I took his hand and we walked to his red Ferrari. It had started snowing, and the temperature had plummeted below freezing. Sixty-five yesterday, I remembered, and now 30. Welcome to Colorado. My mood was plummeting along with the temperature.

On my front steps we held each other while snow fell romantically around us. "I'm sorry," he whispered against my lips.

"I had such interesting plans for this evening, too," I whispered back. I felt his smile against my mouth.

"Tomorrow?" he asked.

"Mm-hmm," I breathed, wishing with every nerve ending that he would stay with me tonight. I pushed him away. "Go," I said, "Before I do something you'll regret."

CHAPTER 3

I called Detective Marshall again the next day and was told that he was again unavailable. But on the plus side, the window company called to ask would it be OK if they came this morning, say in a half hour, instead of this afternoon. I readily agreed, and so, after a lot of banging and drilling at my bedroom window, accompanied by a rendition of "Tu Éres Mi Amor," I was out the door and was headed once again for the light rail to Mineral Avenue.

Technique Cameras is one of those wonderful small businesses run by someone who knows how to run a small business. The service is prompt and knowledgeable, and none of the staff practice the snarky condescension common among camera sales people. The owner, Tom, greeted me by name when I arrived, and deftly passed the customer he was working with to one of the other clerks. Several of the other customers turned to look at me, thinking maybe I was some kind of celebrity. They were disappointed.

Tom came out from behind the counter and gave me a peck on the cheek. "I'll just go get those cameras — they're in the back," but he was too late, because Micke was emerging from the curtained doorway with two boxes. "Oh! Thanks, Micke."

Micke nodded a greeting to me.

"So you were robbed?" Tom asked, as he handed me the boxes for the Nikon and Sony. I described the way the burglars had gotten into my apartment while I opened them. Tom tut-tutted. "That's tough," he said. "Insured, I hope?"

"Yes. But I'll buy these now and let the insurance reimburse me. And I'd like you to get me a D5 as soon as you can. I'll keep this D4 till then, then I'll turn it in for a credit. Is that OK?"

Tom waved a dismissive hand. "Oh sure. I've already ordered you one. I'm just sorry I don't have one on hand. Not much demand for that much camera." And from there we launched into a discussion of replacement lenses, a star filter I used occasionally and better straps.

"So you said on the phone that you were at that light rail murder. Can you tell me about it?" he asked when I'd packed everything into my backpack and he'd sucked my credit card dry.

"I can show you, if you like," I said, and got out the little plastic box with the Nikon's SD card in it. He plugged the card into his computer. We went through the Confluence Park photos, discussing possible markets for them, and then looked through the train photos. "This is her," I pointed to the victim's head resting against the train window in one of the photos. "And this. And this."

"Huh." he said. "When did she get on?"

"I don't know, but the time stamp indicates maybe around I-25 and Broadway? Or a little earlier?"

"Go back," he said. I scrolled back through the photos. "There! Stop! OK, hang on a sec." Tom pulled up the RTD C train schedule on his computer and ran his finger down it. The time stamp on the first appearance of the victim was about two minutes after the 10th and Osage stop. "So it looks like she got on at 10th and Osage. Interesting. She doesn't look like she came from the projects. Too well dressed. Maybe she was coming from lunch at the Buckhorn Exchange. "

"More likely," I agreed. "But check it out. She had this blue nylon gym bag ... here ..." I pointed at the photo of her with the fainting RTD guard.

"Hmmm. A change of clothes?" asked Tom. I tilted my head noncommittally. "Oh, well. I guess the cops will figure it out," he said, closing his computer and handing me back my SD card. I realized he was aware that the shop was filling up, and he was needed. "I'll text you, huh? When I get the D5 in?" I nodded and waved to everyone. A chorus of 'Bye, Clare' followed me out the door.

My phone sang "◈ Email!" as I left the camera store. It was from Apple saying that my new iPad had been FedEx'd to my apartment, and the manager had signed for it. So that was good, but I needed the iMac for editing any photos I was going to send out. And, checking my phone, I saw that I'd received another earlier email from the city asking for some night shots of Downtown for an advertising campaign they were floating in France. Of course they wanted them like yesterday. I knew I had a bunch of stock photos that would fill the bill, but that meant going home and then fussing with the old laptop to get them ready to send along. It might be easier to just go downtown tonight, but ... I'd still have to process the new photos and send them out, so ...

I decided to go home, pick up the broken iMac and Uber over to the Mac store in the Cherry Creek shopping Mall. I put the plan into action, and an hour and a half later I was lugging the iMac downstairs.

It was at that tricky moment when you're carrying something very large, heavy and awkward, such as a 27-inch iMac, down some worn sandstone steps to your waiting Uber when it happened.

Out of nowhere, a person in black jeans and hoodie hurtled into me, knocking me off the bottom step. I landed hard on my right hip and shoulder; the iMac went flying and skittering down the sidewalk; the Uber driver looked up from his phone; the hoodie person scooped up the iMac and stampeded down Pennsylvania Street.

I was so astonished I couldn't even shout for help.

The Uber driver hopped out of his car, helped me up and started to dust me off before remembering about potential sexual harassment suits, so the dusting became a vague waving of arms.

"What the in hell that is about?" he panted when he was sure I was not going to fall over again.

"Shit! I don't — OW! — know," I panted back. I rolled my shoulder, but it seemed it was just sore. "But he's going to be very disappointed when he gets a look at what he's got."

Mohammed (his name tag said) looked puzzled. "You big computer, yes?"

"Big busted computer, yes," I smiled. "I wanted you to take me to Cherry Creek Mall, so I could get it fixed at the Mac store."

Mohammed regarded me with large, intelligent brown eyes. He was good looking in a rugged Middle Eastern way. He was about forty, I thought, with abundant wavy black hair just starting to silver, strong features, skin creased and toughened by hard times, and plenty of cologne. "OK, so I driving you to Mac store is out? Cancel?" He raised his eyebrows and made palm down flattening motions with his left hand. He wore a heavy gold wedding band.

Well, what should I do? Without the iMac I couldn't work, and just then my phone sang its email song again. This time it announced the Business Relations department at the city wanted photos of the Convention Center for the same French campaign. It was no good taking or finding the pictures if I had no way to process them. My laptop was seven years old, and the screen resolution wasn't good enough. Even if I used my existing stock photos, still saved on the many-terabyte drive, they were going to need some work to fulfill what the city was looking for — cropping, and adjusting the colors for printing ...

Mohammed was looking impatient and reaching into his back pocket for his phone. I made up my mind.

"No," I said, "No, I still need you to take me over to Cherry Creek Mall."

"Oh, OK!" he smiled broadly showing large white teeth. How do they do that, I wondered, what with drinking all that tea? "That is very excellent! Hop yourself in!" He opened the back door of the Ford Crown Victoria — *Wo!*

"This is quite a car," I said, once I'd struggled into the marshmallow soft leather seats, and we were underway.

"Luxury car," he nodded, looking at me in his rearview mirror. "Too bad they do not make them since 2007. This is 2007. It pay for itself in one year! One year only!"

"Really," I said, and wondered if this could be true.

"Yeah, really. Buy it at what you call? Cop sale?"

"Police auction?"

"Yeah. That. I only pay three thousand dollar." He held up a thumb and two fingers. "I make trip to airport mostly. Need bi-i-i-g trunk. Lots of leg room for big Americans to fly in tiny little airplane seats!" He laughed at the irony of it all, so I laughed along with him to be polite."

"Pay for itself in one year!" He repeated, nodding with evident pride. "OK, here you are!"

He pulled into the circular drive on First Avenue. A doorman came out and opened my door.

"I'm gonna stay here for maybe 30 minutes," Mohammed told me as I clambered ungracefully out of the enveloping back seat. He held up two cigarettes in explanation. "If I am still here when you come out, maybe you let me take you back?"

I nodded and smiled. "Great!" I said. "See you in 30."

The doorman went over to Mohammed's window and said something that made them both laugh, then they high-fived, and Mohammed drove a short distance away and parked.

The Mac store is on the second level of the Mall, toward the end. The Mall had replaced its Christmas decorations with very beautifully made copper flying geese hanging from the ceiling at slightly different heights. The ceiling lights had been adjusted to catch their copper wing and tail feathers and their comically dangling feet. The geese were smiling. They were charming. I looked over the railing down to the first floor. Under the geese was a large seating area with a coffee kiosk and comfortable chairs. Quite a few people were sitting there, talking, drinking coffee, lulled by the comfortable light and the greens, blues and tans of the chairs and rugs. I swung my new Sony around on its new strap and snapped a dozen photos of the people and the geese. You never knew: Maybe the Mall would buy them.

The Mac store was the usual madhouse, but there were lots of sales people with their iPads listening carefully as affluent Denverites tried to explain what they wanted or what the problem was. I drew the young woman with the very tight blue Apple-logo'd tee-shirt and skinny black jeans. I was going to make her day.

"Hi! What can I help y'all with today?" she asked in cheerful Texan.

"Hi..." I squinted at her name hangar, "... Jenny. I need a 27-inch iMac, the 512 gig with the retina display."

She tapped her iPad without turning a hair. "OK, hang on a sec." She disappeared through a door to the left of the Genius Bar where seven or eight senior citizens were trying to explain what they didn't know how to do while the Geniuses listened patiently.

Jenny emerged three minutes later carrying a large, slim white box by its white plastic handle. "OK, here you go," she said, still bright as a penny. "Do y'all need us to set it up or anythin'?"

I shook my head. "No, thanks," I smiled as I took it from her and handed her my credit card. Thirty seconds later I was a lot poorer, and Apple Corp. was a lot richer. As I was pushing open the heavy glass doors into the Mall, an entering man in his 60s looked at my box with naked longing.

"Hey Miss!" called Mohammed when I emerged from the Mall. He pinched out his cigarette and put the stub in his breast pocket before meeting me and carrying the box to his car.

"Big brand new computer, hey?" he asked. "You get insurance?"

"Not yet," I said, truthfully, thinking I'd be filling out yet more paperwork tonight. "But I need the computer now."

"Too bad," said Mohammed darting into the jockeying traffic on First Avenue. "I know a guy gets those ones cheap. You want me to call? He maybe get it tomorrow or day after? Then you take back that one?"

I'll bet, I thought. "No thanks. I'll just keep this one. I really need it now."

Mohammed harrumphed, and I heard him mumble "expensive" under his breath. "Say," he said, looking at me in his rearview mirror, "You take Uber pretty often?"

"Now and then," I said. "I don't have a car, so I take the bus or light rail most places, but sometimes that's too hard, so I use Uber."

"Listen," he said. "You call *me* next time, OK? I take you anywhere you want," he waved an arm in a circle. I give you discount fare and you pay cash, like today. OK?" he said, pulling up to my building on the wrong side of the street, not bothering to park.

"I'll think about it," I said. "Would you be available tomorrow afternoon to take me out to Greenwood Village to see my brother, then bring me back a few hours later? You know the Blue House? I'd call you a little before I'd need you to pick me up."

"You bet! Here, you gimme a call this number." He handed a card over the back of the seat. "Mohammed Alazir, it said in red ink, and a cell phone number. "Be careful!" he called as I clambered out with my big white box.

I spent a boring afternoon loading up the iMac with all my photos, apps and programs from the many-terabyte drive. I got the iPad from the building manager but didn't do anything with it. That would wait till I had more time. I called the police, then my insurance broker and explained about the now stolen iMac. He sighed and emailed me the forms to fill out. I gathered he was going to have to redo all the paperwork at his end, too. The police said they'd stop by in the next couple of days.

Daniel called and said he was still tied up with whatever the situation was at the Blue House, so wouldn't be over tonight, how about a rain check? Sure — I just hoped the flowers would last until he showed up. I wasn't sure the Prosecco would. The black hole of depression was starting to pull at me.

It was probably OK that he couldn't come over, I rationalized as I sorted through my photos of nighttime Downtown and daytime Convention Center. Some would work, but most were taken at Christmas and didn't really show what the city was looking for. So, after staring out my front window at the lighted Capitol dome, I thought I'd head out to Larimer Square and the 16th Street Mall. It was Friday night after all, so things should be jumping. Bradshaw yawned and said he'd like to come too.

By the time I'd preset and packed up the Nikon and my tripod and packed Bradshaw's backpack with all the smaller bits and pieces I'd need, then buckled his wriggling body into it, it was dark. I fastened his leash to a belt contraption I'd put together for hands-free dog walking, and out we went. Most professional photographers have assistants; I have Bradshaw.

I had decided to walk down the 16th Street Pedestrian Mall and take some shots of people and lights, the restaurants and micro-breweries. Perhaps there would be people playing the gaily painted pianos placed in each block. But first things first.

Bradshaw and I stopped at Alfred's hot dog cart. Alfred was a German immigrant we often visited, who sold the very finest hot dogs, bratwurst, and Polish sausage on the Mall. Or maybe anywhere. Bradshaw preferred his two hot dogs plain and without a bun, but I went for the full Monte — Bratwurst, sauerkraut, mustard and hot pickled peppers. I got a Coke to keep me perky for the long evening ahead. Alfred gave Bradshaw a bowl of his finest water.

"You doin' OK, Clare?" asked Alfred as he dished up our supper.

"Yup," I said. "The city wants photos of nightlife. Can I take some of you?"

"Oh sure!" Alfred seemed pleased. "Get the umbrella with the logo, OK? Who doesn't want free advertising?"

I set up the camera on the tripod and took several snaps. There was Alfred dishing up my bratwurst. There was Alfred talking to another customer. There was Alfred smiling. There was the umbrella with his logo and the black, red and gold stripes of the German flag.

"ZO!" said Alfred between customers, "What gives with d'dead woman on the train? I seen them photos of yours on d' news. Whachu know about it, huh?"

"I don't know anything about it. I was just going from Union Station to Mineral and at Mineral the RTD guard found her. She was stabbed under her left breast with what looked to me like a boning knife."

"Oh, yeah?" Another customer interrupted. Polish sausage on a pretzel bun. "So one of my regulars said she was some doctor. I think maybe I knew her, if it was the doctor this guy was talking about."

"You did?" I couldn't keep the amazement out of my voice. Denver was still just a small town, I thought. "How did you know her?"

"Oh, you know. I think maybe she was the bratwurst and mayo." He shook his head in disgust. "She got some attitude on her, like everybody owes her. She act like I am dirt under her feet. Zo!" He held up a sneakered foot, "I ain't cryin.'"

"Did you know her name?"

Alfred shook his head. "Nah. Just the bratwurst and mayo is all. Like dis guy coming along here is the hot dog, lemonade and chips, and you're the one with the dog dat likes dogs!" He chuckled at his own pun while he dished up for the new customer.

"Well, is anything going on in the Mall that would be photogenic tonight? Other than you, of course," I said, changing the subject.

"Oh, Sure! Dey got a guy down on d'Arapahoe block doin' magic tricks. He's pretty good! Gets the audience to give him their watches and stuff. Pulls in a big crowd most nights. You can prob'ly find him if you listen for a lot a *volk* laughing."

I thanked him, and Bradshaw and I sauntered on down the Mall. The winter-bare trees were laced with tiny white lights. Music was booming out of the breweries, the brilliant lights of the restaurant windows showed crowds of 20-somethings and 30-somethings and the occasional 60-something standing around laughing, talking, and generally enjoying themselves. Each time I stopped to set up the tripod for a series of shots, Bradshaw sat patiently next to my right foot and smiled at the world at large.

The magician was everything Alfred had said he was. A circle of thirty or forty people surrounded him and did everything he ordered: clapped on command, laughed at his jokes, handed over their watches, wallets and girlfriends with the simplicity of children at a Punch and Judy show. The series I shot of him, though priceless, eventually ended up in *Conde Nast Traveller* and made me a couple of months' rent.

I finished up in Larimer Square, laced overhead with strings of big vintage lights and filled with strolling, well-heeled suburbanites. The crowd here was decidedly older, richer and less fun, but highly photogenic from a public relations point of view. John Hickenlooper's Wynkoop Brewery, the one that started Denver's love affair with micro-breweries, was no longer owned by the former engineer, mayor, governor and now senator, but it was jumping all the same. Stylish couples were drinking beer and cocktails, leaning on the iron railings of the concrete loading dock that had served the brick warehouse fifty years ago. A mix of loud gossip and Sheryl Crow's "All I Wanna Do" poured out the windows and doorways as waiters in long aprons threaded their way through the crowd, loaded trays held high overhead.

The evening had been a photographic feast.

Around midnight and exhausted, Bradshaw and I caught the Mall Ride homeward. The fluorescent lights on the trolly cars made all the riders look tired from the night's fun. I leaned against the luggage rack and looked around.

A young person in tight black jeans and a black hoodie was sitting on the bench seat directly across from me. Was it the same tight black jeans and hoodie? I didn't know. I chastised myself. I spent my waking hours *looking* at things, through a lens or not, but I couldn't tell if this was the same black hoodie and tight jeans who had been on the train and the platform at Mineral Station, behind me on Colfax, across the street from my building or knocking me over and stealing my iMac.

Bradshaw and I gratefully let ourselves into my apartment with its familiar fragrance of pizza and dog. But when I opened the new iMac, it had magically been restored to factory settings. Everything I'd just loaded up was gone. Luckily, I'd already backed it all up on the many-terabyte drive. As I set about reloading everything, I chatted with Bradshaw about glitches and power outages. But my technical expertise began and ended with cameras, so ...?

Bradshaw sniffed around the apartment, but came to no conclusions, then looked up at me and yawned.

Acting on impulse, I copied all my photos of the light rail car onto a new card. I put the that into a plastic case and a padded envelope, wrote Detective Marshall's name and address at the Littleton Police Department on it, weighed it on my kitchen scale, and stuck on some stamps. Then I put the original card, that I'd hidden in the "secret drawer" and also had the photos of Confluence Park, in another plastic case and an envelope with similar postage, scribbled a short note, and addressed it to Mohammed, the Uber driver. I took both envelopes down to the mailbox on the corner of Pennsylvania Street and shoved them through the slot. Say what you want about the U.S. Postal Service. It's still safer than a bank vault.

CHAPTER 4

The following day was my day to visit my twin brother, Joshua, at the Blue House where he'd been since our parents were killed in a car crash when we were 14. This meant getting an Uber out to Greenwood Village, a suburb of Denver. Greenwood Village has no green woods and no village, but there are many McMansions, white-fenced chunks of prairie full of horses, and carefully graveled dead-end streets with "no trespassing" signs on them.

There's also one huge four-story mansion clad in blue glass, standing on a wrinkle in the prairie with a view of the mountains to match any corner-office CEO's. After a tech entrepreneur's zillion dollar video game crashed into the canyon of yesterday's news, Daniel's consortium bought and turned it into a home for people with trauma-induced disabilities and Alzheimer's. It's a gorgeous place, twenty-second century modern with every gadget and mod con still in place after the techie departed. Joshua loves it there, but I often get into a guilt loop about how he should be with me.

The loop goes like this: *Joshua is my twin brother, and he should be with me. But he loves it at the Blue House. He has friends there. He has people who can care for him better than I can. I mean, look at the physical therapy he gets! And the grounds are fabulous — they take him for walks and that's so good for him. He can ride therapy horses and splash in the therapy pool. I can't provide any of that. But he's my twin brother, and he should be with me ..."*

Yeah, well. Around and around it goes. It gets worse on the days I visit him, bad enough that I'm grateful when I pass an open window.

So I was standing with my morning tea and looking out my (closed) window, going around and around the guilt loop, when my phone buzzed. It was Mohammed.

"I got this thing you send me," he said. "What you want me do with it?"

"Just keep it someplace safe where you can find it again if I need it," I said. "It's just some photos I took that day the woman was murdered on the train."

"Yes, I know. I look at them."

"Be careful!" I said, alarmed, "Don't delete any accidentally!"

"No, no. I am careful. OK, um, do you want me take you to see your brother today?"

"Yes, I do. Thanks for remembering. Like around 1:30? And come back at, say, 5:00? Will that work for you?"

"Oh sure. That work very excellent. I come by around 1:10, OK?"

I thanked him and hung up, but the phone immediately vibrated in my hand.

"Detective Marshall," said his cigar-roughened voice. "What the hell is this you've sent me?"

"And good day to you, too, Detective. Yes, I'm fine, thank you, how are you?"

He grunted and waited.

I sighed. "It's a copy of all the photos I took on the light rail before we got to Mineral. I had to take off some other photos that I want to sell. I can't lose control of my work, so there you are, and you're welcome."

"Why didn't you tell me about these when you gave me the other card? I could charge you with withholding evidence in a homicide investigation. The murderer's picture could be on here. Serious infraction of the law, Miss Standish." There was a long pause. I didn't say anything. He sighed, then coughed. "I want you to come down here *today*. I need to interview you."

"I can't," I said. "I'm visiting my brother today who's in a rehab facility. But I can come tomorrow morning. Does that work? I'm not under arrest, am I?"

Another long silence. I heard the Zippo click and a deep breath. "No. OK, get here at nine." he hung up.

I spent the next couple of hours processing the photos of Downtown Nightlife and uploading them to Drop Box for the folks at the City's tourism office. They would pick the ones they wanted for the French campaign, then I'd remove the watermarks, substitute a subtle copyright, and delete the rest from Drop Box. I also uploaded some stock shots I'd taken of the Convention Center because I hadn't had time to take any new ones. If the City's business promotion guys didn't like them, I'd take some new ones around sunset tomorrow after Marshall had put me through the bright lights and thumb screws.

When I arrived at the Blue House, I was surprised at an unusual hubbub — a quiet hubbub, it's true, but a hubbub all the same.

Joshua was in his wheelchair in the solarium fingering the leaves of a seven-foot Ficus. I went over and kissed the top of his head.

"Hi Sissy!" he said, genuinely happy to see me. Joshua has a round face and a pudgy body, the latter always encased in sweatpants and shirt. His legs are in braces so that if he wants to take a few steps, he can, as long as someone is walking with him. Falling is a real danger for him. His motor skills are poor, and gravity is not his friend. If he fell, there's no guarantee that he wouldn't fall on his head: a disaster. His head is about as sturdy as an eggshell.

He looks like my father, if my father had just gone six rounds with Mike Tyson. One of his eyes is blind, and tends to wander, the lid to droop. His mouth and nose are askew, and he tends to breathe through his mouth because his nose couldn't be completely repaired. He has many scars that run like train tracks through his hair and on his cheeks. I'm probably the only one who can see my father in him. The recognition always causes a painful twist in my solar plexus.

We chatted comfortably for a while, or chatted as much as Joshua is able. The head injury robbed him of most of his vocabulary, and his speech is deformed to the point that you can understand him only after long familiarity. He tires easily, his attention wanders, and he has sudden, unpredictable outbursts of anger and tears. I miss him: my womb-mate, my crib-mate, my playmate, my best friend.

A couple of orderlies scuttled by the door to the solarium. A nurse trotted by the other direction. "What's all the hubbub about, do you know?"

Joshua shook his head, then stopped suddenly. "Naw jus sumpin I dunno." He paused. "Since Wen'sdy I sink."

"Wednesday was four days ago. Since then?" He nodded once. "Huh." I said. "I hope it's not important, I mean, I hope it doesn't affect you. Did Daniel come here yesterday?"

Joshua thought hard about this. "Dunno," he said at last, then, thoughtfully, "I don't see Dan'l." A pause. "Maybe." a sigh. "I dunno." He looked at me with one sad, brown eye, our dad's eye and mine, as if to say he was sorry to be so useless.

"Never mind," I said, patting his hand. "Let's go outside. I'll spot you while you walk, yeah?" Joshua nodded. I pushed the button to call one of the orderlies. When he arrived, I asked him to get Joshua's coat, hat and scarf from his room.

Josh's wheelchair is motorized, and he enjoys driving it, so I rested one hand on a handlebar and followed him out into the cold.

"Let's look at the roses!" he exclaimed in his deformed speech.

"I don't think there are any roses now," I said, chuckling. He may be damaged but he's far from stupid, so I figured he was joking.

I was right. He laughed delightedly. "No roses now!" he chortled, "Just sticks! But let's look at 'em anyway. We a'ways like to look to see if they are ...." he stopped. His face crumpled like a baby's, red and wrinkled, and he burst into tears. I waited for the storm to pass — there's no point asking why. Something just sets him off. When it had passed, when he was down to just snuffles, I said, "Come on, you lazy dude. Let's go for a walk." I helped him up onto his feet and held his arm tightly. We staggered along the graveled path for perhaps fifty steps, remembering that we had to go back fifty steps to his chair.

As we turned, he said, "Summun died, Sissy."

"Someone died?" I translated, "Who?"

Joshua shrugged and again looked ashamed. Then, "Summun I like."

"Hey, you two, what're you doing out here in the cold?" called a familiar and adored voice.

"Daniel!" I called back, trying to keep a lid on my joy. He was standing next to Joshua's empty chair, relaxed and elegant in brown slacks, an open-necked shirt and a Broncos starter jacket.

"Present!" he said, raising his hand. "Here, let me bring Josh's ride over to him. He'll be running the 100-yard dash pretty soon." Joshua's smile was worth a hundred bad days.

"Hey Mr. Co'dewel! You get in my chair and drive over here!"

Daniel laughed and did just that. "Here you go, A.J. Foyt." He climbed out and formally presented the chair to Joshua. "Take your sister for a spin, why don't you?" I laughed and sat on Joshua's lap. He fumbled one arm around my waist and pushed the joystick forward. Daniel trotted alongside to keep up. Joshua was laughing so hard I had to put my arms around his neck and kiss him.

We arrived back at the solarium breathless and ruddy from the cold. Joshua's good eye was shining, and his laughter put a smile on his nurse Shiela's face, as she helped him out of his coat and gave us all hugs. Shiela is Josh and my oldest and dearest friend. It was Shiela I was supposed to meet downtown the day our parents were killed. While I was getting wasted on the streets, she was becoming a nurse, and now I was happy she was one of Joshua's nurses.

"You tell C'are who died, Sheeya!" Joshua demanded.

"What? I ... I don't know, Joshua. No one ..." But I could tell she was lying.

"She died!" Joshua interrupted. He was yelling now. He banged his fist on the arm of his chair. "I like her!" His anger was about to explode.

I gave Shiela a look that said, "*WTF?*", but she said, "They're having ice cream in the dining hall," unwinding his scarf.

"'Nilla an chocolate swirl?" he asked, mollified. "Can Sissy and Mr. Co'dewel come?"

Shiela smiled, nodded, and pushed him toward the door. Daniel looked at me, then hooked an arm around my neck. "Chocolate swirl for me. What about you?" and Daniel and I followed Joshua down the hall.

As we went along, I asked, "The place seems unsettled today. Is this the thing you had to take care of the other night? Or what?"

Daniel nodded. "Yes, one of our staff had an accident, and it's upset everyone. But things will settle down soon." He kissed my ear, causing my legs to wobble. "Tonight?" he whispered.

"Mmm," I smiled. "a Prosecco-and-you swirl, please." But I wondered: *Who died?*

Daniel brought a pile of Indian food to go with the Prosecco. Afterwards we adjourned to the big claw-footed tub where we sank gratefully into the lilac-scented bubbles. I lay back between his legs and into his arms, my head on his shoulder.

"Who died?" I asked lazily.

He kissed the back of my neck. "No one you know. One of the doctors."

Huh. I thought. But I was distracted. "You seem glad to see me," and wriggled my backside against him.

"Mmm," he said into my hair. Heaven.

I didn't tell Daniel about my difficulties with Detective Marshall. The subject just didn't come up, so to speak. After our pleasant interlude in the bath, we slept, and after another pleasant interlude in the morning, Daniel left.

"Breakfast?" I asked.

"No thanks, my love. I'm off to Steamboat Springs to put out another fire, this one at the Elkhorn. There's a family threatening a negligence lawsuit. The mother fell down the basement stairs after she insisted on going home." The Elkhorn was another of his consortium's nursing homes. Steamboat is about three and a half hours from Denver, assuming no blizzards get in the way. Daniel was looking out my window at the sky to the northwest. "Looks pretty clear at the moment," he mused, "but I heard a front is coming in. I'd better get going." He rinsed his coffee cup and gave me a swift kiss. "I'll be back as soon as I can, OK?" I nodded. He smiled as he pulled the door closed after him. I went over to the window and watched him stride toward his car, his black coat flapping like a raven's wings in the cold wind. Bradshaw sat down on my right foot, ready to be comforted.

The Littleton police station is in a low-slung red brick complex a few blocks north of quaint downtown Littleton: six or so blocks of mostly pretty shops and good restaurants, with the Brutalist buildings of Arapahoe Community College squatting in its playing fields to the south. My light rail train from Colfax Avenue deposited me at the downtown Littleton stop, so I window-shopped the few blocks along Prince Street and arrived at the police complex ten minutes early. All the same, Marshall was waiting for me out front, cigar between teeth, wearing a shapeless, cheap navy suit that made him look like a scarecrow. His skin looked worn and dusty, like he hadn't been sleeping well.

"Come with me," he said without any greeting. I followed him down several corridors to an off white, off-the-shelf office. "Sit," he said, pulling a cast aluminum chair next to his own desk chair and adjusting the screen of his computer so we could both look at it.

I wondered about the special treatment. I wondered why I wasn't a suspect. "No interrogation room? No thumbscrews?"

"No, we keep the thumbscrews out back. I need you for something more important. Also, I doubt you could've murdered her with that monster camera. And why would you have given us these handy pictures? Finally."

He pulled up the first of the photos I'd taken of the train car somewhere between Union Station and the Pepsi Center. A young man stood with his bicycle at the front of the car, facing the camera. The backs of heads and shoulders in assorted headgear sprouted from the seats along both sides of the aisle. Other people sat in the seats facing me: a woman reading a book, a couple with blank looks and large suitcases who were probably coming from the airport, a sharp-faced woman staring into space and clutching a large cloth bag, a young person in a black hoodie staring at a cell phone.

"So our vic isn't here yet," said Marshall, pointing with his unlit cigar at the seat she would have been in, now occupied by somebody wearing a blanket and a pink and green pom-pom hat. He slid to the next photo. No one had left the car, but a few people had been added: a student with a backpack and earphones leaned against one of the doors and an African American man with an attaché case on his lap sat in one of the seats facing me. We slid through several more photos. And there she was. Though her back was to me, you could make out her red coat below her crisp silk turban. She was sitting upright; the strap of the blue-gray gym bag lined her left shoulder.

Marshall pointed. "The time stamp indicates she most likely got on at the Tenth and Osage station."

I nodded. "Yeah. I already figured that out with the timetable."

Marshall gave me a surprised look. "You did? Good work. That's a confirmation, then. So we need to take a real close look at who gets on and off between there and Mineral."

I nodded again, but warned him, "Keep in mind, though, that I was just snapping photos at random. It's a long ride, and I was just goofing around."

"Yeah, I know," he said. I detected disappointment in his voice, as if I'd been shirking my responsibilities. "Like here," he scrolled back and forth between two later photos, "you've got almost ten minutes and two stops between these two." He seemed annoyed and stuck his cigar between his teeth. I decided to ignore it.

"Here," he said, handing me the mouse, its prehistoric cable getting caught on the corner of the screen. "You scroll; I'll write."

"They have wireless mice these days," I said, untangling it.

"Yeah, yeah. Not in the budget."

For the next half hour we worked together, one image at a time. He drew a schematic of the car with the seats numbered, then he added and crossed out people from the car, people with names like "5a kid with scooter" "RTD guard aisle between doors" and "12w woman with hardware store bag."

By the end, only the African American guy with the attaché case, the bicycle guy and the kid in the hoodie were in the car from when the victim got on until the end of the line. And me, of course. But toward the end of the series, sometime during the long gap between the Evans Avenue and Oxford Street stations, our victim's head went from upright to leaning against the window.

CHAPTER 5

"Maybe that's when she was killed," I said.

Marshall grunted. "Maybe. Or maybe she fell asleep. No way to tell for sure. Let's see if any of these folks show up on the platform later."

He fed the Sony's card with my platform shots into the slot, and we looked through them. Sure enough, there was the guy with the attaché case, checking his watch, the guy with the bicycle, and the kid in the hoodie still looking at his phone.

Marshall sighed, rubbed his hands over his face, and lit his cigar. I decided against mentioning the NO SMOKING sign stuck to his one and only window. "So now, all we gotta do is find these three unsubs," he groaned. I raised my eyebrows. "'Unknown subjects'. We have the interviews etcetera with all the passengers on the platform — we won't have too much trouble locating them. And when it turns out they had nothin' to do with it, we start again."

I thought about that. "Hey!" I said, suddenly realizing, "You do know who the victim is, though, don't you?"

"Oh, sure," he sighed. "But I can't tell *you* before we can notify the family etcetera ..." he waved the cigar vaguely toward the window. "We're having trouble finding them, but we know where she worked and what she did. We've talked with her colleagues. Not a popular gal, apparently."

He paused, his cigar forgotten between thumb and finger in his right hand. "You gotta give me those original photos, Clare. I'm not kidding."

I made a face. "Why do you even need my photos? Don't you have the CCTV footage from RTD? And you had a police photographer there — I saw him, tall skinny guy with a man-bun."

"Sheldon Davis, Yeah. But the CCTV wasn't working, of course. Seems like it hardly ever is."

"OK. But isn't Davis any good?"

"He's terrific. But he didn't come till later. You were right there in the train car at eye level all the way from Union Station. We might need your photos if we catch the perp and it goes to court. If we use the photos you sent me, which you've processed, the defense will be all over them like a cheap suit, screaming about chain of custody."

"Speaking of which," I said, looking pointedly at his cheap suit.

He yanked down the jacket where it had ridden up around his shoulders. "Yeah, yeah. No point wasting a good suit on tracking down miserable pieces o' shit perps. I have a good one for court." He must have just come from court at the crime scene, I thought, remembering his good suit, Rolex and English shoes.

"TV detectives are always dressed to the nines," I observed.

"TV detectives make in a week what I make in two years. Also, nobody vomits on 'em."

"True," I said, smiling. I was starting to like the guy in spite of myself.

"But back to the damn SD card. I still need the untampered-with original. How much do you like subpoenas?"

"OK, here's the thing, Marshall. The original card has a bunch of photos I took for commercial purposes, in other words, they're my living, and some of them are already sold. I can't lose control of them and then just hope they don't show up in *Skinny Tires* magazine. The photos you have, of the train car and the murder scene, are a perfect copy of the originals ..."

"Don't you have them watermarked with your copyright?"

"Of course! But there's software out there that will remove the watermark. The point is, you have exact copies of the originals. Can't you just use those? If this goes to court, I'll provide the original SD card for you to use as evidence." I gave him my best winsome smile.

"Won't work," he shook his head and ignored my winsome smile. "The chain of custody is tainted."

"Well, in that case, what are we talking about? I can't rewind the tape and somehow not have kept the card. If the photos are already tainted evidence, why the hell are you making such a fuss?"

"Because I don't want to arrest you," he said, surprising me, "for withholding evidence in a murder investigation. You gotta give me that card, Clare." He was serious, very serious. The wise guy was gone, and in his place was a guy who didn't want to arrest me.

I sighed. "OK, OK. You can have it. But at the moment my Uber driver has it."

Marshall's eyebrows shot up. "*WHAT*?"

I shrugged. "I'll get it from him as soon as I can. Tomorrow maybe. I sent it to him so it wouldn't be stolen. My apartment was burgled a few days ago."

Marshall looked stunned. "You've been burgled? Why didn't you report it?"

"I did. But they didn't take anything that can't be replaced. Just my cameras and iMac."

"Huh. Do you think they were after your photos?"

I shook my head. "Nope. They busted the iMac before they stole it. But I always back up everything, so I still have every damn photo I ever took. The rest was insured. Nobody knows about Mohammed. You already have the Sony's card that I gave you at the scene, and all the earlier car photos are on this card here."

Marshall shook his head in disapproval and rubbed his face so hard his features stretched like a comic strip on Silly Putty. "I wish you'd told me this before. You could be in danger."

"I doubt it." Why was everyone so worried? I'd lived rough on the streets, and I was still here.

"OK," but he didn't look happy. "I want you to see Sheldon's official crime scene photos and yours side by side."

"OK." What was this?

He pulled an envelope-style file folder out of his briefcase, spread Sheldon's eight by tens on the table, and we sorted them in chronological order. Then he pulled up my photos of the murder scene on his computer, and we compared them with the Sheldon's. Like mine, his were watermarked, © *2019 Sheldon Davis*, in the lower right-hand corner. There were a lot more of his, and they were good. Very good. Every detail stood out in the sharpest of sharp focus, even the particles of dirt on the floor. In one, the name on the gym bag was partially visible in a fold of the nylon: "...th Street Pilates."

Of course, he hadn't been taking photos for his own amusement or adjusting the settings for effect. The only effect he was trying for was detail and accuracy. "He must have been using a lens flash, right?" I mused.

"How the hell do I know?" Marshall grumbled.

"Didn't you watch?"

"Nope." he leaned back in his chair and scratched his head. "I was talking to you, remember?" I did. Marshall sat upright again and pulled one of Sheldon's prints out of the line. "See that mark there on the floor, almost under the seat?"

I squinted. "No."

"Here." Marshall tapped the print with his big index finger. He wore no jewelry except the battered Rolex.

I held the photo up to the light from the window. I could barely make out an oval smudge in the dust on the floor tiles, half under the aisle seat. "OK, yeah," I said. "What is it?"

"Footprint," said Marshall happily. "Just the toe of a left shoe."

I looked at him in wonder. "So? And how do you know?"

He shrugged. "Been doing this a long time. You get to recognize these things. Anyways, it's a fairly pointed toe of a left shoe, the pointed toe suggesting a dress shoe. The way it's positioned — see how it's turned toward where the vic was sitting?" I didn't, but nodded anyway, "That suggests that it could have been someone leaning over the aisle seat while he shoved a knife into the person in the window seat."

I stared at him with my mouth open.

Marshall laughed at me. "I love doing that. My Sherlock act."

"Impressive," I said. "Fingerprints?" He shook his head. "So you probably can also tell that he wore glasses and had red hair and a cold, right?"

Marshall laughed again. "Not quite. But here's the thing. This," he tapped the photo again, "is why we need *these* kinds of photos, and not *your* kind. Get it?" I nodded. "Can you take these kinds of photos?"

I bristled. "Of course! Just because I *didn't* doesn't mean I *can't*." I paused, wondering if I should go on.

"Do you have any training? Experience?"

"I've taken every kind of photography course you can name, including forensic and crime scene. This guy — Sheldon," I tapped a photo, "you're right, he's terrific. I'd like to talk to him. I sometimes free-lance for Denver police and the Sheriff when their guy is too busy. So I can do this if that's what I'm supposed to do."

"Good. Then I have a proposition for you," he interrupted. I waited. "I want you to come with me while I interview people about this case, and take pictures for me." I started to object, but he held up his hand to stop me. "Wait. I can't drag Sheldon around with me — he has to do stuff all over Douglas County which, as I guess you know, is about the size of Bahrain. Littleton doesn't have a regular photographer. We have about three free-lancers we can call, but ... well, you can see the problem. *I* can't take the pictures — I don't have the skill or the equipment, and I need to concentrate on what people are saying and how they're acting and all that cop shit. This is a big case, and I need your help — your eye, your skills, your equipment."

I was stunned. Marshall waited, smoking quietly, one long leg twisted around the other.

"Don't you have a partner?"

Marshall shook his head. "Not at the moment. I, uh, prefer to work with women. Always have. With guys you get all that testosterone etcetera getting in the way. But there aren't many women detectives. My last partner, Cody James, got herself hired by Denver a month ago, and they haven't assigned anyone to me yet. So ..." he shrugged, "I'm not asking you to partner — you can't, you're not a cop. But I can hire you as a photographer. You have the skills, training, experience, etcetera." He waved his cigar, smoke ribbons curling up to the ceiling.

I was speechless for a minute. "Would I get paid?" I asked, finally recovering myself.

He nodded. "Eventually."

I thought about it. On the whole, I was intrigued. It was a new opportunity, a change of scene, maybe even a reason to go on living.

"OK." I said.

Marshall smiled and blew smoke at the ceiling.

CHAPTER 6

*M*om and Dad are talking in the front seat. Dad smiles over at her as he pulls up at the stop light. We're at a crossroads, the one ahead goes up the canyon to Central City and Blackhawk, to the left, to Red Rocks Park, and to the right to Golden and Boulder. We wait for the light to turn. We're first in line. We're going to go left to Red Rocks. Joshua and I want to climb up to the top and look out over the prairie to the Denver skyline. A super-sized black pickup truck is coming down the drive from Red Rocks. It's going pretty fast! Too fast! The driver doesn't seem to see us. I yell to Dad that he's not going to stop! But Dad doesn't hear me. I yell at Mom, but she doesn't hear me. I grab Joshua's arm and try to pull him away from the door. The driver isn't stopping. Joshua is too heavy. I can't move him. The driver looks familiar. He comes right for us. He's going to hit us! But Dad doesn't notice. I can't move Joshua. I have to move Joshua. Joshua won't move!*

I wake at the sound of my scream.

It's dark, and Bradshaw is licking my hand. My clock says it's 2:34. My heart is pounding, my mouth dry, my head hammering. I start to weep.

This is no good, I think, but I'm sweating and shaking and nauseous as I throw off the bedclothes and clamber out of bed. In the bathroom, I turn on the light and concentrate on looking at the solid white objects around me — sink, toilet, tub, chair, hamper. I turn on the cold tap, splash my face and pour a glass of water, then take it out to the living room to look out the window. The street and Capitol lights have been dimmed in the city's effort to walk the thin line between reducing light pollution and hiding muggers and drug dealers. But I can still see the Capitol in all its reassuring gold and granite solidity. I focus on the brick and stone buildings around mine. There is a light on in the building across the alley. A man in his pajamas is sitting in a straight-backed chair, playing the cello.

Good idea, I think, and now that my heart rate has decreased, I switch on my iMac and start to look through this afternoon's photos of the Convention Center. No, yesterday afternoon's. The familiar task of editing and culling comforts me, and I gradually stop shaking. Bradshaw sighs and lies down on my left foot. He is soft and warm.

I wasn't in the car when it happened. I was at home talking on the phone with my friend, Shiela, making plans for shopping that afternoon and a trip to Paris on the Platte that evening. I was 14, and sulky at the thought of a *family outing* to climb a bunch of rocks without Shiela or my girlfriends to giggle with and no boys to check out. It was OK for Joshua! He was growing so fast his pants were always *too hilariously short*! His voice was an uncertain yodel, and he was *just a child, really,* even though my friends thought he was cute. I thought he was a geek. And Mom and Dad were so ... so *last millennium.* I wanted a black RAZR flip phone like Shiela's! But *no*! They got me a crappy beeper. So *embarrassing!*

I had figured that Mom and Dad and Joshua would be home in time to give me a ride downtown where I would meet Shiela and my friends, and we'd go to the Paris. When they didn't show, I waited around for a while, and then I called Shiela (on her coveted *RAZR!*) to see if she'd be able to meet me at the light rail. But just then the doorbell rang, and when I looked out, there were two Denver cops on the doorstep. I opened the door, and my world crashed around me like three priceless porcelain vases in an earthquake.

No more giggling with girlfriends. No more laughing at Joshua's high-water pants. No more Paris on the Platte. No more begging my parents for a phone. And not much more school, either. I skipped more days than I went, rode the bus downtown and wandered around. Drank vodka when I could get it; discovered what boys *really* wanted; smoked pot or took XTC when I could trade for it. Then on one of my rare days in school, I threw a book at a teacher and a chair at the wall and just started screaming, unable to stop. It was Shiela who grabbed me and held me tight.

And that was that. My Gramma, Dad's mother, had come to take care of me and get everything sorted out. She figured out how to sell the house and set up a trust fund for me and Joshua with the house money and the insurance money and the money Mom and Dad had left, and then a bunch more money from her and my other grandparents and Medicaid and Social Security and I don't know what all else. She found a good counselor for me, and she homeschooled me, so I wouldn't have to go back to school. I got my high school diploma at 17, and then she moved to Arizona. I'll always be grateful to her, but by the time she'd left, we'd both had enough. I visited her a few times before her death in 2011.

I'd been fascinated by photography since about the age of eight, first with my father's cameras, then with my own, gradually buying more and better equipment. I learned every kind of photography I could at a local art college that also taught me how to market and sell my work. So by age 22, I'd turned pro and was reasonably self-sufficient. But the black hole of depression that had appeared at 14 still pulled me in, especially on days like today, when the combination of visiting Joshua and the recurring nightmare of the crash left me wrung out and sleepless.

I decided to think about something else, so I called Shiela, because now I was thinking there might be a connection between the two dead people I'd been hearing about, and I was concerned about Joshua's outburst yesterday.

"So you know what Joshua said yesterday?" I asked her.

"No," she said, "What?"

"Yes you do. You were right there. He said somebody died. Somebody he liked."

"Oh," she said. "What about it?"

"Well, you lied about knowing about it, for one thing. So ... Who was it?"

Shiela was silent for a minute. "I don't think I'm supposed to say. But since it's you, it was one of our doctors — Dr. Pleasant. Although we called her 'Dr. UN-pleasant.'

Anyway, she died on Wednesday under 'suspicious circumstances,' according to the police. Apparently she was just coming back from a Pilates class. Don't tell anyone I told you."

The hair on the back of my neck stood up. "Oh, yeah? How did she die?" I was trying to make my voice sound as natural as possible.

"Well, it sounds like she was murdered. But the cops weren't saying. I think they were trying to see if anyone here acted suspicious, so they weren't giving much away. Anyway, they were asking about if she had any enemies or whatever. And of course she had enemies. Plenty. She's a tyrant. *Was* a tyrant. Nobody is going to be sad she's gone. Except her family, maybe. If they haven't disowned her."

"Did the cops say anything about the light rail?"

"Jeez! Yes! How did you know? They asked everybody if they'd taken the light rail anyplace on Wednesday. I didn't, but a couple people had. I drove down to Littleton on my lunch hour to get some curry powder at that nice spice store they have there. Parked in that big RTD lot by the Nature Center? And then I came back."

I looked out the window. The morning was getting darker, and it was starting to snow. The big flakes floated like little parachutes, but the temperature was dropping, so it might go on for a while. "So around noon? What time did you get back?"

"About one-ten. I figured I was going to get a big UN-Pleasant hiding for being 10 minutes late. When that bitch takes you down, there's nothing left but a pile of ashes. She was due in at noon for the noon-to-ten shift. She's on four tens. Was on four tens." I understood that Dr. Pleasant worked four ten-hour shifts per week. "But when I got back, she wasn't here. And never came in. So there was a Gawd-awful scramble to get all the docs rearranged to cover all the shifts, so nobody noticed I was late getting back. And the next two days, too, the day you were here."

So that was what all the hubbub was about. For some reason, maybe because I was going to be working with the police, I didn't mention that I'd been a witness, sort of, to Dr. Pleasant's murder.

"So how did Josh know she'd died?"

"Oh, by then the cops were on their second day here, and he'd already noticed she wasn't here. He's not stupid. He doesn't talk very good, but he listens just fine." I smiled. This was true. "Listen Cas, I gotta go." She'd always called me that, my initials. Clare Annette Standish. My folks had thought this hilarious. Me, not so much. "Let's get coffee next time you're here, OK?"

I considered what she'd told me. It didn't sound like her. Why would she need curry powder? I knew she ate most of her meals at the Blue House and the rest at Burger King. Why would she lie? But Marshall would have cleared her. He would have checked. And she was my best friend, after all.

As if on a direct telepathy line, my phone vibrated, and I saw Marshall's name.

"What are you doing today?" No hello, no chat about the snow.

"Sending some pictures of the Convention Center off to the Denver business liaison people."

"Christ. Aren't there enough pictures of that thing? Of the Blue Bear, etcetera?"

Few people actually said "etcetera" I mused. "Well, you'd think so, but the boys in business liaison don't, luckily for me. They're sending them to France. Special photos for a special French orthodontist convention."

"OK, well how long is that going to take?" He sounded aggrieved, like I was once again shirking my responsibilities. "I need you to come with me to chat with some special American folks."

"About an hour, I guess. Can you pick me up? I don't have a car."

"No. Get that Uber guy to drop you off at the Blue House in Greenwood Village — he'll know where it is — where our vic was an unpopular doctor. A Dr. Pleasant. We'll go from there. You can get him to bring that SD card, too. Two birds etcetera."

I considered things. "My brother's a patient at the Blue House. He was the only one who liked her."

"Huh. You're starting to sound more like a suspect," he said. I hoped he didn't mean it.

CHAPTER 7

When I got to the Blue House, Marshall was in the director's office trying to get the Assistant Director, a fiftyish woman holding middle age at bay with an asymmetrical haircut, too much makeup, and a body starved to perfection under her tight pink suit. Her name, Alison Klingman, was engraved on a plastic and brass name plate at the front of her desk. Detective Marshall was wearing the silver-gray suit I'd seen on the rail platform after the murder. He was also wearing his Rolex watch and the English leather shoes. His court uniform, I surmised. He introduced me as his "assistant." I'd brought my small Sony that looked like a point-and-shoot with its stubby 55-millimeter lens. I hoped it would be fine for what I thought Marshall wanted without being intimidating. I had it set on silent and "AUTO" to reduce any fiddling around, and I snapped a quick one of Klingman that included her name plate. She hardly noticed.

After some official-sounding blather featuring the words, "murder investigation," Marshall prompted, "I believe Dr. Pleasant had some trouble recently with some parents of a disabled kid she treated? He pretended to consult his notebook. "An Alan Demidov?"

"Where did you hear that?" asked Klingman, clearly rattled. Marshall didn't answer. "Well, if she did — and I'm not saying she did, OK? — *If* she did, that information would be confidential."

"Why?" asked Marshall in a neutral tone.

Klingman fidgeted with a pencil and rolled her chair back from her desk a few inches. "*Because!* Doctor-patient confidentiality. Perhaps you've heard of it?"

Marshall remained impassive. "But the parents weren't Dr. Pleasant's patients, were they? In fact, the kid wasn't *her* patient either. She was just standing in for another doctor. And since both Dr. Pleasant and the Demidov boy are dead, I think the point is moot."

"Who told you all that?"

"How fond of subpoenas are you, Ms. Klingman?" A favorite phrase of his, I guessed.

Silence.

"OK," Marshall scribbled something in his notebook that might have been *get a subpoena* but wasn't. "May I have a look at your shoes, Ms. Klingman?"

"What!" she squawked. "What for?"

Marshall sighed as if the answer should be obvious. "The killer wore pointed-toed shoes. I'm checking everyone's." I almost laughed but stopped myself in time. Pointed toes, yes, but a man's, if I remembered correctly.

Klingman grumbled but took off her high heels and put them on the desk. Her toenails were painted pink to match her suit. "Turn them toward my assistant," said Marshall, waving to me. I got up and took four closeups of the shoes from different angles. "OK," said Marshall when I'd finished, "You can put them back on."

Fear had replaced officiousness on Klingman's face as she slid her bare feet back into her shoes. She brushed the longer side of her hair back out of her face in an effort, I thought, to regain her self-regard.

"Right," said Marshall. "Now how about those names? I can get a subpoena, and frankly, once that can of worms is opened, there's no telling where those worms will go."

Klingman wasn't happy. But she stood and opened one of the blond lateral filing cabinets behind her desk and, after a quick search, found the correct folder. "Are you going to tell them I gave you their information?" she asked.

"Probably not," Marshall shrugged. He looked at me and pointed at the folder. I waited until she'd opened it, then stood and quickly took snaps of the pages.

"HEY!" blurted Klingman and gave me a hard look. I sat down.

"Any photos my assistant takes will be destroyed once this case is closed," Marshall said. Klingman wasn't reassured. "The names?"

Klingman sighed. "James and Elizabeth Demidov," she said, and slapped the folder closed. She rested her folded hands on top of it as if to protect it from further prying.

"Address? phone?"

"You can find those out yourself," she snapped. *She* wasn't giving away any more information, *so there!*

Marshall got up to leave. "Thank you Ms. Klingman. You've been very helpful," he lied. "Have a nice day!" I followed him out her door. We walked down a hallway and turned left.

"What was that bullshit about the shoes?" I asked.

"Wanted to scare her, etcetera. It worked."

"Could you have gotten a subpoena?"

"Not a drunken gambler's chance. But she didn't know that, and she's the type who won't risk making a mistake."

I nodded but wondered how he could tell. "And *can* you get the address and phone number?"

"Oh, sure," he said. "In fact, I'll bet it's right there in that camera of yours."

I scrolled back to the photos of the file and pressed the enlarge button a few times. "Yup," I said, handing him the camera. "You knew she would stonewall you on that, didn't you." He nodded.

"And you had me take the photos mostly to intimidate her, right?"

"Gotta have some fun in this job," he grinned, pulled a cigar from his breast pocket, and jammed it unlit between his teeth.

I followed him until he stopped in front of a door that had an X of yellow crime scene tape blocking it. The plastic sign on the door said, "Dr. Marla Pleasant." Marshall pulled a key out of his shirt pocket, opened the door and disconnected two of the arms of the X from the jamb. "I want you to take a bunch of pictures in here," he said, holding the tape aside for me. "Sheldon Davis already took the official photos yesterday, but I want some of my own. I'll tell you what I want."

He lit the cigar and pointed to various places around the room. The desk, one of the filing cabinet drawers, a low-angle flash shot of the carpet, a dusty palm print on the windowsill, and then some general shots of the room from all angles. I realized right away that I needed to always bring along a lens flash and a lens that could get the extreme detail Marshall wanted. I hadn't been prepared today, but I had what I needed at home, so I'd figure it out tonight. The trick was going to be to have maximum flexibility with minimum fuss. I didn't want to have to change lenses while Marshall was trying to question people. I thought about what I needed while Marshall relocked the door behind him and started back down the hallway.

"OK, now I want you to take some pictures of the staff," Marshall said, walking quickly. "Just snapshots. Go for fast, not pretty. And get the name tags."

We walked all over the facility, and whenever we saw one of the staff, I'd say, "excuse me," to make them turn, and I'd snap a quick face-and-shoulders portrait. I now had about 125 snapshots — the facility, the staff, Ms. Klingman and her shoes, the file and Dr. Pleasant's office. By the time we stepped out into the snow, the evening sun was shooting long golden rays out from under gray clouds. Marshall turned up his collar and lit another cigar.

"Can you drop me off at the light rail station?" I asked.

Marshall considered. "I don't think so," he said. "I live out in Columbine."

Oh, for Crissakes, I thought. Columbine was way out of the way. I'd have to Uber home, which I'd hoped to avoid. I checked the time. Rush hour. "OK," I said. "But Bradshaw will worry."

"Who's Bradshaw?" he asked.

"My dog. He keeps a tight schedule and he'll be expecting his walk and dinner before I make it home."

"Can't have that," said Marshall, surprising me. "I can detour as far as Orchard Road, I guess." He led me to a Littleton Police cruiser, a white Ford Escape complete with light bar, parked illegally in a handicapped space. I raised my eyebrows. "I have a Porsche Cayenne at home," he said. "But I don't drive it on business. No point when I can drive one of these babies." We climbed in, pulled out of the parking lot, and he turned on the lights and siren. I clocked us at 62 mph all the way up University Boulevard, stoplights be damned. Not surprisingly he drove like a cop, silent, aggressive and sure.

"The Demidovs tomorrow?" I asked, a little breathlessly when he pulled up at Orchard Road. He nodded and held out his hand, palm up.

"I need the card with today's pictures and the one you're withholding," he said.

"I'm not *withholding* it. Mohammed didn't have it when he picked me up. But here's this one. I'll get you the other one ASAP." I handed over the one from my Sony. And he surprised me by handing me a new card, still in its cardboard hanger. "Thanks," I said.

"Yeah, yeah. I got two goldfish and a Lean Cuisine, etcetera waiting for *me*. See you tomorrow." And he sped off, lights and siren receding fast into the falling snow.

Marshall picked me up at the Oxford Avenue station the next morning at nine. It was a diamond-bright, blue-sky day, the sun sparkling off the new snow that squeaked under foot in the freeze-dried air. I had a backpack and my newly organized Sony over my shoulder, having discovered a good lens for both macro and portraits, and a lens-ring flash in the bottom of my equipment stash. I had more lenses, a remote flash, spare batteries and SD cards in my backpack. Bradshaw had been disappointed when I'd left him at home. When I'd started packing camera equipment, he figured he'd be assisting, and he'd brought me his leash and vest to be helpful.

"So how did you get into this photography thing?" asked Marshall as we sped up Oxford Avenue into darkest suburbia. No lights and sirens today, just expert speed.

I shrugged. "My dad loved cameras and had a bunch of them, all kinds — a Nikon 35 millimeter, an old Kodak press camera, a Hasselblad, a tiny Minox spy camera. He let me borrow them when I got old enough to learn how to use them. Film cameras mostly, but also an early Kodak digital. So after my parents were killed, I couldn't think of anything else to do, so I went to the Colorado College of Art and learned how to work professionally."

"Your parents were killed?"

I nodded. "In a car crash in 2005. Some guy speeding in a big pickup truck ran into them out by Red Rocks. They were both killed, and Joshua was ... well, damaged."

"You weren't with them?" I shook my head. "Did they catch the guy?" I shook my head again. "How did he happen to run into your folks?"

I shrugged. "I don't know. Drunk, maybe. I don't like thinking about it. Why do you want to know?"

I took a quick snap of his profile. He was steering with his right hand and leaning against the driver's side door, his eyes fixed on the road ahead. His not-quite-regulation hair lay on the back of his collar, and his lean profile featured a prominent nose and strong chin around a thin straight mouth. The scar on his eyebrow gave him a piratical look. He was attractive in the way some un-handsome men are. "I'll tell you some time," he said, turning onto Highlands Ranch Parkway. No ranch, no park. Just a former cattle ranch with about a million houses in a maze of cul-de-sacs.

Somehow Marshall pulled up unerringly in front of a big beige split-level with street-facing garage. We walked up to a windowless front door, and he punched the Ring button with a blunt forefinger. I tagged along. After a minute, a disembodied voice came out of the doorbell speaker.

"Identify yourself," it said. The sound quality wasn't great, but I thought it was a woman. Marshall identified us and held his badge up to the little camera above the bell button. I heard several unlocking noises and a very thin woman with perfectly white hair bundled into a butterfly clip at the back opened the door a crack, then wide enough for us to enter. We all stood crammed onto a small square of beige carpet between a short stairway going up and a longer one going down.

As soon as we were inside, I took her picture. The review screen showed that the ring flash had lit her perfectly. I smiled to myself. I have an unhealthy amount of professional pride.

"Why are you taking my photograph?" she squawked. Her voice was high-pitched and strung tight. She turned to Marshall. "You didn't tell me you were bringing a photographer!" Her left hand with a glittering sheath of diamond rings was pressed to her thin chest.

Marshall explained that I was assisting him with interviews. His voice carried a comforting authority.

"Well, can't you ask her to wait outside? I don't like having my picture taken. And we have Things here I don't want people to know we have. Valuable Things." You could hear the capital letters. She waved up the short flight of stairs towards the beige and cream living area. I could see beige furniture and carpeting, cream walls. Pathologically clean with expensive-looking gewgaws sitting on various surfaces. But nothing personal, nothing old, no books. A space to look at, not to live in.

Marshall didn't answer but followed her up the steps into this neutral territory and waited for her to sit down. She perched on the edge of a beige sofa facing two beige chairs across a white coffee table. "James will be up in a moment," she said. "He's in his snug."

I wondered what his snug looked like.

Just then, a short, rounded man with military cut silver hair appeared through the arch that I assumed led to the dining room. Marshall stood and held out his hand. "Mr. Demidov," he said. I took a quick snap of him.

"Stop that!" piped Mrs. Demidov. "Mr. Marshall, make her stop that!"

"Detective Marshall," he said. "Mr. Demidov, please have a seat." We all sat down. "I just have a few questions about Dr. Pleasant over at the Blue House."

Mrs. Demidov leaped to her feet, nearly losing her balance. Mr. Demidov steadied her by taking one of her thin hands. "Sit down, dear," he said softly and tugged gently on her hand. His voice was soft and cracked like old leather, as if from disuse. "The detective just wants to help. Dr. Pleasant was killed two days ago. It was on the news."

"Well!" said Mrs. Demidov, sitting down again. "That certainly is good news. I hope she suffered."

Marshall ignored this. "Would you please tell me about your association with Dr. Pleasant?"

Mrs. Demidov pursed her lips, smoothed her skirt and looked at her husband. I turned off the flash and held the Sony in my lap. Using the tilt-up screen and silent shutter, I took several snaps of husband and wife, side by side.

Mr. Demidov sighed and rubbed his eyes with his fingertips. "Our son, Alan, was a patient over at the Blue House. He had Brugada Syndrome, a rare disease that nearly killed him several years ago. He'd had a cardiac device implanted to regulate his heartbeat, but he still required several drugs to be administered regularly, and he had to watch his diet, exercise, electrolytes ..."

Mrs. Demidov made a distressed motion with her hands. "He needed expert care."

Marshall nodded.

"He wasn't doing awfully well, and we were very frightened, but the nursing staff and doctors at that place were very well-regarded, and we really had no complaints. Alan had been there a little over two years when it happened."

Marshall nodded encouragingly. "Take your time," he said. He had placed a tiny digital recorder on the chair seat next to his thigh. I don't think the Demidovs noticed.

"Then That Woman started interfering in his case. She was very pushy and kept trying to talk us into changing Alan's routine, his room, his food ... I don't know why, maybe she was trying to save money? Or just throwing her weight around. Anyway, we wouldn't agree to any of it. Alan was comfortable with the way things were, and we didn't think the changes would help him." Demidov paused.

Tears were running down Mrs. Demidov's thin cheeks. He took her hand. "And then one night he died. Just" he snapped his fingers, "like that. One day playing chess with one of the other patients, the next day dead." Another pause while he visibly collected himself and squared his shoulders.

"Dr. Pleasant wasn't his regular doctor, but his regular doctor, Dr. Early — she isn't there anymore — had been called away to an emergency, so Dr. Pleasant gave him his afternoon medications. The administration said he'd had 'sudden cardiac death,' caused by a malfunction of his Implantable Cardioverter-Defibrillator," Demidov did finger quotes. "We wondered why no one had picked up on the ICD malfunction, so we tried to bring a malpractice suit, but the lawyers ... well, anyway, it came to nothing. But we thought, and still think, that That Woman did something that killed our son — overdosed him, or changed his meds, or changed or added something to his food or something. But we couldn't prove it. So ...," he shrugged, and seemed to shrink into himself. Mrs. Demidov caressed the back of his hand with her thumb.

"What did the doctors say was the cause of death?" Marshall asked gently.

Demidov waved his hand impatiently. "Cardiac arrest. But it was That Woman who signed his death certificate."

"Wasn't that a conflict of interest?" asked Marshall.

"Probably. But she was the only doctor on duty that morning. We asked for a second opinion, and another doctor confirmed her diagnosis."

"Of course," whispered Mrs. Demidov. "They were all in cahoots with each other. Now, will you leave us alone?"

"Just a couple more things," said Marshall. "I need to know where you were last Wednesday between eleven a.m. and three p.m."

Mrs. Demidov shot to her feet, eyes blazing. "We were right here, of course, just like we always are! Now would you please leave!"

"Sit down, Betsy. Obviously the Detective has to ask us that." Mrs. Demidov sat down with bad grace. "As Betsy said, we were here. We don't go out much anymore. We have very few friends left. After Alan ... passed, it seemed that most of them were reluctant to spend time with us. Maybe they were afraid ... Maybe our grief was uncomfortable for them. We don't blame them. It's horrible to think about the death of your children, and maybe we reminded them how close to the razor's edge we all are. Whatever. And Betsy ... You don't go out at all now, do you dear?" She shook her head. He patted her knee. "So I do all the shopping and all that. But more and more, I'm having stuff sent to the house. So anyway, we were here. And before you ask, no, nobody else can vouch for that."

"Did you talk to anyone on the phone? Or work on your computer? Watch a movie?"

Mrs. Demidov nodded. "Yes, I talked for about half an hour with our daughter in Austin." Mr. Demidov nodded, remembering. "I think that was about one o'clock."

"Can you give me yours and your daughter's phone numbers?" Mrs. Demidov nodded and bustled out of the room, returning with a slip of paper. Marshall pocketed it and stood up, surprising me. "Thank you both. I think that's all for now. But please let me know if you think of anything else." He got a card out of his breast pocket and handed it to Mr. Demidov. "And I may have to come back and ask you some more questions."

They showed us out. Standing, they were about the same height. I wondered how it would be to live confined in such a hothouse of anger and grief. And I thought about my own vicious circle of wanting, and not wanting, to take care of Joshua.

"Well, that probably eliminates the Demidovs!" sighed Marshall when we got into the cruiser.

"Probably," I said.

"That means I'm going to have to go back to the office and dig up some phone records and death certificates, etcetera. Brugada Syndrome? What the hell is that? I'll drop you at Littleton station."

When I got home, Bradshaw was sitting in the middle of the living room with his back to me. "Hey Bradshaw!"

I greeted him. He turned and gave me a dirty look, then went back to staring at the couch. His feelings were hurt. So I went over and scooped him into my arms and gave him a good scratch, rub and tussle, after which he was far more cheerful and accepted with good humor a meatball from the bag in the fridge, a favorite snack. I felt better too, Bradshaw having lifted the Demidovs' anger and grief from my solar plexus.

I downloaded the photos I'd taken of them and went through the usual culling and cropping and correcting and sent the remainder off to Marshall. In one of them, Mrs. Demidov was attempting to incinerate the camera with her eye-beams, and Mr. Demidov was looking at her with sadness and compassion. A perfect statement, I thought, of their relationship to each other and the world.

CHAPTER 8

Daniel called just as Bradshaw and I were finishing up our macaroni and cheese. I was having mine in a toasted hamburger bun with a sliced tomato, but Bradshaw was having his with some asparagus I'd cooked for us both. Bradshaw loved asparagus.

"I'm going to have to stay up here for a few more days," Daniel told me after a few pleasantries. "In the first place, Rabbit Ears Pass was closed by that blizzard yesterday, and now another problem has come up. So I probably won't be back until Monday or Tuesday."

My heart sank. Something about the interview with the Demidovs had brought the blackness closer, I felt myself gliding toward my black hole in its hiding place just below the horizon. I needed to be with Daniel, to feel his warmth and light. He would tell me a funny story and kiss my neck, run his warm hand down my back ...

I shut down that line of thought. It would just bring the blackness closer. "Oh?" I tried to disguise my disappointment, "Can you tell me about it?"

"It's just some relatives of this woman who was a former patient here. They're raising hell because we let her go home — she insisted on going home — and then she died suddenly a couple of weeks later, so they're blaming us, threatening a lawsuit. I just need to sort it out, that's all, but it's going to take a couple days."

"Why don't I come up there? Keep you company?" I was caught up on all my assignments, and Marshall didn't seem to need me right away. And I could take some skiing photos, which were always in demand.

"No, Love, don't do that. There's another snowstorm forecast for tonight. It's not worth the chance."

"I'll rent a Snow Cat!" I laughed. Daniel laughed, too, but he didn't seem to think it was as funny as I did. "I miss you," I pouted.

"I miss you too! But I'll be home Monday or Tuesday, probably Tuesday, and we can do something then. OK?"

I was imagining the "something" we could do, but there was really nothing else to say. After we'd hung up, I wandered restlessly around the apartment with Bradshaw watching my every move.

"You're right," I said to him. "Let's go visit Joshua. Go get your leash."

Joshua loved Bradshaw, and the feeling was mutual. Bradshaw believed that *all* humans should be confined to wheelchairs so he could sit in their laps and be petted without interruption. We found Joshua in the dayroom playing chicken-foot dominoes with Shiela and another patient named Roger, a Desert Storm vet, who was blind and whose legs had been amputated above the knee. Though only in his forties, his pudgy face was lined and scarred, and his hair was pure white. He occasionally had intense bouts of PTSD. But he and Joshua were best buds. You could tell because they constantly insulted each other.

Needless to say, the game was not going according to Hoyle's rules. There was enormous hilarity when Joshua lied to Roger about where to put his domino, and Shiela was constantly having to correct Joshua's lies and guide Roger's hand to the correct place. Roger accused Joshua of "lying all over your Frankenstein face," which made everyone laugh because, of course, Roger couldn't see Joshua's face, Frankenstein or not.

In the spirit of the game, Bradshaw peered over the table and inspected the layout. Joshua boosted Bradshaw up onto the table so that all the dominoes scattered under his big feet.

"OK, OK, that's it," laughed Shiela. She slid the scrunchy off her cornrow bun, then smoothed the cornrows back and rewound them, deftly securing them with the scrunchy from her wrist. She started gathering the dominoes to put them back in their battered cardboard box. Roger reached out and patted Bradshaw on his rump, which Bradshaw didn't mind, and returned the favor by licking Roger's face. Roger started laughing and trying to hug Bradshaw, who just licked him harder. Everyone was having a really excellent time. The blackness slid back below the horizon.

I pulled up a chair between Shiela and Joshua and helped Shiela put the dominoes away.

"They wa' coss here t'day," said Joshua. Unconsciously, I translate Josua's difficult speech into normal English in my head.

"Cops here today?" I asked, surprised. "I thought they'd questioned everyone already."

Shiela nodded. "Round three," she said. "They spent a good long time on me, that's for sure."

"Not me! I was not on that train." Joshua smiled around at us, proud of his joke.

"Me neither!" giggled Roger, and Joshua gave him a friendly slap on the arm.

"What did they ask you?" I asked Shiela.

"Well, they didn't buy my story about going to Littleton on my lunch hour."

"Neither do I," I said.

Shiela rolled her whiskey-colored eyes at me. "Yeah, well, I'm sticking to it. But mostly they were interested in who had a grudge against Dr. UnPleasant and whether I knew of any 'disgruntled employees' who'd left recently. It's a long list. Nobody hangs around taking crap from her for very long. We've lost a lot of good people."

"Omar," said Joshua. Roger nodded.

"Right. I told them about Omar. And Dr. Early."

"Who's Omar?" I asked. All three of them started talking at once until I shushed them.

Shiela explained, "Omar was a doctor here. We called him 'The Doc-o-mar,' which he loved. But UnPleasant didn't like him because he was some kinda Arab — "

"Syrian," said Joshua and Roger at the same time, correcting Shiela.

"OK, Syrian, then," continued Shiela, then stopped. "Wait! How did you know?" she asked Joshua and Roger.

"He taught me how to do Cat's Cradle," said Roger. "He said it would be good for my eyeless-hand coordination."

Joshua snorted.

Roger was offended. "Wanta see?" He pulled a loop of string out of his breast pocket and with amazing speed made a Cat's Cradle. "And he tried to teach Joshua a tongue twister, but that didn't work so well because Joshua's tongue is already twisted!"

Joshua blushed. "Naw. Woodchucks and she-shells and all that," he continued in his difficult speech, "but he was nice. I like him a lot."

"He told us some stuff about Syria, and we were glad we weren't there." Roger said, agreeing. "Kuwait was bad enough, but Syria sounds like pure hell." Joshua nodded enthusiastically.

"*Anyway,*" continued Shiela. "UnPleasant watched him like a hawk until he made a mistake. I caught it, something to do with a fever over in the gaga wing."

"Old folks," clarified Joshua.

"So she wrote him up for that, and then got the relatives all riled up, calling Klingman, and Daniel and the Medical Board, and who knows who else. The upshot was he had to go. They gave him a golden handshake, but it was a horrible experience for him. He had a *terrible* time getting another job. Practically ruined his career. I think he's someplace out in Rio Blanco County now."

Rio Blanco County is way out in the northwest corner of Colorado. It's a county that is larger than Connecticut with a population about a tenth the size. It's beautiful, but it's in the far back of the Far Back of Beyond. "That's a strange story," I mused. "I wouldn't think Daniel ..."

"Oh my God! You have no idea." Agitatedly, Shiela once again reorganized her cornrows. "One time she gave a patient the wrong meds and denied it and then blamed another doc for it —"

"Doctor Kim!" said Joshua and Roger together.

Shiela looked at them, clearly shocked. "How do you know that? You're not *supposed* to know that!" Joshua and Roger, a little intimidated, I thought, just shrugged. Shiela gave them a hard look, then turned to me. "No offense, Cas, but *none* of us can understand why Daniel kept her on. Really! He just kept saying she's good at her job. I just wished she'd be good at her job in *Hell*." She clapped a hand over her mouth. "Oops. Well, that was cringeworthy."

She giggled. Then I giggled. Then Roger and Joshua giggled, and it was one of those times when something is so not funny that you can't stop giggling. Like laughing at a Bible name in church — Og, the king of something — as Shiela and I had done years ago. We laughed until we were all out of breath. Bradshaw took the opportunity for a short nap in Joshua's lap.

I was feeling much better when my phone woke me the next morning at 7:14. Beside me, Bradshaw grunted his disapproval.

"Get your skis on," growled Marshall. "We're off to interview the guy with the attaché case."

I opened one eye and peered out the window. It was just barely light, and snow was falling gently. "Where?" I asked. And after a moment for thought, "When?"

"Nine-thirty a.m., his office in the Capitol."

Well, that was doable. The Capitol was only three blocks from my apartment. I sat up and rubbed my eyes. "OK. Who is he?"

"State Representative Bernard Johnson. Represents District 39 in Littleton. He's my own representative, in fact. Coincidence."

When I got to the Capitol at 9:26, I waited under the great dome in the second-floor rotunda for Marshall while men and women in suits streamed by along the balconies on all three floors, heading to their offices from the Senate and House chambers. It reminded me of class changing time at Hogwarts Castle. I looked over the brass railing to the marble floor below, and up at the ribbed dome above. The Colorado Capitol is a gorgeous Victorian monument to precious stones and metals from the mountains surrounding the towns they're named for — Marble, Golden, Silverton, Redstone, Leadville — the sources of the state's early wealth. It's virtually impossible to photograph because of its scale. But, of course, I tried.

"Hey," said Marshall, beside me.

"Hey yourself," I said, covering my surprise. I hadn't heard him because of concentrating on light and angles and colors. "Where to?"

We climbed dished marble stairs to the second tier of balconies then down a marble hallway. Office doors were open with the usual office sounds of laughter, chatter and machinery leaking out. As we entered one on the left, a college-age girl dressed in a tweed skirt, black boots and black sweater greeted us and ushered us into Johnson's inner office.

Representative Johnson, an impressive African American man in his late thirties, stood as we entered. Well over six feet tall with a quarterback's build gone only slightly to seed, his face showed the high cheekbones and prominent nose of some Sioux or Cheyenne ancestors. He'd dressed his impressive stature in an obviously custom-tailored black suit, white shirt and red and blue striped tie. A tiny Colorado flag was pinned to his lapel. He shook each of our hands, called us each by name, smiled into our eyes, and gestured to the two Denver University armchairs on the visitor side of his desk. He was wearing the same gold watch I'd seen him consult on the train platform, and the same attaché case was open on his desk. He was wearing a Columbine High School ring, class of 2000. So he'd survived the shooting.

"What can I do for you?" he asked importantly, in a voice like aged bourbon. A practiced politician, he checked his watch and wrote something on a notepad in front of him. "I'm sorry to tell you that I'm due in a committee meeting shortly."

Marshall looked meaningfully over at me. "May I take your photograph?" I asked Johnson. This was not a man you snapped a quick one of. Substantial, self-important and very dark, he was going to require my best portrait skills.

"Of course," he boomed. "Where would you like me?"

Marshall had read him right, of course. He was flattered. *I'd better make this good.* I arranged him against a peach-colored wall with the Colorado flag on his left, then set the slightly telephoto lens with a wide aperture to highlight his skin and take some weight off him. I took about six photos using the ring flash, which lit him perfectly. I showed them to him.

"Great!" he enthused. "Would you send me copies? I'd like to use them in my next campaign."

"Of course," I said, "Just include my credit and copyright, if you would."

He nodded, puffed up his chest, flattened his stomach, and reseated himself behind his desk, smoothing his tie. Marshall looked down at his notebook, and I thought I saw a smile trying to bust through the rough cop face.

Marshall explained why we were there and asked about Johnson's train trip on the C line between Union Station and Mineral Avenue on Wednesday last between the hours of approximately eleven a.m. and two o'clock p.m.

Police jargon puts people on the defensive. I suddenly saw that this was the point. In Johnson's case, his defensiveness became self-importance.

"Well, I talked with one of your officers on the platform that day. I assume you have her notes?" His tone indicated that we were wasting his valuable time. "What more would you like to know?"

Marshall nodded but gave Johnson an unreadable look. "I have read the notes of your interview. I'm looking for whatever you can remember about the woman who was stabbed and the behavior of the other people on the train," Marshall almost scolded. "I'm looking for details here. I've got the big picture, but as a witness, you may have seen something that you forgot under the stress of the moment."

I was interested that Marshall didn't mention that Johnson was also a suspect by the simple fact of having been on the train.

Johnson nodded and looked very serious, doodled something on the notepad, and gave Marshall a hard look. "I don't know anything about the woman," he said, defensively. "Just because we're both Black doesn't mean we had tea and crumpets together."

Marshall didn't react. Johnson sighed. "I got on at the Auraria West station. I'd been talking to a poli-sci class in the King Center at Metro State College, and that is the closest stop. I take the train whenever I can because with the current mayor's refusal to improve the highway traffic flows, it's more convenient than driving. I leave my car at the RTD lot at Mineral Ave. and drive home from there, which is what I did that day. But before going home, I had another appointment that afternoon to meet some constituents in Littleton who were concerned about construction noise and pollution on C-470, so I finished up at Metro, and went on down. I might add that I had to miss a meeting here as a result." He'd added that to tell Marshall how important he was, I thought.

"As I'm sure you already know, the woman got on sometime after I did," Johnson continued, pedantically. Marshall nodded. "I'm just reminding myself, trying to get a good picture." His sense of his own importance was now in full bloom. "Anyway, I was working on some paperwork and getting through a few calls — you know how it is — so I wasn't paying much attention to the other riders. At some point there was a young White man standing with his bicycle at the end of the car, and I *think* he sat down with her for part of the ride. I did notice that he seemed very nervous, maybe even a little angry. Then there was a young person in a black hoodie ... maybe with a skateboard? Also a young woman taking pictures." He turned to me. "Was that you?" I nodded. "Then you probably know better than I do about the other people. I'm not sure why you think I have anything to add," he bristled.

"We're just trying to fill in some blanks, etcetera," Marshall said. He was also testing Johnson's story against my photos, I realized.

Johnson thought and doodled a little more. "And of course, an RTD guy came through checking tickets. I think he stopped briefly while the woman was — I assume — looking for hers. In any case, he leaned over to speak to her."

Johnson stopped again and squinted at the ceiling. "But I will tell you one odd thing. The RTD ticket guy came through twice. Once before Alameda station and again ... maybe sometime after that stop between Evans Avenue and Oxford Street where they change drivers? They usually only come through once, or sometimes not at all. RTD is shamefully under-funded, so there's only enough for random checks, but maybe someone screwed up the schedule." He spread his hands open on his desk. "I think that's all I remember."

"Can you describe any of these folks?"

"Well, the RTD guy was medium height and a little overweight, with sunglasses and a mustache, I think. The bicycle guy was ... medium — height, weight, brownish hair

— I didn't really pay attention. And the hoodie kid? No idea. Just a kid in a black hoodie. There were some others, of course — a woman with some shopping and another with a kid, a Hispanic guy in work clothes ... Obviously, I can't remember everyone."

"Obviously." Marshall lowered his pen and looked up at Johnson earnestly. "Did you happen to notice at any point in the journey whether the victim changed her posture — her seated position, I mean — in any way?"

Johnson looked up at the ceiling and closed his eyes. We waited. After a minute, he returned his eyes to Marshall and said, "You know, I think she did, but I couldn't tell you when. I was taking an important call and only looked up now and then. But it seems to me she started out sitting up fairly straight, and then later she was leaning against the window. I assumed she was taking a nap. But I would think you have photographs...," he looked over at me as if I might be holding out in an important police matter.

Marshall put his hand on my arm to stop me from speaking, then looked down at his notes. Johnson was fiddling with his pen and looking at his watch. "I'm sorry, but I'm due —."

"Just a couple more questions, and then we'll let you go. Was it the same RTD guard both times?"

"Yes, I think so," said Johnson.

Marshall was writing furiously in his little spiral notebook. I still couldn't figure out why he didn't use his phone to record. Today I didn't even see the little digital recorder.

"Can you tell me who you called?"

"Oh, yes. It was only two calls." Johnson wrote on the bottom of his note pad sheet and tore the slip off, handing it over to Marshall. Marshall looked at it, folded it in half, and stuck it in the little pocket in the back of his notebook. He also took out a card.

"If you happen to remember anything else, please give me a call," he said, standing. "We won't take any more of your time today." He stuck out his hand. "Thank you for being so cooperative. And for all your good work, here."

Johnson stood to usher us out. "Are you one of my constituents?" Marshall smiled and nodded. "Did you vote for me?"

"Nope," said Marshall, still smiling. "Maybe next time."

CHAPTER 9

As we left the building, we stood on the Capitol steps for a few minutes looking at the City and County Building. The mountains behind it were partially shrouded in an icy silver mist shot through with golden sun that lit up a crag here, a white peak there. Suddenly a ray of light shot through a hole in the clouds and lit up Red Rocks Amphitheater, looking like a red castle. Marshall lit a cigar and pulled the digital recorder out of his coat pocket.

"So you did record him," I observed. Marshall nodded. "So why don't you use your phone?"

Marshall reached into his breast pocket and pulled out — I couldn't believe my eyes — a RAZR flip phone. "Don't use it for that," he said shortly.

I didn't even know they still made those things. "But ... doesn't the police department provide you with a phone?"

Marshall nodded. "Yeah. This one. I don't use it for anything except a phone."

"But ... What about texts? And email? And directions to places?"

"I get texts on this," he opened it to show me, "and send one if I want to, but I don't want to. I pick up my email from my computer. I have maps, etcetera. This is good. It's small and does what I need it to."

"Listen," I said. "Johnson was right about that bicycle kid looking nervous or angry."

"Yeah, some other people mentioned that, too." He stopped talking and looked at the City and County Building. I sensed he had something else to say, so I waited. He seemed ... *embarrassed*, of all things.

"Would you take my picture?" he blurted. "I liked the ones you took of Johnson."

"Sure," I said, again surprised. "Let's go back in and I'll get you looking heroic on one of those balconies. The light's great in there."

Marshall smiled an amazingly sweet smile, stubbed out his half-smoked cigar and put it in his pocket. We went up to the second tier of the rotunda balconies on the side where a shaft of silvery morning light shone down from the windows in the dome. I had him lean his shoulder against a pink marble pillar with one hand on the brass banister, adjusted the aperture so as to pick up a suggestion of the many flags ranged around the open circular space. I took a couple of his left quarter profile, emphasizing his strong jaw and narrow mouth. Then a few full profiles of him looking out over the open expanse, his cigar in the fingers of his right hand, again resting on the banister. I'm not sure why, but the cigar seemed to say something about him that was important.

"Can I see?" he asked anxiously. Inside every man is a 9-year-old boy wanting to get out.

"Nope." I said. "I'll send them to you tonight once I've fixed them up. But listen, I need to tell you about my visit at the Blue House last night." He raised his eyebrows, relit his cigar, and I followed him back outside. "I talked with my brother and his friend Roger and a friend of mine who's a nurse there."

He nodded. "Go on. I know who Roger is. Who's the nurse?"

"Shiela Jackson. We grew up together." He raised his eyebrows again, but I plowed on. "They told me about two incidents between Dr. Pleasant and two other doctors. One was a Dr. Omar Something — "

Marshall nodded and puffed his cigar. The smoke mixed with the little cloud from his breath. "I know about Dr. Omar. Omar Hussein. He's way the hell out in Rio Blanco County now. And unfortunately for him, he was here in Denver at a conference the day Pleasant was killed. I'm going to have to go out there to interview him even though I didn't see him in any of your pix. Who else?"

"I don't know. Shiela said Pleasant gave someone the wrong meds, then blamed it on another doctor. That's all I know."

Marshall nodded and smoked for a minute, gazing at the homeless camp in the park across from the Capitol. "I don't know how people can live like that," he said, his mouth turned down. "OK. I'll look into it." He started down the steps. When he got to the one engraved "One Mile Above Sea Level" he stopped and walked back up.

"Almost forgot to give you this." He scrounged two fingers into his left-hand breast pocket and pulled out a slip of paper. For a second, I thought it was the slip Johnson had given him. But it wasn't. It was a check, drawn on Marshall's personal account, an address in Columbine. The amount was correct for my hourly rate. I knew because I'd filled out time sheets for my accountant to claim a pro-bono deduction. I looked at him, again astonished. "You've done a good job," he said, embarrassed. "and I notice you're going through something difficult. So I've applied to put you on the payroll, but that can take a while. So ... Well anyways, there you go."

"Thanks," I said, also embarrassed. "You really didn't need to do this." Marshall shrugged. I put the check in my pocket. "Listen, do you want to get a cup of coffee?"

"Thanks, but not today. Research." He waved as we parted at the bottom of the stairs, him to his illegally parked cruiser, me to my apartment.

As I watched him walk away, I realized I knew nothing about him, but he knew a lot about me.

CHAPTER 10

When my phone buzzed on Wednesday, I was pretty sure it would be Daniel telling me he'd been delayed again. It was another bad day preceded by another night of nightmares. I was not smiling, and the world was not smiling with me. In fact, I was stretched out on my sofa with a warm Corgi on my chest watching the Weather Channel with the sound off. Bradshaw was sending positive vibes my way, but they weren't working.

It wasn't Daniel. It was Marshall.

"Where did you say your parents were killed in that crash?" he asked without greeting.

"Near Red Rocks Park. That intersection with Colfax." Silence. "Why?"

"Well, I thought I'd look it up. That'd be Jefferson County, so not my turf, but I went over there anyways to take a look at the report, etcetera. Just curious."

"Oh," I said.

"Yeah, but here's the thing, there's no record of it in JeffCo. 2005 you said, right?"

"Right."

"And also Colfax doesn't intersect with Red Rocks Parkway. That would be Sixth Avenue. Or Alameda Parkway."

Suddenly I felt my heart beating very fast, and tears were pressing against the backs of my eyes. I couldn't speak because I couldn't breathe.

"Clare? Are you there?"

I couldn't answer. My mind was in turmoil. How could that intersection not exist? They had been going to Red Rocks. It was 14 years ago, and I was 14. I could see it clearly in my mind's eye even though I wasn't there. I could see the car, my mother's face turned toward Joshua in the back seat, the back of my father's head, the flashing left-turn signal, the big pickup speeding toward us ...

"Clare! Are you all right? Answer me!" Marshall's voice was urgent, commanding, coming out of my phone, which was now on the floor where I'd dropped it. I scrabbled around trying to reach it, disturbing Bradshaw who was looking at me with his ears and whiskers pushed forward, concerned.

"Yes, yes," I panted. "Hang on a sec." I took a deep breath and closed my eyes tightly to squeeze back the tears. "OK," I said, once I'd gotten myself and my phone in hand. "That's impossible. It has to be there, the record, I mean. The intersection ... maybe that's wrong ... but I was so sure. I've dreamed about it so many times ... They were going to Red Rocks. I didn't want to go ... wanted to hang out with my friends ... I would have been there too, if ..." I couldn't go on. The horror and shame were rising in my chest.

"Are you OK?" he asked after a bit.

"Hm? I guess so."

"I can narrow it down if you remember who informed you of the death."

"Two police officers from Denver. A man and a woman. Don't know their names."

"OK, well, I think I'll keep looking. You've got me curious."

I didn't say anything. I didn't want him to keep looking. I wanted to forget the whole thing. I knew I would never forget any of it.

"So, I also wanted to tell you that we can't find the kid in the black hoodie."

"You can't? I thought one of your ... um ... officers had talked to him. Or her."

"Her. She did. She gave a false name, address, phone number, you name it. She's completely disappeared."

"Didn't she ask for some ID?"

"Of course she did. She gave her a fake one."

I thought about the many kids in hoodies I'd seen lately. *Had* she (or he) disappeared? Or was she following me around? Or were those all different kids in hoodies? I didn't know. "Well, I'll keep an eye out for her," I sniggered.

"Not funny," scolded Marshall. "She could be our stabber."

"Yeah, sure, OK," I said. "By the way, did you get the photos of you I sent?"

"Yup. Pretty corny. I think I'll run for Sheriff. I'll win by a landslide."

I smiled. First time today. "What are you doing today?"

"Paperwork. Going through the interviews at the Blue House. But tomorrow I'm interviewing that doc she blamed for giving a patient the wrong meds. A Dr. Kim. Want to come?"

"Sure," I said. "When and where? Not too early, I hope." I was still hoping I might see Daniel tonight, and I wanted to spend as much time with him as I could.

"At the Blue House. Not till after four when he gets off."

I'd like to say the day went better after that, but the blackness returned in force after I clicked off. I finally got off the couch and got Bradshaw something to eat, but I had no appetite, and I couldn't shake the feeling of shame and bewilderment. How could I have imagined an entire crash? *I couldn't have,* I told myself. Fact: my parents were dead. Fact: Joshua was permanently damaged. Fact: the Denver Police had come to the house to inform me. But inform me of what? Had I imagined what they'd told me? I couldn't remember my grandmother talking about it at all. She'd grimly refused, grief-stricken and silent. And now, sadly, she was dead too, and I couldn't ask her about it.

But in the late afternoon, Daniel *did* arrive, blowing in like a breath of mountain snow. I'd made New Mexico Chili in the crock pot and grilled some tortillas. There was beer in the fridge and clean sheets on the bed and soon there were Daniel's warm hands on my body, calming and comforting. The black hole again dipped below the horizon as we made love. He was a lovely lover, intuitive, correctly reading my responses so that nearly every time was mind-blowing pleasure for me and, it seemed, for him, too.

I lay warm and sated in the crook of his shoulder, my hand on his belly, my leg wrapped around his, stroking his other ankle with my toe.

He kissed my hair. "Did you miss me?" he whispered. I nodded. "What did you do with yourself while I was gone? I've blabbed on and on about my week, but I don't know what you've been up to."

I told him about Marshall and the photos and the interviews with Johnson and the Demidovs. "But the strangest thing is that Marshall can't find any record of my parents' car crash."

That got his attention. He shifted to look at me. "What do you mean?"

"He's checked all the Jefferson County records for 2005 and there's no record of that crash."

Daniel craned his head to look at me, his blue eyes filled with concern. "Is that where you think it happened? In Jefferson County?"

I nodded. "Yes. Near Red Rocks Park. But he says that the intersection I described doesn't exist."

"What intersection?" he asked. I told him. He nodded. "He's right. You've got it mixed up with someplace else. Is that what you're so sad about? I'm worried that bringing all this up might trigger your ... um ... depression. I want you to be happy." He turned toward me and ran his hand from my waist to my breast, kissing my neck.

"Don't worry," I said, enjoying his touch. "It was just a shock, that's all."

He pulled me closer. "Let's explore a closer intersection," he whispered.

The next day, at four o'clock sharp, Mohammed dropped me at the Blue House. What's more, he had remembered the SD card, so I could at last hand it over to Marshall.

Marshall showed up ten minutes later. I handed him the card in its little plastic case. He didn't thank me, just dropped it into a Zip-lock evidence bag too big for it and stuffed it in his pocket.

"There are about 56 pictures of people enjoying themselves at Confluence Park on there," I warned him, "And if even *one* of them shows up on the Web, I will personally see to it that you become an *ex*-detective. I've already sold two of the bicycle shots, so don't you lose control of those, OK?"

Marshall saluted and clicked his heels. I rolled my eyes. "You wouldn't smirk if somebody stole your notebook. It's the same thing."

"OK, OK, untwist your panties. The doc is waiting for us this way," he pointed down a hallway with his cigar.

"I'm glad she's dead," said Dr. Kim when we'd settled in the canteen with tea for Marshall and 7-Up for me. Dr. Kim was, photogenically that is, the opposite of Johnson. Pale, with tired circles behind his military issue glasses, about five foot eleven and slim, he wore his straight black hair sticking haphazardly out of a bowl cut. There was no way I could take a good picture of him, so I didn't try. I already had one of him looking quizzically at my lens from my last visit here with Marshall.

But I put the camera on the table with a remote shutter release in my lap, just in case.

"I know that's a stupid thing to say," he continued. "I suppose I'm already a suspect because of what she did to me, so frankly, I don't care." He rubbed his eyes beneath the glasses, then pushed them back up his nose with a middle finger.

"You look beat," said Marshall. "Can I get you something to eat?"

What? This was certainly a different tactic than he'd used with Johnson, whom he'd tried to antagonize.

"No, I ..." Kim pushed his bangs off his forehead, leaving them sticking up in all directions. I'd never encountered anyone so lacking in vanity. "OK. I wouldn't mind a hamburger."

Marshall went up to the cafeteria counter, picked up a tray, and started loading it up. When he returned, it contained two cheeseburgers, a bucket of fries, a green salad and a slice of chocolate cake. He unloaded it in front of Kim, put the tray on the floor, and sat down.

Kim looked at the food, then at Marshall. "I doubt I can eat all this," he said flatly.

"Not a problem." said Marshall. Kim began eating, and it soon became clear that he was famished and would, in fact, finish everything.

How does Marshall know these things? I wondered.

Marshall lit a cigar. Kim looked at him, and then at the NO SMOKING sign. Marshall ignored him. "Tell me about Dr. Pleasant," he said.

Kim sighed and rubbed his eyes under his glasses. "She appointed herself head honcho about a month after she got here, then got lead physician officially after the Demidov kid died and Dr. Early left."

"Where did she come from?" asked Marshall, puffing contentedly.

"From Browning Hospital, I think. She was chief of something there and *said* she was looking for a quieter billet. She had recommendations up the wazoo. Maybe a bit *too* highly recommended."

"Trying to get rid of her?"

Kim shrugged. "Probably. Anyway, she started bossing the nurses around, bullying them, really — I mean, any good doc knows you don't treat the nurses badly. You depend on them *all the time* and if you treat them wrong, they'll get even somehow, someday."

"How?" asked Marshall.

"Oh, I don't know. Not murder, obviously. Just little things. They won't do anything to endanger a patient, but you know, mislay things, 'forget' to tell you about an appointment or a consult until you'll be late. Enough little things, and it can really screw up your day."

"So did that happen with Dr. Pleasant?"

Kim shook his head, chewing, then swallowed. "At first, yes, but then no. She was a terror on the floor. Once I saw her dock a nurse's pay when she was slow in answering a page. Another time, she wrote up a doc in the gaga wing for a minor mistake. It wasn't even clear whether it was him or her that had made the mistake. He ended up out west somewhere. She'd cut into nurses' coffee breaks, lunches, that kind of thing. Again, small stuff, but she made their lives miserable if they tried anything against her. Harassment."

Kim pulled the chocolate cake toward him. "I didn't realize how hungry I was. Thank you."

Marshall waved the cigar, dismissing it. "OK so we've got Genghis Khan on the wards. So tell me about what happened between *you* and her."

Kim stopped eating and twirled his fork. "I had a kid who'd been smashed up pretty good in a motorcycle crash. Spinal injury, both legs broken — one with a spiral fracture, the other a broken tibia — a broken arm and collar bone. He was young and mending pretty fast, so I was pulling him off the opioids. He'd been on them long enough to become addicted, but we were gradually lowering the doses so he wouldn't withdraw, and so that by the time we released him, he'd be clear. It's tricky — you have to keep the blood levels high enough to control the pain and decrease the withdrawal symptoms, but kind of step the dosage down slowly so the body doesn't notice." He looked at Marshall. "Understand? That's an over-simplification, but fairly accurate."

Marshall nodded. "Yep." he said.

"Right. So one afternoon I started coming down with the flu. You don't want to bring flu into these areas. Most of the patients are immune-compromised one way or another, and a case of the flu could bring some of them down. Kill them, I mean." Marshall nodded. "So I stayed home that day, called in, gave myself a shot of Tamiflu, checked in on all my patients remotely — The Blue House has all its records on a secure link — wrote up reports. All that. I felt like shit and eventually went to bed. Two days later I felt good enough to return to work."

Marshall nodded. "And?"

"When I got back, the kid was gaga. She'd upped his meds to such an extent that he had to stay with us for over a month longer than his insurance would pay for. *He* couldn't pay, of course, so ... it was a dead loss financially. But more importantly, it was absolute *hell* stepping him back down. And frankly, I don't think it worked. It wouldn't surprise me at all if the first thing he did when he left here was go looking for some Oxy." He pounded on the table, causing the plastic plates and cutlery to jump, his grief and fury all over his face. I snapped a couple of photos.

Marshall said nothing.

"So I got called on the carpet. It was money, after all," he sneered. "She claimed I hadn't provided adequate dosage instructions, which was bullshit. I damn near got fired, sued for malpractice, you name it. Luckily for me — but obviously not for him — the kid had no functioning parents to sue me, so ... But I'm still under a cloud around here. They don't give me anything too difficult these days," he added, sadly.

"Do you think she did that on purpose?" asked Marshall, tamping out his cigar.

"Maybe. Well ... actually, yes I do. About a week before this, I caught her dressing down a nurse in the hallway — Shiela Jackson, one of our best in the disabled wing. Pleasant had reduced the poor woman to tears in public, in full view of staff and patients. Completely unprofessional. So I called her on it, suggested strongly that she was behaving unprofessionally. She just stood there and gave me that stone cold stare of hers. So, yeah, I think it was revenge." Kim stopped to take a sip of tea. He was shaking, with fury, I think. "I did leave correct instructions, you know. I told her what dosage to give him, and the records were right there on his chart. And every doc knows how critical this is. Shiela Jackson testified on my behalf at the Board review, said everyone knew the protocol. But the Board knew that the nurses had it in for Pleasant, and Pleasant said that I hadn't provided instructions." He sighed. "Ultimately, it was my word against hers, so they didn't fire me."

"So where were you the day she was killed? We know you were off duty. What did you do?"

Kim sighed again, a tired, tired sigh, and looked at his cake. "I was home in bed. I can't provide a witness."

"No phone calls, texting, emails? Computer time? Did you stream a movie?"

Kim shook his head, then looked up and I thought he was angry. "No! Look at me! When I get a day off, I rest. I sleep. That Woman had control of the duty roster and put me on such a grueling schedule that I basically have no life other than sleeping and working. I don't blame you for being suspicious. I would be suspicious of me too!" He was almost shouting now, moving his shoulders aggressively. "I *hated* that woman! But I fucking well wasn't riding around on the light rail, and I fucking well didn't kill her!"

Marshall waited.

"Listen," said Kim, and the fight had gone out of him. "I really need to go home now. I've been on duty for 20 hours, and I need to get some sleep before I have to be back here at seven tomorrow morning. Thanks for the meal. It helps."

"Just one more question," said Marshall, "then go with my blessings. Do you know anything about the Alan Demidov case?"

Kim yawned convulsively, shaking his head. "No, not first-hand. But my own opinion is that her license should have been suspended or even revoked over that. It's clear to me that she hastened his death. Of course, he didn't have long to live in any case. He was already outside the normal survival range for that illness. But no, I don't have any first-hand knowledge, and before you ask, I don't know where Dr. Early went when she left. She was Alan's doc, and she got fed up with Pleasant when he died."

Marshall waved him off. "OK. Sleep tight," he said. "But I may need to talk with you again." Kim nodded, then hoisted himself to his feet, hands braced on the table. He sketched a wave as he left.

"Wow!" I said.

"No kiddin'" said Marshall. "I'd call that motive. Lemme see those pictures of him." I held up the camera and scrolled through the ten or so snaps. "Poor fucking do-gooders," he said. "They can't believe what shits people can be." He pulled out a new cigar but didn't light it. "I don't think he did it, but we can't ignore the lack of alibi or that level of anger."

"No," I said. "But he's not in the train pictures."

"Nope." said Marshall getting up. "One thing we learned, though."

I followed him out into the early winter dark. The sky was indigo with a smattering of stars, Orion high and clear. I looked at him and his belt. "What?" I asked.

"Well, Kim's case is a different case from the Demidov kid. The Demidov kid was Dr Early's patient, not Kim's. So that's one more thing I'll have to investigate."

Dr. Kim had said something that bothered me. "He said Pleasant came here from Browning Hospital, right? Well, Joshua was at Browning before he came here," I said.

Marshall gave me a sharp look. "You think she was there then?"

I shrugged. "Maybe. I don't know. We could ask Joshua, I guess ... I mean, 14 years ago? He has trouble remembering what happened last Wednesday."

Marshall put his cigar back in his breast pocket. "Worth a try," he said.

CHAPTER 11

Joshua was in the dining room tucking into a chicken pot pie. His smile when he saw me broke my heart. "Hey, Bro," I said, leaning down and kissing him.

"Sissy! Who's dis?" he asked, looking at Marshall.

"This is Detective Marshall with the Littleton Police," I said.

"Cool!" said Joshua and stuck out his hand. Roger was at the same table and looked up sightlessly from his supper.

"Hi, Clare!" said Roger. "Is he your boyfriend?"

"No," I laughed, "He's a detective."

"Excellent!" said Roger. "I listen to lots of detective stories. Is he here to gather us all together and tell us who done it?"

Marshall laughed. "I wish! No, I just need Joshua to tell us something if he can." Joshua looked receptive. "Joshua, can you remember if Dr. Pleasant was at Browning Hospital when you were?"

Joshua stood up suddenly, pushing his wheelchair back violently, then threw his fork across the room like a pitcher practicing his fast ball. It bounced against the far wall and clanged to the floor. "SHE'S DEAD!" he shouted. Instantly, two orderlies rushed over to the table and gently — how could they be so gentle and so forceful? — took Joshua's arms and lowered him into his chair. But Joshua wouldn't stop shouting incoherently, tears streaming down his flushed cheeks, so the orderlies pushed him in his chair out of the dining room, the doors swinging shut behind them. I could still hear Joshua's shouts, muffled by the doors.

"Interesting," said Marshall calmly.

"That went well," Roger commented. "Joshua really liked Dr. Pleasant."

"Clearly. Do you know why?"

"Nope. He never said. And I didn't ask because ... well, because of *that*. He was very touchy about her. Protective, I'd say. One time somebody said something mean about her and he screamed and rolled his chair away so fast, it fell over, and he couldn't get up. So the nurses just shut up about her after that."

"Roger," said Marshall in his sweetest voice — I was beginning to realize that Marshall read people with lightning speed and adjusted his attitude for maximum advantage — "Is Joshua totally crippled?"

"Naw," said Roger. "He can walk some."

"Thanks," said Marshall and turned to leave the room.

"I have to go check on Joshua," I said angrily as we exited the swing doors. *Why did he ask if Joshua could walk?*

"I'll wait for you outside."

"No way," I said. "I'll call Mohammed."

"*I'll wait for you outside*," Marshall repeated quietly, giving me a look that would melt glass. "You're a paid consultant, and I need to consult. Don't be long."

Joshua was calm when I found him in his room. Shiela had brought his partially eaten supper in on a tray and was sitting with him, stroking his back. She gave me a tiny shake of the head. I wasn't to bring up Dr. Pleasant, it said. I stroked Joshua's hair and kissed his cheek. "See you, Bro," I said. He nodded and attended to his food. I left him and went out to where Marshall was smoking by his cruiser.

"Why did you ask Roger that?" I hissed when I got to him.

"I'm just dotting I's and crossing T's, etcetera" he said. "You have to admit, his reaction was interesting."

I did have to admit that, but I wasn't going to admit it to him. "OK, so I'm here. Consult."

"It's not so much consulting as listening," said Marshall, climbing into the cruiser. "I need to bounce some stuff off you. You listen and correct me if I'm wrong."

"OK. Bounce away."

Marshall started the engine but didn't put it in gear. We just sat there in the parking lot adding to Global Warming. "So we've got a dead doctor on a light rail train. She gets stabbed somewhere between the Tenth and Osage and Mineral Avenue stations. A witness says she went from sitting up to possibly napping against her window sometime during the ride, possibly between Evans and Oxford Avenues. Supposition, she fell against the window after she was stabbed." I nodded.

"A young white man with a bicycle may have sat down with her for some part of the ride after the Auraria West stop and got off at Mineral station. That makes him a suspect. We have his photo and contact information, but that's still to do." I nodded.

"An RTD guard checked tickets twice, once around Alameda station, the stop after Tenth and Osage, and once, maybe, after Evans Avenue and Oxford Street where the drivers change shifts. Unusual, and coincidental with when she may have fallen against the window."

"Right." I said. "He's in one of the car pictures — you'll see him — wearing a name tag. I think it says, 'Martinez'. Can we assume that they were both the same ticket checker?"

Marshall nodded. "Yes. We interviewed Martinez — Martin Martinez his name is — at the crime scene. We asked RTD for the duty roster, and they confirm that Martinez was working that train at that time. They don't know why he checked the tickets twice, so I need to follow up. But he hasn't shown up for work since then." I looked at him. "Yeah. Strange, right? But I heard his mother was sick, so maybe that's why. But I need to find him."

"Do you think he and the Hoodie Kid are — I don't know — connected?"

He thought for a minute. "Could be. We can't find either of them, so that's suggestive. Now we know of four other people who were on the train all the way from Tenth and Osage to Mineral — you, Representative Johnson, and an unidentified kid in a hoodie and a bicycle guy," He continued. "And Johnson, the guy with the bicycle and the kid in the hoodie are all in your photos, with the correct time stamps, which corroborate all of Johnson's statements." I nodded again. "But there are gaps in the photos," he continued, "For instance, we only see the RTD guard twice —"

"Three times," I said. "There's one where he was standing in the aisle between the doors, one next to the victim when he discovered her, and one when he was on the platform behind the coroner. He's blurry, but there, in the background.

Marshall wrote a note in his little notebook. "Not the Coroner, the Medical Examiner. Coroners are elected; MEs are hired."

So what? I changed direction. "Did you record Dr. Kim?"

"Of course."

"Are you recording me?"

Marshall gave me an uninformative look. "So that's the murder scene. Now, it turns out that Dr. Pleasant was coming from a Pilates studio — we've checked that based on the bag she was carrying. And she was universally disliked by her colleagues at the Blue House."

"Putting it mildly," I said. "And maybe at Browning, the facility she came from."

"Yes, true." Marshall made a note. "She had several pretty serious enemies. Dr. Kim who she blamed for a misadministration of opioids, Dr. Hussein who she hounded out to the equivalent of Siberia, several nurses who she humiliated in public, maybe your brother ..." I squawked, but Marshall ignored me, "the Demidovs whose son she may have killed, possibly the Blue House administration because of causing some serious financial difficulties ... and who knows who else." It seemed daunting.

"There's one other thing. The bag contained, as you'd expect, yoga clothes, toiletries, etcetera, but also five thousand bucks in used fifties in three Ziplock snack bags."

I goggled. "That really is odd. So where —? Had she just come from her bank?"

"Not that we can tell."

"And who has a bunch of snack bags ... She doesn't have any kids, does she?"

"Nope. Good point. Or maybe they were from her lunch."

I shook my head. "She's a doctor. She wouldn't put her money in a bag she'd had her lunch in. Money and mustard don't mix."

Marshall shrugged. "We talked to the Pilates receptionist on duty the day of the murder, and she said that Pleasant had a personal locker at the studio — had it for years, had her own padlock on it and everything. So I'm assuming she either brought the money in the bag, or it got put in the bag while it was in her locker. But where it came from — we just don't know."

I rubbed my hands over my face. "Can you take me home now?" I asked. "I'm done for today."

"Sure," he said. "But we've got the bicycle guy tomorrow noonish. He's a bicycle courier downtown. We'll catch him during lunch." I nodded tiredly. Marshall put the cruiser in gear, and we scorched Santa Fe Drive all the way to Denver, pulling up with a screech at my apartment sidewalk. Marshall put a hand on my shoulder. "See you," he said.

I opened my door and stepped out onto the curb. "Not if I see you first."

I would have given anything if Daniel had been with me. But it was just me and Bradshaw. We enjoyed a family-sized Stouffer's Swedish Meatballs with Noodles. Then I stripped off my jeans and sweater and fell into bed in my undies. It was early, only eight o'clock, but honestly, I didn't give a shit. Bradshaw joined me, resting his soft muzzle on my chest and peering up at me through his eyebrows. I covered my eyes with my forearm and sobbed. Hard. All gone. Everyone gone. My twin — gone. My parents and grandparents — gone. Taken from me by who knows who. *And I alone am left to tell the tale.* I remembered the line from something I'd heard in a high school English class. I only remembered it because it touched something in me. I was so alone. So alone. And somehow, it was my fault.

Oh, Fuckit, I thought. The black hole began to pull on me. I fell asleep before I fell in.

CHAPTER 12

Bradshaw and I met Marshall at Alfred's hot dog cart on the 16th Street Mall at 11:30 the next day.

"Who's this?" Marshall asked, looking at Bradshaw.

"This is my assistant, Bradshaw," I said. Marshall reached down a hand and let Bradshaw sniff his palm. Bradshaw gave it more time than usual, then sat down on my right foot and smiled. "You're approved," I said.

Marshall scratched Bradshaw on the top of the head. "I had a Golden Retriever once," he said. "Robin. I miss her." I made a sympathetic noise and took the three bratwursts Alfred handed me. I gave Bradshaw the bunless one. I handed the other to Marshall. We all ate in companionable silence while people came and went at Alfred's cart. It was busy. Lunchtime.

Finally Marshall dusted off his hands and said, "Well, let's go find this guy Dylan ..." he consulted his notes "... Humboldt." We started down the Mall. The sun had returned, and with it, the lunchtime sun worshippers sitting on the benches with their faces turned skyward. With temperatures in the forties, the melted snow on the paving stones was steaming gently and sparkling streams of water were running in the gutters. I took a few photos.

We found Dylan inhaling a large multi-meat sub and a 16-ounce Coke at the Italian sandwich bar in the Dairy Block. We sat down on either side of him, and I asked his permission to take a couple of snapshots of him without his mouth full. Marshall got out his little notebook. Bradshaw lay down under my stool and fell asleep.

The kid was good looking, medium height and very lean and muscular, in cargo shorts and a tee shirt. He looked dried out, almost mummified, I suppose because of riding a bicycle full tilt eight hours a day in all weathers. Bristly light brown hair was brushed up and heavily gelled into a peak on top of his head, giving him a Smurfish look. He had white "raccoon" sunglass patches around his eyes, like skiers often have. At the rate he was eating the sandwich, he clearly was not going to give us much of his time. I supposed, in his business, time really was money.

Interested, I watched Marshall size him up, then lean back, increasing his distance from Dylan, and draping an arm over the back of his stool. *Relax — I am*, it said. Dylan's eating slowed slightly.

I should really be taking pictures of Marshall, I thought. *A series called Marshall Investigates or something.* I wondered if he were in any of my earlier photos. I'd check. But for right now, I put the camera on the counter and aimed it at Marshall, the shutter silenced, the remote release on my lap, Dylan visible to one side, slightly out of focus. The light coming through the Block's glass walls was perfect, and the whole place was beautifully lit by halogen bulbs high up in the rafters. Above us, a gigantic wooden hand was suspended from the ceiling.

Marshall pulled a cigar out of his breast pocket and held it, unlit, between his fingers while he assessed Dylan. I snapped a photo.

"So you were on that train when the woman got killed," said Marshall.

Dylan shrugged. "I guess."

"I need to know what you saw." Dylan started to protest, but Marshall held up his hand. "I know, I know, you gave your statement to the cop on the platform." Dylan nodded. "I've read that, but now I need to know more. Who else did you see on the train?"

"Her," Dylan pointed his thumb at me, "And a big black guy with a briefcase, a couple of gangsta wannabes, a lady with a bag ... Can't really remember. I was texting with my girlfriend." He took another bite of the sandwich.

"Did you see an RTD guy come through?" Dylan nodded, chewing. "Did you happen to see his name tag?" Dylan shook his head. "Did he come through once or ..."

"Yeah, right! He came through twice. After the first time, I stuck my pass in my bag, so the second time I had trouble finding it. Stupid. They usually only check once. I figured something was going on."

"So why were you on the train?" Marshall managed to make it look like he was just curious. "I mean, instead of working?"

"I wasn't working that day. I was in classes. At Metro. Engineering."

"So you got on at Auraria West?" Dylan nodded. "Were you coming home from classes?" Dylan nodded again. "I thought you lived ..." Marshall pretended to consult his notes, "over on The Highlands."

"I do."

"OK so what were you doing on a train to Mineral Avenue? That's a long way from The Highlands in the opposite direction. You could have biked to The Highlands."

"None of your business," mumbled Dylan, taking another bite of sandwich.

Marshall leaned forward into Dylan's space. I snapped another photo. "Oh, but it *is* my business. There was a dead lady on that train with a boning knife stuck in her heart. And I have a witness who says you sat down next to her for part of the ride."

Dylan chewed and swallowed. "I don't want to say," he mumbled. Then more clearly, "Yeah, I did sit next to her for a few minutes. My legs were killing me. But then she's all, 'That seat is taken, young man.' I mean really nasty, 'taken' my ass. So ... Whatever. I got up. I was pissed off though. She pissed me off so much that I missed my stop in Littleton and went all the way down to Mineral ... and then you guys held me up some more ... and I was late ..." He stopped talking suddenly, as if he'd said too much. Which he had.

Marshall pounced. "Late for what? What was in Littleton?"

Dylan took a long drink from his enormous Coke. "I don't want to say. Am I a suspect? Do I hafta to say?" Marshall didn't answer, just looked at him. Dylan sighed. "OK OK, I was supposed to be in court for a DUI. I went right over there to the Littleton Courthouse as soon as I could after you guys finished grilling everyone, but by the time I got there the judge had already issued a bench warrant and now ... ," He shrugged again, "My folks are all pissed off and my girlfriend ditched me and I don't have the money for a lawyer ... I wasn't going to fight the DUI, just plead guilty and do the community service or whatever. But now ... I'm fucked. I can't afford a fucking lawyer, and they're probably gonna throw the book at me. And then I won't be able to finish my degree. And I need to get back to work so I at least have some money." He looked fiercely at Marshall, who put a hand on his arm to stop him from leaving.

"Don't worry about the bench warrant. I'll talk to the judge. You were being questioned about a homicide, and I think that will be excuse enough." Dylan just stared at him. "Also, I know about the DUI. I just wondered if you'd lie to me."

Marshall smiled like a shark. Dylan's mouth dropped open. "Shit," he said. I snapped a photo.

"Right," said Marshall. "Now maybe you'll tell me this. Did you see anyone, anyone at all, stop next to her seat or sit down next to her, etcetera, for the rest of the ride?"

Dylan shook his head, then thought better of it. "No, I mean, just the RTD guy like asking for tickets. But I was like texting my girlfriend, you know, telling her about the way the woman was so nasty, and like I said, I missed my stop, so then I was like trying to figure out when the next train *back* was so ... I didn't really pay attention to who was doing what."

Marshall leaned back again, out of Dylan's space. "Did you see her fall asleep? Lean her head against the window?"

Dylan shook his head. He was still scared. His eyes were huge and round in their round white sockets.

"Can you remember anything else about anybody on the train?"

A minute passed and Dylan's eyes unfocused and grew distant. "I don't think so," he said.

"Did you notice a kid in a black hoodie?"

Dylan laughed. "You kiddin'? They're everywhere for Chrissake. It's hard not to run over them sometimes. So yeah, maybe. Yeah, like sitting across the aisle and a little way back? But he was facing away from me, so I didn't see him, you know, to like describe or anything."

"OK, Dylan. You've been very helpful," Marshall lied, "If you think of anything, give me a call." He handed over his card. Dylan inhaled the rest of his Coke and jumped down off his stool. He was out the door before Marshall had time to light his cigar. Bradshaw jumped up with a startled bark.

"You can't smoke that in here," said the counter girl. She had an Afro halo held back with a sunshine yellow bandana. Marshall waved at her, and we went outside.

Bradshaw trotted happily along beside me, smelling the thaw-dampened air.

"Kid's useless," said Marshall, puffing. The sunshine had brought out everyone's cabin fever and the traffic on 18th and Wazee Streets was heavy. The sidewalks were crowded with everyone who'd managed to escape a cubicle. "Let's walk," said Marshall.

We headed toward 16th Street and turned the corner onto the Mall. It was only 2:30, but the breweries and restaurants were already gearing up for the evening, anticipating cabin fever. Marshall smoked quietly as we walked along.

"We need to find that kid in the hoodie," he said as we approached California Street. I figured he'd pick up the light rail there to go back to Littleton, but I was wrong. As we crossed the tracks, he continued, "But I'm going to have to go out to Glenwood Springs to meet this Dr. Omar ... whatsisname."

"Hussein," I supplied.

"Yeah, him. He's off next Tuesday and agreed to meet me halfway in Glenwood Springs. Are you free?"

"I have an assignment this weekend, but I'm free Tuesday." He nodded and looked critically at the end of his cigar. "But wasn't Hussein at a conference when Pleasant was killed?"

Marshall puffed hard on the cigar, getting it going. I took a photo. He didn't seem to notice. "Well, I've been to a lot of conferences, and they're not real good as an alibi. They're about as secure as a cobweb. You can usually leave and come back, and nobody will know the difference. All's they do is keep a record so the attendees can show their bosses and the IRS that they were there."

I nodded. I'd been to a lot of conferences, too. "So do you think this kid, Dylan, killed her?"

"Maybe. He was pissed off at her and blamed her for missing his court date, etcetera. He's real physical and real strong. I didn't think he was too bright at first, but engineering isn't for the feeble-minded, so maybe I'm wrong. And he's the only one so far who we know got close enough to her for any length of time. So yeah. Probably him and Dr. Kim are our best suspects so far."

"But there aren't any pictures of Kim on the train," I pointed out.

"True, but you said yourself that you weren't shooting all the time."

He was right. I could've missed him. When we got to the corner of Court Street Marshall said, "Well, I'm off. My car's here." I looked where he pointed and, sure enough, there was a Littleton Police Blazer parked in a loading zone. I rolled my eyes. Marshall didn't notice.

As Bradshaw and I turned the corner onto Pennsylvania Street, I saw a kid in a black hoodie and jeans sauntering ahead of us past my building. I thought a trip to Glenwood Springs might be a good idea. But this weekend I was on my way to Aspen.

CHAPTER 13

Each year for the last four years, the Rossignol ski company had offered me an assignment to photograph their sponsored ski racers in Aspen's giant slalom races in February. This year it was the Master's Cup races, and Rossignol had offered me an assignment to shoot the women's giant slalom. The idea was that they'd use my photos in their various advertising campaigns. I'd also landed a piggyback assignment with *Colorado Alpine* magazine, for which I would photograph as many other racers as I could manage.

Aspen would be packed with not only the best ski racers in the world, but also with former Olympians, skiers' coaches and celebrity "commentators." These would be some of the most important ski races before the 2022 Winter Olympics.

So I dropped Bradshaw off with my downstairs neighbor, Marlon, for a couple of days of spoiling with lots of walks and hot dogs. I put about fifty pounds of photographic equipment into a suitcase and backpack, and Mohammed Ubered me out to DIA to catch the small plane to Aspen. On board, along with the usual tourists, were race personnel, a retired Olympic contender, journalists and fellow photographers, all working different races for different magazines, news outlets and equipment manufacturers.

As usual with these junkets, the flight was convivial and fun. In my swag bag — a nylon grocery bag that folded up into its own ski hat-shaped pocket — I found a pair of green sunglasses and neck strap and a green bandana with the race name on it that would look great on Bradshaw.

A former Olympian, Sallie Teller, sat next to me. I'd seen her ski a number of times and win the Olympic Giant Slalom on television twice. But the last few years had not been kind. She'd been a lithe, sparkly-eyed redhead, the darling of the international press because she always showed up for competitions in full makeup, thematic nail polish, shining hair and her trademark green bandana. Now the long days in the wind and sun had freeze-dried her skin, she'd gained too much weight in her backside and thighs, and the cover-girl grooming had been replaced by no makeup and her hair bunched into a take-it-or-leave-it bun. She fell asleep almost before we left the runway.

But the rest of the party was in excellent spirits. I traded seats with a tourist and went to sit with one of the skiers whom I knew from other outings.

Jamie was tall for a skier, but she had the right leg-to-torso-ratio, abundant blonde hair, and the sparkle that comes from athletic, outdoorsy good health. She also knew a little about photography, so we chatted about that and her upcoming role as one of the Forerunners, who ski the course first to make sure it's correct and safe.

"I'm not good enough for the Cup," she frankly told me with a laugh. The pure white peaks of the Continental

Divide's Fourteeners were passing below us, seemingly close enough to touch. I heard some of the tourists gasp.

"I wanted to ask you something," said Jamie about twenty minutes before landing at Aspen's airport. I looked receptive. "I think I heard that you know Daniel Coldwell?"

I was surprised. "Yes, I do. We've been together for a few years."

"Yeah, that's what I heard. Well, my grandmother is in one of his assisted living places. The one in Golden? And I just wanted to ... I don't know, maybe get your thoughts on how things are there. I mean, if you know. Or wouldn't mind my asking."

"I don't mind at all. But I don't think I can be much help. As far as I know, all Daniel's places are fine. My brother is in one, and he seems happy enough."

"It's just that ... forgive me for saying this ... but two of Gran's buddies left to go back to their own houses, which seems — I don't know. Odd? Gran is pretty upset about it. I guess one of them died recently from a fall downstairs. Does that seem unusual to you?"

I shook my head. "I don't know. I haven't seen anything like that happen at Joshua's place. But Joshua is in a special wing for people with disabilities. I don't know about the other wings, like the Oldies part."

Jamie nodded. "It's just that Gran is so upset. She seems to think maybe the fall downstairs wasn't ... um ... accidental?" She looked over at me anxiously. "You know?"

I needed to be careful here. I didn't want to say anything that would cause problems for Daniel, or God forbid, be actionable. I decided not to answer directly. "So ... why do you think your Gran's friends decided to go home? I mean, I know people sometimes don't want to stay in a nursing home or whatever, but what set them off?"

Jamie shook her head. "I don't know. But Gran said they were excited because somebody offered to fix up their houses so they could go home. I don't know the details. Gran couldn't remember exactly." She smiled. "Oh, well. Forget I asked. It's probably *just my imagination running away with me*." she sang the last seven words. She had a strong, true, contralto. I laughed, and we sang the rest of the old Temptations song until the plane landed.

But her story troubled me. It seemed to me that Daniel had described something similar happening at the Steamboat facility. A fall downstairs? I couldn't remember. And I forgot about it in the bustle to do my job.

Rossignol had booked me into a no-frills room in a no-frills motel where a lot of the other people on the flight were also staying. The women's Giant Slalom started at about 10:00 a.m., so I parked some of my stuff in my room and hustled over to the base lodge for my ID hangar and the lift to go up to Thunderbowl to stake out my "spot." I needed a place on the course where the skiers would be making a left turn around a gate so that it and their skis — and more importantly the Rossignol name — would be visible. I wanted the sun to be behind me, but I was also looking for some open shade and maybe a time display. All the other photographers were looking for all the same things.

I got everything except the time display. I side-stepped down to a position about 40 feet from a gate in the bottom third of the course where the skiers would be going hell bent for the finish. They'd be clocking over 50 mph, which meant I needed my 300 mm lens and a shutter speed of at least 12 frames per second. I waited in my spot until one of the Gate Setters skied down to double-check the gate. I focused manually on her skis, checked that the composition included her and the gate, and took a few practice shots. Next down were the Forerunners. As my friend Jamie and the others rounded the gate, I snapped a shot of each to make sure that the manufacturer's name on their skis was in sharp focus and the composition was right. A few of these came out well, and I hoped I could sell them to some magazines or the skiers. I'd give Jamie hers, of course.

Then I waited. Re-checked my battery and the camera's motor drive. Swung the camera right to left, over and over, to get my muscle memory calibrated. I could get about 14 shots per swing. Fourteen for maybe one good one. Maybe.

A Ski Patrol guy on stubby Head skis hockey-stopped next to me and stood for a minute. I knew him slightly — Brandon Something — from previous races, a guy in his early thirties with a Russell Crowe build and a mullet haircut. With his tight black ski pants, bulky red Ski Patrol parka and red Ski Patrol hat, he looked like an Anjou pear on sticks. However, he had perfect confidence in the power of his chick-magnetism. He squinted out over the course, trying, I thought, for a philosophical look. "How're you doin'?" he said. A greeting, not a question.

I nodded. Standard response.

"Snow looks good, Dude," he said.

I nodded again. "Pretty good."

"Dude, there's a party at the Lodge after. You going?"

"Maybe," I said. "I'll need to get these photos off to Rozzi before I can do anything. How long do you think it'll last?"

He shrugged. "The racers need early beddy-bye, so probably not late. You should come." He leered over at me, but his eyes were calculating. "*I'll* show you a good time."

Tempting? *NOT!* But I said carefully, "Maybe I'll see you there."

He nodded and skied off down the hill, showing off his tight turns and tighter ass, looking, no doubt, for a more willing conquest.

The pre-race traffic around my spot was heavy. Besides Brandon Something, other Ski Patrollers came by to check for hazards. Coaches, referees and other photographers sidestepped past. Diane, a photographer for *Downhill Sports,* stopped by, and we talked technicalities for a few minutes. We both greeted Ted, from Reuters, with his video camera and wind-proof microphone. He'd be shooting uphill from a spot down by the finish, getting the skiers coming in, interviewing them, and hoping for a spectacular fall for the evening's news lead.

At 10:22, I heard the buzzer sound at the top of the run and gathered myself and my camera for the Big Test. Bib Number 1 sped toward me, swooping, tucking, and flying around the gates, poles planting just past the moment of arc, shoulders perfectly perpendicular to the fall line, skiing only just this side of out-of-control.

I lifted my camera and pointed the lens at the ten feet before the gate, got my shutter finger out of my glove, adjusted for the light, and waited, keeping both eyes open, until I could see Number 1 just before she came into the frame. I pressed the shutter. The motor drive clicked, and I panned with the skier as she rounded the gate, her face contorted with concentration, one pole planted and the other pulled close to her body, knees and skis three inches apart. Her form was perfect. But at the last second, her outside ski caught an edge, and down she went, tethered skis flying out of their bindings. I heard the announcer babble something sympathetic as she reattached her skis and dejectedly drifted down to the finish. I paid no attention. I wasn't here for wipe-outs that didn't involve a tragedy. Besides, Bib Number 2 would soon be in the gate.

The buzzer buzzed, and I did it all again. And again. And again. By the twenty-ninth skier, I felt like my knees were going to telescope into my ankles, my shutter finger would fall in a frozen lump into the snow, and my head would fracture with the strain of focusing my eyes again and again on people moving at over fifty miles per hour against the brilliant whiteness.

But I was also elated. Eyes watering, heart thumping, split-faced grin ecstatic — as hyped up as if I'd skied the race myself. I repacked my backpack and skied illegally down the wide run until I pulled up in the icy area where the skiers were milling around. I took photos of as many racers as I could (skis held beside their heads so the name was visible), especially any who were displaying Rossignols. Then the bus came that would take me to the no-frills motel.

I dropped my stuff on the floor, and collapsed, exhausted, onto the bed. For a few minutes I just lay there enjoying the room's warmth and the absence of weight on my aching legs. Apparently I dozed for a bit but awoke to take off my ski boots and change into comfortable sweats.

Then I got out my MacBook Pro and downloaded the day's photos. All 486 of them.

I scrolled through them all, deleting the bad ones and depositing the ones with the Rossignol skis visible into a separate folder ready to edit. Rossignol would want these as soon as possible to send out to all the news outlets, hoping for free advertising. And if one of "their" skiers made one of the Olympic teams, or won the World Cup, the image would flood every news broadcast, magazine, newspaper, billboard, poster, and 30-second ad from Archangel to Antarctica.

Good for them and great for me.

I opened the folder and got to work.

By the time I stood up and stretched my back, I was ready for a drink, a snack, and a little partying. I'd done pretty well with the Rossignol shots and sent the best ones off. They'd already been texting me obsessively, the first text timed at 4:12 p.m. my time, ten minutes after the last race. I would go through the rest later tonight and tomorrow, looking for the salable ones.

But for now, I thought, dinner, a cocktail and some good company were needed — stat. So I headed out into the sparkling high-altitude darkness to participate in whatever was left of the party.

The Milky Way blazed overhead in a sky like black glass, along with Mars and trusty Orion. The new snow that was falling dampened all sound except the crunch of my footsteps and the occasional laugh from a passing group of après skiers.

The party had reached that stage when all the hell-raisers had gone to raise hell elsewhere and those who were left knew each other well enough to be friendly but not well enough to be hostile. Most of the competitors had gone back to their rooms to bed, some alone, some not, to prepare for tomorrow's events, the last of the races.

The exception was Alain, who was virtually guaranteed a spot on the French Olympic team, as he had been for the last three Olympic cycles. He was lounging comfortably in a corner booth, alone except for a blonde woman of about his same age — pushing 40 — and a pair of half-full brandy snifters.

Alain was a handsome six feet, slender and long-muscled, with thick blond hair that made him look like some deposed aristocrat. He waved me over to join them and somehow got the attention of one of waiters and ordered the same all around. He introduced me to the blonde. "This is Magda, Clare. She is my biographer."

I laughed, but apparently it wasn't a joke. "Really!" I recovered myself.

Magda nodded. "Yes, Alain is a great celebrity in France. The book will sell very well. Especially as he is going to include some skiing instructions in it." She had a deep sandpapery voice laced with guttural French.

"Do you need any photos of him?" I asked, cravenly. I had a lot of him from the previous year.

Alain laughed this time. "I think we have enough. Me skiing, Me drinking, Me with girls. Me skiing and drinking with girls." Smiling, he buried his aristocratic nose in the snifter, then took a large gulp.

Just then, Sallie Teller stood up across the room holding a piece of paper. A darker, less ropey version of Alain was at her side. I recognized him as one of the French coaches. Sallie now looked like her old self — flawless makeup and glossy hair with the trademark green bandana knotted jauntily at her neck, the tails floating at one shoulder.

"We have the semi-finalists for the French men's slalom and giant slalom teams. We'll have the women's, downhill and other teams tomorrow evening."

I looked over at Alain. "They announced the U.S. men's team earlier. Your team looks promising, I think," he said, complacently.

Sallie rattled off several names, but Alain's wasn't one of them.

Alain and Magda exchanged a look that said, 'fix this.' Alain got up and walked without haste over to where Sallie and the coach were standing, surrounded by three or four racers.

Magda explained, "We need him to ski this Olympics to ... um ... enlarge the sales for the book. It is a ... how do you say? A *condition* of the book contract." She looked mildly embarrassed. "There will be a great deal of free advertising if he is in the Olympics."

I nodded, understanding. After all, I'd just taken over sixty photos of people on Rossignol skis with the same purpose. "Is the book finished?"

She shook her head. "Well, almost. We wait for the last chapter, you see."

"Oh, of course," I said. The last chapter would have to include whatever triumphs Alain could pull off in the 2022 Olympics.

Alain returned and slid gracefully into the booth. Unworried by being passed over, he was a man whose success was already legend. "Well, that is settled, then. They have me in first alternate position. So it is certain I will ski in the Slalom and GS. No question. Someone will always get injured or drop out ..." He waved a lean hand at the room. "So now let's drink up and go to bed."

After they'd left, I went over and rehashed the day with Diane, the Reuters guy and the Head Skis photographer.

"Did I see one of your pix in the *Post* of that murder on the train a couple of weeks ago?" asked Diane. I nodded. "So that doctor who was murdered, you know she allegedly disabled one of the cross-country team, right?"

My breath caught in my throat. "What? Who?"

"Can't remember his name," said Diane. "Do you remember, Ted?"

"Martin something," said Ted, the Reuters guy, shrugging.

"That's right! Apparently this Martin, I guess was training up Winter Park, fell down a double black and broke his leg pretty bad. St. Anthony's Flight for Life brought him in, but this doctor —"

"— Pleasant," I supplied.

"— messed up somehow and he had to quit the team. I don't know what he's doing now. This was a while ago."

"Wow," I said, unnecessarily. "Was his last name Martinez?"

Ted, a veteran, who'd shot wars and disasters and a photo essay about Engineers Without Borders, was sliding gently into retirement doing candy-ass assignments like this one. Balding, with a bowling ball stomach, he had a pudgy face full of dark humor. He shrugged again, fingering an empty shot glass with a mangled wedge of lime in it. "Just gossip. Maybe I heard it from one of the guys at the *Post*." He snapped his fingers. "Not Martinez! Bradley, I think."

I was disappointed, but here was yet more evidence of Pleasant's murder-ability. We had a few more snacks, but we were all tired, so after one more drink we left. I texted the story about Martin Somebody to Marshall, then after two more hours of editing photos, I fell into my no-frills bed and dreamed of Alain gliding down the Olympic GS slope in 2022.

But in my dream, at the end of the run he somehow became my father, crashing into a huge black pickup driven by Martin Martinez.

My phone vibrated in my pocket as I was unlocking my apartment door on Sunday evening after picking up Bradshaw from Marlon. The weekend's shooting had gone well, and I'd sent off a photo to both Rozzi and *Skiing High Country* of one of the U.S. team finalists screaming past the next-to-last gate on Rossignol skis. The photo was one of the best I'd ever made, brilliantly colorful, red, white, blue and black, perfectly focused, showing the intense effort of the skier as she fought centrifugal force around the gate. Rozzi and *High Country* would fight for it. And Alain had said he'd include one of my photos of him in his biography. I was feeling pretty smug.

I pushed and pulled myself and Bradshaw inside and juggled the phone out of my pocket to answer it.

"You home yet?" asked Marshall.

"Yes, I just —"

"OK, well, I finally got hold of the Sheriff's file and the hospital report etcetera on your parents' crash." A pause. "Do you want to see them?"

"You did?" I asked, more than surprised. I didn't know he'd been looking for them.

"Yeah," I heard the clink of his Zippo and a breath. "The records officer at Jefferson County got them for me from Denver."

I was totally discombobulated. 'Hang on,' I said, dropping my travel bag on the floor and unhooking Bradshaw's leash. "I just walked in. Can you ... I mean ..." I was looking around for a place to put my backpack and camera bags so I could take my coat off. Also, I needed to pee. Also I was hyperventilating.

"Let me call you back," I said, "when I catch my breath. I just —"

"OK," he said, and clicked off.

CHAPTER 14

As I bustled around the apartment, Bradshaw sat in the middle of the living room watching me closely. The bustling was mostly nerves. I was having trouble catching my breath, I needed the bathroom, a glass of water, a big tumbler full of Chateau de Box, and to call Marshall back ... I was having trouble deciding what to do first.

When I finally got it all straightened out and called him back, he asked, "So do you want to hear this or not?"

"I guess," I said. *Did I? It was mostly going to depress me and make me cry. I had loved my family, and I was still grieving after all this time. Would knowing what really happened to them help me or hurt me?* Suddenly I heard my mother's voice, as clearly as if she were in the room. *The truth will set you free.* I knew she was right. But I didn't want Marshall with me when I read it. I didn't want him to see me cry.

"Would you rather read it yourself? I have a copy of the files." he said, reading my mind.

But the other thing was that I didn't want to be alone. I knew I was headed for a deep black hole, and someone was going to have to hold on to me so I wouldn't slide in and hit bottom. I needed Daniel.

"Can you hold on a sec?" I asked Marshall. He grunted. I put him on hold and punched Daniel's number.

"Clare!" he said when he answered. He sounded happy to hear from me. "How was Aspen?"

"Great. But listen, Daniel, I need you to come over as soon as you can. Now if possible. Marshall's found the police files on my folks' crash. I'm ... I'm scared ... Can you come?"

"Really? That's ... amazing! Where did he find them?"

"I don't know, Daniel, Denver, I think. But I need you to ... come hold my hand. Can you? I really —"

"Denver, huh? That's a surprise. I can be there in, say, an hour? Is that OK?"

I sighed, tears starting from relief, or fear, or ... I began to feel sick. *I will not throw up,* I thought. "Yes," I whispered.

"OK — but don't start without me!"

"I won't," I said, and clicked back to Marshall.

Getting control of my voice and stomach with an effort, I said, "Still there?"

He grunted.

"Listen, can you send them to my drop box? I'll give you my —"

"What the hell's a drop box? No, I'll just bring them by. I need to come that way anyways. There's something I need to check with DPD."

"They're in hard copy?" I asked, astonished. That must have cost a fortune.

"Yeah. Sure. Twenty minutes?"

As good as his word, Daniel arrived in just under an hour. The two fat folders containing all the reports and gory details of my parents' deaths and Joshua's destroyed life were lying on the dining table. I'd spent the last forty minutes wearing out the oak flooring from the table to the window and back. Each time I'd stop at the table and look at the folders. I wanted to open them immediately. I never wanted to open them.

Daniel brought hot Thai soup and some saki that he warmed in the microwave. He sat me on the couch, pulled me close, and opened the first file, the one about the crash.

As he read it to me, I sobbed into his shoulder. He stroked my back. And when he'd finished, he tucked me into bed, climbed in next to me, and held me close. Bradshaw joined us on my other side, so I was in a cuddle sandwich. Things began to get a little bit better.

"So there's nothing in there about the driver of the truck?" I asked at last. "No description or anything?"

"Never identified, I guess."

"Does it say who referred Joshua to the Blue House?"

Daniel opened the second folder and leafed through the pages with his free hand. "Well, now that's interesting ..." he mumbled.

"What is?"

"It looks like it was Dr. Pleasant. Small world."

"Well, what did you think?" asked Marshall, when I called him the next day. After Daniel left, and we'd had our coffee, toast and sausages, Bradshaw and I had taken a cold, windy walk around the neighborhood. The sky was Wedgewood blue with white puffy clouds scudding through, the sun too bright. I finished editing and sending off my Master's Cup photos. The terrible black hole I'd feared had kept its distance, and though I had a headache from crying, or possibly too much saki, on the whole, I felt relieved — and something else, something burning in my gut.

"I think," I said, "That I owe Dr. Pleasant a thank-you note."

Marshall chuckled. "I wondered if you'd catch that."

"Coincidence?"

Marshall groaned, and I heard him light a cigar. He was walking someplace. The cold wind kept blowing into his phone, and I could hear street noises. "Maybe," he said, but he didn't sound convinced. "Do you think you could look into that? It's Denver's case, and I don't want to step on their toes. But you could go over to St. Anthony's and the Browning nursing home where he was at first and ask around to see if anyone remembers Pleasant or your brother. Maybe you could find out how both she and Joshua were connected and got to the Blue House."

"I'll think about it," I said carefully. "I barely got through those reports without diving out my window, and I don't know if I can handle talking to anyone who ..." I struggled to steady my voice, "who ... um ... actually remembers them."

He paused to let me get control, then continued. "I visited with Denver PD's cold case unit yesterday to see if they had any evidence left from your folks' crash. They said this morning that they had dug out a hunk of that burned pickup truck with the VIN number on it. Apparently the perp missed it when they scraped the rest of them off. Easy to do. They stamp the VIN on a lot of hard-to see places." Marshall exhaled sharply, then coughed. "They might be able to recover the number with acid now. They either didn't or couldn't back then. Long-shot, though."

Wow! "That's great! If they can recover the number, then ... What?"

"Then they can try to trace the truck's owner. From the witness descriptions, we think the truck was probably new, so it would only have had one owner. Of course, there's no guarantee that it's the same truck that hit your folks. But what with it being burned and found on Green Mountain, which is consistent with the witness statements saying it headed west, it seems likely. Obviously that's not enough evidence to stand up in court, but it's a start. Excuse me a sec." I heard him muffle the mouthpiece and cough repeatedly. It was a rough cough, with a little gurgle in it. *He should probably quit those cigars,* I thought, listening.

"OK, sorry about that," Marshall said, returning. "And then, of course, there's that guy who came into St. Anthony's later that day."

"What guy?"

"The guy who came into St. Anthony's that afternoon. Didn't you see him in the file?"

How had I missed that? I'd been pretty upset, so maybe that's why. "No," I said, "I must have missed that part."

"Well, some guy came into the St. Anthony's emergency room at about four o'clock, several hours after the crash. He was pretty banged up, had a broken wrist, mild concussion, contusions and abrasions, etcetera. Said he'd been in a fight. So they patched him up and sent him on his way."

The line was quiet for a moment.

"And?"

"Well, his injuries are suggestive — another long shot. Of course, the nurses and docs didn't have any description of the driver at the time. They only remembered the guy the next day when they were interviewed by Denver PD."

"But didn't they have his name from his insurance or credit card or whatever?"

"No. He paid cash. Your actual folding. The name he gave them turned out to be ... well ... false. So Denver wasn't ever able to find him. It's all in the file."

"So I guess Denver didn't try very hard to find him, huh?" I felt the unmistakable stirrings of anger in my solar plexus. It felt good, which surprised me.

"Well, probably not. They have a lot more serious stuff to investigate than a guy who pays cash at a hospital."

"OK, fair point." But the anger stayed put and still felt good. "Why are you doing this? Why are you so interested in a 14-year-old hit and run case?"

Marshall inhaled sharply, then coughed. He didn't answer right away. *What's up?*

"My wife was killed by a hit and run driver three years ago."

Oh.

"The difference is, they caught, prosecuted and sentenced the guy. I can't imagine what it would be like to ... know he was still out there. Free. Going on living when ... she's dead."

The anger ballooned again in my chest, bigger and fiercer now. *Yes! They're dead and he's ... somewhere.* To distract myself, I said, "So when are we going to meet the Doc-O-mar?"

"Doctor Omar Hussein? So you'll come along?"

"You bet. I'd rather do that than sit here fuming about stuff that happened 14 years ago."

CHAPTER 15

I met Marshall in the parking lot of the Littleton Police Department on Rio Grande Avenue. It was a lovely day, with predicted highs for Glenwood Springs in the mid-forties, and I could tell Marshall was looking forward to the drive — about two and a half hours, he figured, though I thought it was more.

Bradshaw looked up at him with his slightly bulging brown eyes, and Marshall bent down to give him a scratch behind the ear. "Ready?" he asked me.

I nodded. "Looks like a great day," I said, turning my face to the early morning sun. "Do you think we'll have time for a soak in the pool?"

"Maybe," said Marshall, and, to my surprise, led the way to a black Porsche. It looked like a thoroughbred among cattle in the herd of Littleton PD Blazers. He pushed a button, and with a chirp, the car's top folded down into its trunk.

"Not a patrol car today?" I asked. Honestly, he just made me laugh sometimes.

"Nope. This baby will outrun a patrol car any old day. We'll have some fun on the passes. Does Bradshaw get car sick?"

"I guess we'll find out," I said, hoisting Bradshaw and my backpack into the tiny back seat. I knew Bradshaw wouldn't get sick. I was just yanking Marshall's chain. Bradshaw settled himself on the seat, tongue out and smiling, looking forward to the ride.

"I can't wait to get this baby onto I-70 where I can open it up and really show it off." Marshall was clearly enjoying himself. He drove sedately enough through the I-70 on-ramp, but once he'd navigated into the far-left lane, he gently pushed the needle up to eighty, keeping the tachometer in the green. He glanced over at me.

I had just taken a picture of him with my phone. I'd caught his expression of intense concentration mixed with what I could only describe as joy. "What were you thinking?" I asked, pulling on my red and yellow ski hat. The wind was getting colder as we climbed into the foothills.

"About cars," he said. "Actually about how some men abuse them. You know, racing the engine, laying down rubber, etcetera. Some of the younger cops do that. Messes up the patrol cars for everyone else. Sometimes I think that a guy who'll abuse a car will abuse a woman."

I was surprised by this bit of philosophy. "*You* drive well, though."

"Thanks. The cruisers are pretty good. They're souped up a bit, customized for police work. But this — this is my idea of a car." A white Honda CRV was ahead in the fast lane, going about 70. Marshall smoothly pulled around it, never slowing. The lane ahead looked open, so he pushed the Porsche up to 85. We were passing cars like they were going backwards. Bradshaw poked his head forward between the seats, eyes squinting, fur blowing.

"He's loving this," I said, scratching him under the chin. "It's like he's running as fast as he does in his dreams."

Marshall chuckled. He was thoroughly enjoying himself, the cold wind, the speed. "Listen, if you get too cold I can slow down to put up the roof."

"Maybe when we get to the tunnel," I said.

We'd just passed Silverthorne and were heading up the steep climb to the Eisenhower Tunnel. Some kind of enormous motor home was in front of us, Iowa plates, laboring mightily with black smoke puking out its exhaust. Marshall was looking for an opportunity to pass it quickly before getting to the tunnel, but the traffic was too heavy. "Shit. See, this is what I'm talking about. People should get their vehicles tuned for the altitude. They'll be lucky if they don't break down in the tunnel."

Once in the tunnel where we couldn't pass, we crawled along behind the motor home. Marshall pushed the button to raise the top and block out the exhaust. Suddenly it was quiet and a lot warmer. He promptly lit a cigar. "Do you mind?" he asked.

I shook my head. "No, the only thing I mind is that you're probably going to kill yourself with those things."

Marshall made a face. "You might be right. But it beats dying of lots of other things. Alzheimer's, for instance. Alcoholism. Bleeding to death in the street. At least this has an up-side." He waved the cigar. I laughed and took another snap of him smiling wolfishly, holding the cigar.

It was taking forever to get through the tunnel. "OK," he said, settling back in his seat, "Let's talk about this murder, then." I shrugged. He glanced over at me. "Come on, you probably know as much about this as anyone. Other than me, that is. Plus, I like women's perspectives on these things."

"Is that why you don't partner with men?"

"Yup. Women read people differently. My last partner was ... well ... she usually could see the *reasons* why suspects behaved the way they did. So even though I don't put much credence in motive — opportunity is a hell of a lot more important — it's definitely useful to consider *why* someone would kill someone else."

We stopped suddenly. The motorhome had stopped and was flashing its hazard lights. "Shit," said Marshall, and looked for an opening to squeeze past it on the right. Somebody let us in, and he charged around the McMansion on wheels. "See? I knew that would happen. Idiots. Good motive for murder right there."

"Absolutely," I said. "Should you call it in?"

He shook his head. "No signal in the tunnel. There's a pretty big mountain on top of us. Somebody will call it in on the other side. So what did you think of our suspects?"

"Well, it seemed to me they all had a good reason to want her dead. Except for Dylan, the bike messenger. And that state representative, Whatsisname."

Marshall nodded. "Johnson. But Dylan had the opportunity. He sat with her for a while before she was dead." Marshall was happier now that we could see the end of the tunnel and the traffic was speeding up. "So tell me about your friend, the lovely Nurse Shiela."

I looked at him in surprise. "I've known her forever. I was going to meet her downtown the day my folks were killed." Suddenly we were out of the tunnel, and Marshall let the Porsche have its head on the long downhill before Vail Pass. I watched the speedometer ease back up to 85. "She's a good friend. I can't really be objective about her." *But I do know that the story she told about going to Littleton to buy curry powder was bullshit. But I'm not about to tell him that.*

"Look!" said Marshall suddenly, pointing over to our right. An eighteen-wheeler was belching smoke and flames from its brakes. The stink of burning brakes filled the air, and a Cadillac SUV darted in front of us to avoid the slowdown behind the truck. Marshall cursed and slowed the Porsche to let the SUV in ahead of him, then pulled up tightly behind it, willing it to move back into the middle lane. It did. I undid my seatbelt and knelt backwards on my seat, looking back at the truck, which was pulling into one of the heavily graveled run-away truck ramps.

"Jesus! Sit down, Clare! That's how your mother got killed, for Chrissake!"

"*Oh!*" I remembered that from the file. I was shaken by the vision of my mother flying out of the car and landing in the street. I slid back down into my seat and tamely buckled up.

As we approached the top of Vail Pass, a light snow greeted us. Gradually the seemingly endless evergreen forest began to be dotted with houses, and as we got closer to Vail, the houses got larger and closer together. Vail itself, a cluster of restaurants, condos and hotels masquerading as Swiss chalets, rose against the backdrop of the dark conifers and wide white ski runs. I'd once photographed Vail at night during a festival. It was more photogenic than Aspen. I'd taken the following day to ski, and I'd been impressed by the wide perfectly groomed slopes, like a lovely debutante wearing a sparkling white gown.

After passing Edwards, we finally reached the new, two-story highway through Glenwood Canyon. This was the last piece of the Interstate Highway system to be completed, the technical feat of squeezing four lanes into the narrow, steep canyon above the rushing Colorado River had been nearly insurmountable. The river danced and sparkled in the sunlight below the vertical rose pink canyon walls above.

When we'd pulled up in front of the ornate towers that flanked the entrance to the Hotel Colorado, I checked my watch. Yup — two and a half hours.

Dr. Omar was a rangy five-ten, with slightly graying hair, wearing a yellow cashmere V-neck sweater above a pair of loose-fitting khakis, and Nike rubber sandals on his long brown feet. He sprawled — ostentatiously relaxed — on a gold brocade sofa in the turn-of-the-century lobby, surrounded by more gold brocade sofas, dark wood, and green and gold oriental rugs. He rose to welcome us, smiling, as if this were a social call. He gestured to the sofa across from him and to a coffee table holding a coffee carafe, cream and sugar dispensers, mugs, napkins and a plate of assorted croissants. Bradshaw sniffed politely at the edge of the table, then turned his nose to Dr. Omar's knee.

Marshall and I sat on the sofa across from Omar. Marshall didn't touch the food or coffee. I helped myself to both. "May I take your picture, Dr. Hussein?" I asked once I'd filled plate and cup.

"I prefer just Omar, if you don't mind." He had an upper-class English accent.

Deciding to take that as assent, I set the camera and took several photos. Then, as I had before, I rested the camera in my lap with the tilt screen up and the remote shutter release on silent, ready to take some candids.

Marshall was digging things out of his briefcase. "I'm going to record you," he said, placing a folder and his micro recorder on the table. This was new. In the other interviews, he'd pretended to be only taking notes. He'd sized up something about Omar that made the overt recording preferable. Omar squirmed uncomfortably, but then he folded his hands in his lap and looked receptively at Marshall. His large brown eyes were a millimeter too close together over an arched nose. He looked at the folder, then nodded, agreeing reluctantly.

"We've heard from several people that you and Dr. Pleasant didn't get along."

"I loathed the woman and she detested me," said Omar unapologetically. "She made it clear as soon as she arrived that she was going to kick my Syrian ass out the door as soon as she could. From that moment on, it was a cat and mouse game with her. She spied on me, read my charts and email, interrupted consultations in the hope I'd make a mistake, questioned my patients — you name it. When she finally caught a mistake on a patient chart, she raised hell about it for weeks, called the patient's daughter, the State Board till I was well in it." He waved a hand again. "She at last convinced the daughter to file a malpractice suit — it went absolutely nowhere and cost everyone a fortune — but it was enough for the Blue House to suggest I might be happier somewhere else. So ... here I am. Somewhere else." Omar was struggling to remain composed, but his eyes were blazing with righteous anger.

"What did she have against you?" asked Marshall. "How long did this go on?"

"Oh ..." Omar again waved a hand, sweeping things away, "I was at the Blue House geriatric wing for almost seven years.

I wondered if I'd met him. Probably not – geriatric was in a different part of the Blue House from Joshua.

"I have no idea what her problem with me was, Detective Marshall. I thought it was because I am Syrian — Middle Eastern, do you see. Probably Al Qaeda, right? But she had it in for lots of people. Several of the nurses, Dr. Kim ..."

"Do you think she was just prejudiced against immigrants? You're Syrian, Dr. Kim is Korean ..."

Omar was shaking his head. "No, I don't think that was it. She drove away several nurses and another doctor, Dr. Early, none of whom were immigrants."

"How long ago was that?"

"Oh, quite soon after she arrived. They got out rather quickly. Smarter than I am, do you see."

"Do you remember any of their names?"

Omar shook his head again. "No, it was too long ago, and I've made a point of forgetting all that. The Blue House will have records of them, I rather assume."

"OK. So where were you between eleven and two on the day she died?"

Omar looked surprised. "I have already told you that. I was at a conference on geriatric medicine at the Marriott in Downtown Denver. They will have a record of the attendees, I believe."

Marshall leaned forward, elbows on knees, and looked intensely into Omar's eyes. "See, I don't think you were. I think you cut out — easy enough to do — and went someplace else." He opened the folder on the table and pulled out a sheaf of papers. "I've talked to some of your colleagues who are on this list, and they're pretty sure they didn't see you after the lunch break. Not until the cocktail party later that afternoon."

Omar shrugged and leaned back in his chair. "What of it? You can check the sign-in rosters. They'll show I was at the colloquium on pain management from one-thirty to four p.m."

"I have," said Marshall. "And you're absolutely right. But that's easy to arrange. See ..." he pulled out another sheet. "This is a xerox copy of the sign-in sheet, but it's not actually a sign-in sheet. It's a reservation list. So you checked off your name here ..." he pointed at Omar's name on the page. "And then it seems you and most of your colleagues skipped checking out."

"That's because — "

Marshall held up his hand. "I know, I know, because it would have caused a jam up at the end of the colloquium when everyone was ready to head to the bar. I get it. I've been to a fair number of these things myself. But that's beside the point. The question is, where were you between one-thirty, when you checked your name off on this form, and four o'clock when the pain management colloquium ended?"

Omar just stared at Marshall for a long moment. "I was not on the C train to Mineral Station," he said, finally.

Marshall said nothing. There was another long silence. I took a snap of them looking at each other, metaphorical hackles up.

"OK, OK, I did skip out of that colloquium. I did attend the beginning ..." Marshall looked skeptical. "I did! I stayed for, oh, perhaps twenty minutes, then left. There was nothing new in it for me. What I don't know about geriatric pain management would fit on a postage stamp."

"Then why did you sign up for it?"

Omar shrugged. "I thought maybe there might be something new. And it interests me more than any other aspect of geriatric medicine."

"Where did you go?"

Omar looked at me, then back at Marshall. "To my room."

Marshall stood up and picked up the file, seemingly preparing to leave. "Come on, Doctor. You can do better than that. Where did you *really* go? Because if you keep lying to me, I'm going to take you down to the Garfield County Sheriff's office and question you there, in one of those little cinderblock interrogation rooms with the nailed-down chairs and the one-way glass."

How the hell does he do that? I wondered during the long silence that followed. *How does he know what people are thinking? And who is lying? And what the hell does he know about me?*

"Oh, *bugger*! I went to sodding REI!" Omar blurted at last. "I wanted some new boots to wear out there in Butt Fuck, Colorado. Fishing, hunting and hiking, that's about it for hot times out there if you're not fond of horses. No good for the wife and kids — they all took off about six months after we got there. No decent restaurants, no rock concerts, no cell coverage, almost no bloody *internet* ..." Omar hid his face in his hands. He wasn't crying, but his big strong hands were shaking, and he was breathing hard. "That bitch ruined my life. She deserved to die. I'm glad she's dead." he mumbled. "But I bloody well didn't kill her. I took an oath ... And I try very hard *not* to kill anybody no matter what the bitch said."

For some reason, Omar's anger was contagious. I felt my own new anger swelling in my chest, getting bigger and bigger. *Whoever killed my parents ruined Joshua's life. He deserves to die. I would be glad to know he was dead. I would kill him myself if I could.*

Marshall smiled. He put the file back on the table, sat down, and helped himself to a croissant and a cup of coffee. Something had changed in Marshall-world. He waited for Omar to get hold of himself. "These are good," he said to me, and fed half a croissant to Bradshaw. "How did you get to REI?" he asked conversationally, ignoring Omar's angry outburst. The tension in the room dropped about 120 degrees.

"Uber."

"Do you remember the driver's name?"

"No. He was Somali, I think. Didn't speak much English." Marshall waited. "So I don't have an alibi for that bitch's murder, and I hated her guts, and she ruined my life. So — I don't know — do I need an attorney? Too late to ask, I suppose." Omar was rubbing his hands on his knees. His nose was red, and he was still shaking.

"You might want to think about it." said Marshall complacently.

The fight seemed to go out of Omar like a swatted wasp. "Yeah, OK. What's one more thing?" He poured himself another cup of coffee and broke a horn off a croissant, crumbling it on his plate. "But there's something else I need to tell you," he continued. Marshall raised his eyebrows. "I don't think it's anything to do with the bitch's murder. Just something I found odd. I never reported it because ... well ... I had enough troubles." Omar waved away whatever he had been going to say.

"There were these two young men who sometimes came into the geriatric wing." He stopped, seemingly unsure whether he should go on. Marshall stayed absolutely still, looking at him. "Pleasant was chummy with them. She'd show them around and introduce them to some of the ... um ... less competent old dears. Very nice, clean-cut guys, possibly religious, you know? Maybe in their thirties. They would, oh, read to the women or run errands for them or just chat with them. Friendly. I speculated it was perhaps part of their Mission, you know?" I nodded, but Marshall continued to sit perfectly still.

"Anyway," Omar continued, "I began to notice that some of the ladies they talked to later insisted on going back to their own homes. We'd try to convince them to stay, of course — most of them were at the Blue House because they weren't safe at home. But there really wasn't anything we could do. They weren't prisoners, after all. And lots of old people don't like being in care, most of them *would* like to go home, but most can't because their house has been sold, or their families won't let them. Ultimately, a few of these ladies did go home. And I heard of two of them who ended up dying there. One fell downstairs, and the other had a stroke."

"And you think Pleasant was involved somehow?"

Omar nodded. "Too right, I think she was involved somehow." His tone was sarcastic. "All the old dears she introduced them to were not only impaired cognitively, but also their houses were still available. I think she was engineering the whole set-up."

"What would she get out of it?"

Omar shrugged. "Money, I should think. Shouldn't you?

CHAPTER 16

"Close to half the Uber drivers in Denver are Somali," grumbled Marshall when we finally left Dr. Omar, and Marshall had warned him not to leave the state. "And the two hotshots at the Blue House — I'll check it out, but that description is probably useless. If they really were con artists, and Pleasant was involved, she won't have kept a record of their visits. But I would like to get to the bottom of it, eventually. But at the moment, I think my hands are full."

I remembered my conversation on the plane with Jamie about her Gran's friends who'd gone home from the Golden facility. I told Marshall about it.

"Huh," he said. "Interesting."

"Are we going back to Denver right away? I'd like a soak in the Hot Springs, since we're here."

"Sure. I need a walk and a smoke and a think, etcetera. Meet you in the lobby at ... two o'clock? We'll need to get on the road by then."

I nodded. "Will you take Bradshaw with you for a walk?"

Marshall smiled. "I'd love to." I handed him the leash. Bradshaw smiled up at him. He liked Marshall. He had the right smell, apparently. "He can help me think."

"OK. Just so long as he doesn't help you smoke."

Bathing-suited and dropping the towel from my backpack onto a chair, I gratefully lowered myself into the steaming hot water of the big pool and lay back, the buoyant minerals holding me up. The steam smelled of sulphur, granite, iron, and other things I couldn't identify. It was a sharp, cavernous smell that flowed straight out of the hot guts of the Rockies.

I floated contentedly, the water around my ears blocking out the sounds of children playing and people around me talking. The heat from the water was soaking into my bones and joints, easing a tension in my neck and shoulders I hadn't known was there. It was anger, I realized. Pure, hot anger — a big change from the heart-broken depression and survivor's guilt I'd been living with for ... I wasn't even sure how long. The anger felt clean, as if it were cauterizing an open wound inside me. I didn't want to cry — I wanted to yell like a Samurai and rip somebody to shreds.

But who?

Marshall had given me some hints. At least I knew where the crash had really happened and what had happened afterwards. I pictured the intersection where the entrance and exit ramps from I-25 meet the two urban arteries of Alameda Avenue and Santa Fe Drive creating an eight-lane snarl of fast-moving traffic. There's a crash, and several other cars are sandwiched by the sudden stops. And a huge black pickup truck speeds off to the west, to the relative seclusion of the foothills. And some guy with a phony name walks into the emergency room at St. Anthony's Hospital — St. Anthony: the patron saint of lost things. *My lost things*.

If the pickup's VIN number was recoverable, *maybe* it would at last reveal who the driver was — the driver who had stolen my family's life away.

Omar's contagious anger surged inside me again, so strong this time that it made me lose my precarious flotation, and I sank briefly under the almost solid-feeling water. Some got in my mouth. It tasted terrible, bitter and salty. I stood up, and a beach ball hit me on the head. "Sorry!" called an adolescent voice from across the pool. I looked at the big clock on the bath house wall. Time to get out, anyway.

After a shower to rinse all the sticky minerals off my skin and hair, and freshly dressed in my jeans, sweater and down vest, I ordered three roast beef sandwiches from the hotel cafe and waited in the lobby for Marshall. My phone buzzed. Daniel.

"Hey, my love, when will you be back? Can I bring you some dinner? And then can I get you naked?"

I laughed. "Absolutely! I should be home by six. I've got a lot to tell you. After the naked part, though. In fact, let's do the naked part first."

"Or first *and* after, you dirty girl. I'll see you — all of you, I hope — at six."

I was smiling goofily when Marshall and Bradshaw reappeared.

The drive back to Denver was a little faster than the drive up. Vail Pass was clear, and the tunnel was clear of belching motor homes. We didn't talk much because I was thinking hard. I made up my mind.

"I'll go talk to the people at the Browning home and St. Anthony's," I said, at last. "But I don't think they'll have any information after all this time."

Marshall grunted and took the cigar out of his mouth. "Good. It's worth a try." He was navigating the complicated interchange between I-70 and I-25, known since the Johnson Administration as The Mousetrap. "Listen, I'm going to drop you at home. You've got a lot to carry, and Bradshaw, and possible kids in hoodies, etcetera."

"They're probably just kids in hoodies," I said, "but thanks."

"Yeah, well, maybe. But we can't find the one on the train and I'm having a Sherlock Holmes feeling about them. You seem to be attracting them like flies, and I don't like coincidences."

Marshall pulled up outside my building and came around to help me climb awkwardly out of the low-slung seat with my load of camera, bag and dog. I handed him the SD card from the Sony with the photos of Dr. Omar that I'd already downloaded to my phone. "Thanks." he said, "Let me know what you find out. And thanks for today." And with that, he folded his long self into the Porsche and blazed away, anxious to break the speed limit south to his wifeless Lean Cuisine and goldfish.

Clumsily, I unlocked the front door and held it open with my foot.

From inside, somebody in a black hoodie and jeans barreled through me, knocking me sideways and nearly off my feet. I put out a hand to catch myself on the red-stone porch railing and saw the gleam of a blade. Bradshaw barked sharply, growled and lunged at the black-jeaned leg as it went past.

How did they get in?

I felt the blade slice through my sleeve and bite into my upper arm, then my camera fell away as I toppled sideways onto the porch floor. I saw a pale face with multiple piercings — eyebrow, nose, lip — but not much else before my head bumped painfully against one of the stone balustrades. Bradshaw continued barking hysterically.

I heard whoever it was drop a skateboard and the scrape of rapidly disappearing wheels as she put Converse to concrete around the corner onto Colfax Avenue.

She? Was it a girl? I shook myself to clear my head and looked down at my arm. A little blood was leaking through the cut in my sweater. I looked around for my camera, but it was gone. Bradshaw had stopped barking but was whining and looking at the door. Footsteps were running down the stairs.

"What the fuck!?" said Daniel from the doorway. "Jesus! Clare, let me help you!" I was only too glad to oblige. I started to gather my wits and my feet under me as Daniel helped me up. "I'm calling the police, and we should get you to a doctor!" He stooped to examine the cut sleeve of my sweater. "This is a pretty deep cut. Let's get you inside, then I'll make those calls. Bradshaw! In!" Bradshaw obediently trotted into the front hall and over to the elevator.

"No, I'm fine," I protested. Daniel lifted me around my waist, picked up my camera bag, and helped me in. When we arrived at the landing outside my apartment, I noticed that my door was ajar.

Daniel pushed it open. "Welcome home, I guess." He whispered. Bradshaw trotted inside and Daniel slammed the door shut behind us with his foot.

There was a WELCOME! banner across the window, champagne on the table, along with flowers, lighted candles and delicious-smelling something in some cardboard containers.

What's the occasion? I wondered, briefly, before stepping into his embrace.

Sometime later, I lay comfortably in Daniel's arms. I'd refused police and doctors, so he'd expertly disinfected and bandaged my wound. He'd worked a lot with doctors and nurses, after all.

The emptied containers of veal parmigiana, salad and crunchy cannoli rested on the floor next to the bed. The half-empty champagne bottle stood handy on the bedside table along with the glass we'd shared. I nuzzled Daniel's neck, kissing him down to his sternum and hugging him to me as tightly as I could. He was caressing my hair.

"So what's the occasion?" I murmured. "I'm not complaining, mind you. That was about the best welcome home I could imagine. I think I'll leave again, so I can come back. But I'll skip the part about being mugged, if you don't mind."

I heard his soft laughter through his chest. "Well, this is sort of an anniversary." I looked up at him, questioning. "This is the anniversary of the first time I saw you, at the Blue House, five years ago. You were visiting Joshua."

"What took you so long to celebrate?" I asked. "You had me at 'hello.' Do you always wait five years to ... um ... declare yourself pleased to meet me?"

His laugh rumbled again. He disentangled himself from me and leaned over to get something out of his pants pocket on the floor. I missed his heat and pulled the duvet up under my chin. "Come on, sit up," he said, hoisting me up to lean against the headboard beside him.

Then for some reason he knelt on the bed facing me. *No, can't be," I thought.* "Clare," he said in a very solemn voice. "I've loved you since the first time I saw you. I saw – I saw how good you were to your brother. I saw the pain in your eyes. I saw the woman I wanted to spend the rest of my life with."

I looked into his blue eyes, then down at his hand. He was holding out a small, blue velvet box on his open palm.

"Would you do me the very great honor of becoming my wife?"

He opened the box.

Inside was a ring, a central sapphire flanked by two smaller diamonds. Exquisite art deco platinum filigree surrounded the stones. My breathing stopped. Perhaps my heart stopped.

"It was my grandmother's," he said, lifting my chin. "Close your mouth." I did. He kissed me gently. "Will you?" he asked.

I nodded. Took a breath, finally. Daniel laughed with joy, slipped the ring onto the correct finger and kissed it. Then he pulled me back down under the covers and gently wrapped me in his arms.

I was bemused but grinned up at him. "Why?" I asked. "Why now?"

"Why not now?" he asked, nuzzling my hair, "but perhaps we could discuss that a little later."

I was happy to agree.

It was actually much later when we found enough leisure to talk. We were in the kitchen sharing a tub of Cherry Garcia ice cream. Bradshaw was having a couple of meatballs.

"So," I said, "Why now? This is so sudden, Monsieur."

"Well, I love you, and you don't seem to find me repulsive," I shook my head vehemently. "So '*tempus fugit*' as my mother used to say. I want to marry you. We've had five great years together, so ..." He looked at his watch. "We could be in Vegas by tomorrow evening if we leave now." He smiled, and his eyes crinkled up. My heart beat faster. But he saw my uncertainty and rubbed a thumb over my brow. We scooped some more ice cream. "And — OK, I know you're not going to like this, but — I'm worried about you. About these break-ins and thefts and this kid in a black hoodie who seems to be following you around —"

"We don't know that," I said. "There are kids in black hoodies all over the place. Everyone says so."

"— following you around and attacking you." he continued, emphatically. "I want to protect you. I want to be with you, all the time. I want you to move in with me at the house in Greenwood Village —"

"What?! Daniel, I —"

"Shhhh." He put a finger to my lips. "I want you to come and live at my place," he repeated. "It's clear you're not safe here. You know that." I looked skeptical. "You do! Look what just happened! Even when that Marshall guy —"

"Detective Marshall. He's a cop, Daniel."

"— OK, Detective Marshall, when he was with you, that hoodie kid was still able to attack you. You *know* it's a problem, Clare. Don't pretend otherwise. You don't know what the hell she — or he — wants. You're not safe here. Come on. Please?" He looked deep into my eyes, then pulled me against him, wrapping his arms around me. I held the cold ice cream spoon away from his skin.

Was Daniel jealous of Marshall? "OK, I'll think about it," I mumbled into his chest.

On the table where it lay, my phone buzzed. I let it go to voicemail.

CHAPTER 17

It was close to eleven the next morning when I finally checked my voicemail. Daniel had left around nine, still trying to convince me to move in with him, and I'd spent the following couple of hours lying on my sofa with a Corgi on my chest trying to process that and his sudden proposal. I was crazy about him, that was true. I looked at the beautiful ring glinting on my finger. That wasn't so bad either. *But marriage? Hmmm.*

The larger problem was moving down to his house in Greenwood Village. True, it would put me closer to Joshua. But my life and much of my work were here in downtown Denver, with its street life, businesses, sports, people of all kinds. Greenwood Village was a desert by comparison. No green woods, no village — just big houses spaced acres apart, with horses in between. Also I'd need a car. I sighed. I didn't want to buy a car. I didn't want to leave my apartment.

Other than the house in the Baker neighborhood where my parents and grandmother had raised me, it was the only home I'd ever had. Well, other than the streets and flops in my teens — but I didn't want to think about them.

The voicemail was from Marshall — big surprise. He was going to interview Shiela and Dr. Kim again late that afternoon at the Littleton Police complex and wanted me to tag along. "You'll give Shiela a sense of security," he said. I wondered what that meant. I called him back and said I'd meet him there.

With the Sony stolen, I'd have to take the Nikon, I thought. *Another camera gone. What was it about my cameras?* I thought glumly as I once more dialed my insurance agent's number and explained about the mugging. He wasn't happy. But then, neither was I.

I packed a suitcase — Daniel was expecting me at his house this evening — my camera gear, some snacks for Bradshaw, and a big tote bag full of odds and ends. And then I called Mohammed.

"Blue House?" he asked when I'd climbed into the enveloping back seat of the Crown Vic.

"Not this time," I said, and gave him the address of Daniel's house on remotest South Franklin Street. Mohammed looked at me in surprise, but I didn't enlighten him.

The key was under the mat as promised. I asked Mohammed to wait.

Inside, I dropped everything on the ivory carpet, noting the precise lines made by a vacuum cleaner, put Bradshaw's meatballs in the fridge after giving him two and filling a bowl with water, and sat down on the floor to have a chat with him.

"We're here for the duration, Buddy," I said, kissing his soft nose. "No sleeping on the furniture. You know the drill — come and go as you please through your little door there," I pointed to the doggy door Daniel had installed a year ago in his back door, "and don't bark too much." Bradshaw stared at me with his protuberant brown eyes. I wished I knew what he was thinking. I ruffled the back of his neck and pulled gently on his ears.

Daniel's house was one of those modern houses built to look like a very, very large Hobbit house — a pointy turret, oddly shaped windows, pretend half-timbering and a fake shake roof. Inside, it was spacious and light with a big professional-looking kitchen, an L-shaped sitting room large enough to accommodate several "conversation areas," an entertainment center, an exercise room in the basement and three huge bedrooms upstairs. Daniel liked Western Art, so the walls sported lots of paintings, etchings and illustrations of Rocky Mountain landscapes — mountains, cowboys, Indians, elk and wolves in various combinations. Everything was spotless. Daniel employed maid and landscaping services to cover all the maintenance. He rarely ate in, so the stove and oven looked brand new. No sound reached me from outside.

I went upstairs to his bedroom. Our bedroom now, I supposed. The view to the west was stunning — Mount Evans and Pikes Peak shone bright white in the sunlight. The king-sized bed bore a beautifully carved oak headboard and footboard that had been parts of an old bar-back in Central City. Bradshaw came in and sat on my foot, regarding the bed speculatively.

"Don't even think about it," I warned him.

Daniel had made a space for me in his closet, but I made no attempt to move in. *Later* I thought and went downstairs to the waiting Mohammed. "Be good," I said to Bradshaw as I closed the door behind me. He just looked at me.

"OK, now to the Littleton Police complex," I said.

Mohammed pressed his lips together in a line, but he turned and headed west.

Marshall met me at the door and led me into the depths of the sprawling building, stopping at a closed door that said "Interview Room in Use" on a cardboard placard. "Dr. Kim is next door. I'm letting him stew a bit. I want you to chat with Shiela as informally as you can. See if you can get her to tell you what she was really doing the day Dr. Pleasant was killed."

"Oh, so I'm a spy, now? I thought I was your photographer."

Marshall shook his head. "Not today. In crimes of this gravity, we have to find ways to get people to tell us the truth. In fact, let me take that camera from you. If things get rough, I don't want it to get damaged."

I handed him the Nikon. "You expect things to get rough?"

"Not necessarily. Just procedure — we don't take any valuables, etcetera, into interviews." I looked at his wrist. The Rolex was not on it. "And take these in with you." He pulled two cans of Pepsi from his jacket pocket. It was the old blue suit. "A drink makes it informal," he added. "Puts people at ease."

I raised my eyebrows at him but took the two cans and opened the door.

The room was not what I'd expected. It was small and attractively lit with a table and three fairly comfortable plastic swivel chairs secured to the floor. I saw two wide angle cameras high up on the walls and a fisheye in the ceiling. Unlike on TV, there was no one-way glass. I guessed the cameras were hooked up to a monitor somewhere.

Shiela was pacing around in the restricted space. She looked up in surprise when I entered and came over to me for a hug. Her beautiful mahogany skin was missing its customary glow, her whiskey eyes were worried, and she nervously scooped her long cornrows back over her shoulders. She was wearing her own clothes — a pair of purple leggings, a purple and green geometric tunic and gold hoop earrings. I'd always envied her style.

"What are you doing here, Cas?" she asked once we'd settled ourselves. I sat next to her rather than across the table. *Let's be all informal* I thought. She opened and took a sip of the Pepsi.

"I'm supposed to find out what you were really doing when Pleasant was killed," I said. "I'm a police spy."

"I told you — *and* the police — I was shopping at that little spice store in Downtown Littleton. I bought some curry powder."

I raised my eyebrows again. "For an hour and a half?"

"OK, I also, you know, did some window shopping."

"No lunch?"

"No. I'd brought a sandwich with me. I ate it in the car."

"Bullshit, Shiela. Nobody believes you, including me. It's a stupid story. Curry powder? You mostly eat hamburgers at the Blue House. And now you're suddenly making curry?

And eating home-made sandwiches? And driving into Littleton when you can buy all the curry powder in the world at the supermarket five blocks from your house?"

Shiela opened her brown eyes wide and nodded.

"Tell me the truth, Shiela. What were you really doing? I'm your friend, remember? Your best friend? Joshua's and my best, oldest friend? And now you're fucking around with the police. You're in trouble, Shiela. You're a suspect in a murder, and you have no alibi, and I love you, and I'm scared for you." Shiela still looked at me with those wide-open eyes. Beautiful eyes in a lovely face. I wished I could take her picture. "You have to tell me the truth, Shiela. Where were you? Why were you late if you *knew* Pleasant would kick your ass? Did you know she was dead?"

"NO!" Shiela shouted. Then sat back in her chair and looked at her lap. "No, of course not. I just ... I got distracted and lost track of time." She again scooped the cornrows back.

I sighed and got up. I wondered if Marshall was watching us from wherever. "Shiela. *Please.*"

"It's a secret," she said in a tiny voice. I doubted that the recorders would hear her. I went over and sat down beside her, leaning in as close as I could. "We could be fired," she whispered. I stopped myself from asking, *Who?* "There's a non-fraternization clause. I'm a nurse, so I can always get another job, but he ..."

"Who?" I whispered.

"Kim."

"Tell me." I tried to keep the surprise out of my voice. When did this happen?

"We ... we were at his place. Over by the Nature Center — you know those condos there?" She was still whispering. I nodded. "We were ... Well, you know ... in bed. I love him so much, Clare. We were talking about getting married. But one of us needs to go someplace else, and I don't want to leave you and Joshua, so he's looking around the Metro area, but hasn't found anything yet. You can't tell anyone, Cas! If we both got fired ..." She put her face in her hands. When she looked up, I could see that I couldn't out her to Marshall, not only for her sake, but for Joshua's also. "I love him so much. I have to protect him."

Humans. Always trying to protect each other. Daniel protecting me. Shiela protecting Kim. Me protecting Shiela. Everyone protecting Joshua. Where were all the protectors when that truck hit my folks? The rage surfaced again, inconveniently. Shiela picked up on it. "Don't be mad at me, Cas!"

I got my wits under control. "I'm not mad at you, Shiela. I'm mad at ... Well, never mind. I'll try to keep your secret. I get it. I'll try to protect you and Kim. But would they really fire you? Is the place that hostile? Should I be talking to Daniel about this? I mean, he owns the place. Maybe he can ... I don't know ... do something."

Shiela shook her head vehemently. "No. Please. Don't tell anyone."

I nodded. *Friendship über alles!* But I needed to think. We sipped our Pepsis, old friends comfortable with silence. I figured out how to handle this. "OK." I said finally and stood up. When I walked out the door, Marshall was standing in the hallway smoking a cigar under the No Smoking sign.

"What did she tell you?" he asked. "I couldn't hear."

"It's a secret," I said. "I can't tell you." He looked surprised. "All I can say is that she definitely wasn't buying curry powder in Littleton, but she *was* someplace else. And Kim is telling the truth. He *was* home in bed."

Marshall looked puzzled. Then smiled. "So ... *someplace else?* As in alibi? They're each other's alibis?" I said nothing. "Huh! I knew that had to be it."

"What?"

"I figured they were together. We got one of them with a bullshit story and the other with no alibi, no attempt at an alibi. Figures." He turned on his heel and entered the other interview room. I looked around for the monitor and found it in the tiny room across the hall.

Marshall handed Kim a Diet Pepsi, which he refused. They talked for a few minutes about this and that. Their voices, picked up by the recording equipment, sounded thin and tinny. Then Marshall said, "So. You and Shiela were together, right? At your place?"

"Who told you that?" asked Kim, alarmed.

"Nobody. I'm a detective — I detected it. So it's true?"

Kim nodded sadly and rubbed his eyes under his cheap glasses. "I guess we'll both need new jobs now, right?"

Marshall shook his head. "Not on my account, Doc. But I gotta tell you, two people giving each other alibis isn't all that strong. Especially if they have a motive. And they're ... involved, etcetera. Anyways, you're off the hook for now, but don't leave town." Marshall got up to leave. Kim looked at him, astonished, I think. "You should consider getting married as soon as you can," Marshall continued, a little too loudly I thought. "That way, you can't testify against each other, if it comes to that." Kim's head went back as if he'd been struck.

Marshall left the door open as he came out.

CHAPTER 18

"So, for now at least, Shiela and Dr. Kim are off the suspect list," I said to Daniel in his big bed that night. He kissed my hair. "But Marshall is still trying to track down the kid in the hoodie and the RTD guard. Apparently he's disappeared, too. RTD says he just didn't show up for any of his shifts since the murder. Apparently that's not all that unusual. The mystery is where he's gone."

"Mmm-hmm," cooed Daniel. He was caressing my breast.

"Cut that out!" I laughed. "I need to ask you something."

"How about later?" Daniel whispered, easing me onto my back and nuzzling my neck.

It was later.

"OK, so *now* I need to ask you something."

Daniel sighed and pulled me closer. Bradshaw grumbled at being again disturbed on my other side.

I took a deep breath. This question had been bothering me for quite a while. "Why did you keep Dr. Pleasant on at the Blue House? You must have known how many problems she was causing. People say you lost a lot of good nurses and doctors on account of her ... interference, or whatever."

Daniel lifted his head to look at me. "What brought this on?"

"Just ... well you know I've been going around with Marshall, taking pictures. Everyone we've interviewed ... well, not everyone, but most of them ... say she was hell on wheels."

"And all of them disgruntled former employees, right?"

"Well, not all of them. But some, yes."

Daniel pulled away from me and sighed. "When you run a big operation like mine, Clare, when you have literally hundreds of employees and hundreds more clients, you're going to find that some of them are unhappy with the way you run things. Dr. Pleasant was highly disciplined herself, and she expected the same from her staff. If they didn't measure up, they left, or she fired them. Simple. Quite frankly, I thought she was a very valuable addition to the Blue House. And she was, up to a point. So I'm sorry if — I know Shiela didn't like her. Is that where this is coming from? Shiela is a very good nurse, but nobody is perfect."

"Not just Shiela, Daniel. What about the Demidovs' son? He died under her care. And what about the way she harassed Dr. Omar and finally got him pushed out?"

"The Demidovs' son — Alan, by the way — died of natural causes. He had Brugada Syndrome, a particularly severe case. It was just a matter of time. I'm sorry for the Demidovs, I am, but Dr. Pleasant didn't have anything to do with his death. That was well established at the time."

"By Dr. Pleasant! Daniel, that was a conflict of interest, since she was the attending physician."

"Do you really want to do this, Clare? You have no reason and no experience to question me about this. I've been over all this a hundred times with doctors, lawyers, the police and all the people concerned. Enough."

The chill in the room had little to do with the Chinook wind tossing the trees around outside. I moved toward him and hooked a leg over his. "Don't be mad," I whispered, stroking his chest. I felt him start to respond. "But can you tell me about Dr. Omar?"

He sighed but pulled me back into his embrace. "Dr. Omar was prone to small mistakes. For that reason, Dr. Pleasant was watching him closely. The last one was just one too many. He reversed a patient's Celsius temperature reading as 37.9 when it was really 39.7. That's the difference between, um, about 100 and 103 Fahrenheit, or between no big deal and cause for concern. Luckily, Shiela caught what could have been a serious mistake. But not grounds for dismissal. Marla did what she could to make him leave, and he did. I was behind her all the way."

"Marla?"

"That was her name. Marla Pleasant." He sighed again and rubbed his face with the hand that wasn't holding me. "Now go to sleep before I have my way with you again."

He had his way with me again.

I was back at my own apartment, uploading some photos to the stock photo service I used, when Marshall called. I was tempted to let it go to voicemail, since I was right in the middle of assigning search terms and making sure the metadata were accurate and complete for each of the photos, a process that requires concentration. But I answered distractedly, trying to multitask.

"Have you still got all those photos from the train and platform, etcetera?" he asked. Again, no hello or questions about my health or state of mind.

"Yes and hello to you too. I'm fine thanks. How are you? Nice weather we're having." In fact, the Chinook was blowing gangbusters, tossing the trees around and sending debris sailing upwards.

"Yeah, well, not where I am," he said. "Can you pull up those photos? I want you to look at something with me."

I minimized the stock website and opened the folder in Photoshop that was labeled 2019-02-09 Pleasant Murder. I'd gotten a kick out of the contradiction.

"OK. Which ones do you want me to look at?" I heard the Zippo clink and an exhale followed by a cough.

"Look at the photo of the train car with the guard standing in the aisle."

I found it in the Nikon batch. "OK."

"Now look at the photo of the guard with Pleasant's body. Not the one when he's sitting down, but the one where he's standing."

I scrolled through the batch from the Sony. "OK." I said again.

"Look at his shoes."

I zoomed in on the guard's shoes in each photo. I had both up on the screen for comparison. "Holy shit! He's wearing two different pairs of shoes!"

Marshall's chair creaked. "Yup. But which ones look like the shoes those guards wear usually?"

"The second one," I said, peering at my expensive screen. "His are black and look like those squashy leather ones that cops wear. The first one —" I increased the zoom to just before it became pixilated. I increased the exposure and definition. "— looks like he's wearing ... more like business shoes. Brown?"

"I thought they might be, but I can't get the same amount of detail on my piece of shit monitor that you can. Is that what they look like to you?"

I selected and copied the segment of the photo with the enhanced image of the shoes. "Here, I'll send this to you." I attached it to a text message. I heard it arrive on his computer with a ding.

"I'll be damned," said Marshall after a minute. "Whaddya bet they're size 10." We were both silent for a minute. "Can you enhance their faces and send them to me?"

"Yes, a bit. But you obviously can't tell what size shoes he's wearing."

"Dream on."

I sighed. "OK, but in the first photo, his face is partially obscured. I'll do what I can."

"Good. Send them as soon as you can. I gotta go back to the RTD lot in Englewood. That one between the Evans and Oxford Avenue stops. I think that's where the second guy got on." He hung up.

"You're welcome," I said to cyberspace. But I got to work blowing up the two faces and enhancing them the best I could. Both guards had short dark hair, aviator sunglasses, and trimmed mustaches. They were both about the same height and build — about six feet and slightly paunchy. They could easily have been the same man. But on closer study, the first one's face seemed a little narrower, and the second one's a little redder. I sent them at full resolution to Marshall's email.

I completely forgot about the stock photo uploads until it was too late. The link had timed out, and I had to start all over again.

The next morning, Daniel had to go put out another fire at his assisted living place in Golden, so he told me he'd be back late, or maybe not till the following night. Something about a patient who'd been hit by a car. The family were screaming negligence and threatening lawsuits.

Daniel was frustrated. "She insisted! They're not prisoners, for Chrissike! Why didn't her family just ... I don't know ... watch out for her. What was she doing out on her own? They say she was conned. Apparently two young guys befriended her and promised that she could go home if she signed the house over to them. Then they got a loan on the equity of the house and used it to start a downstairs bathroom, but they never finished it. The money's disappeared, of course." He shook his head disgustedly. "What a mess."

"What happens if she dies?"

"More like *when* she dies, the family will only get her savings, and Medicare has first dibs on that. The house will belong to those two — con artists. So the family's livid. They say we're abetting a scam."

"Anyway," he continued, "I gotta find these two guys before they do any more damage. Christ only knows how many of these scams they've pulled. If this gets out, it could sink us. I'll probably have to fire somebody, too. I love you. Let's get married."

"I love you, too," I said, ignoring the marriage part. After he'd left, I looked at the ring. It was gorgeous. I loved it. But marriage seemed ... I wasn't ready. Dismayed by my thoughts, I went back to getting ready for the day. A day I wasn't looking forward to.

Browning Rehabilitation Center is in a brick building, an archipelago completely surrounded by parking structures and the Vineland Hospital complex. Once inside the magnificent entrance off Anschutz Plaza, you're confronted with a fairly ordinary reception area with the usual reception desk, offices and snack bar, like you would find in any late 20th century hospital. Lots of flowers, though.

St. Anthony's had sent Joshua there to start his long physical and psychological therapy. He'd been in a coma so long that his Achilles tendon had shortened, making him unable to flatten his feet out, and thus unable to walk. The head injury had caused other neuromuscular problems that required relearning how to use his hands and form words.

Browning was never able to bring him back to his old self — he'd been a good student and on the track team at school — but they'd at least made it possible for him to walk with assistance, operate his wheelchair, feed himself, and speak with difficulty. They'd been surprised at his emotional resiliency. Unlike me, he'd grieved normally, then accepted his multiple losses. And the Blue House had been an incalculable help. There he'd found a community, counselors and friends, giving him emotional and physical support.

But the Blue House had been in high demand back when he'd been admitted after a two-year stint at Browning. And as a private facility, the Blue House was incredibly expensive. Somehow, Joshua had been admitted on a reduced fee basis. I'd always just assumed my grandparents had known somebody or pulled some strings.

But suddenly I was curious. I wanted to see how his admission to the Blue House had come about. And my newly discovered anger was pushing me to see if anyone at Browning, St. Anthony's or the Blue House could help me find out who the driver of the big black truck had been. I was hoping Denver PD could raise the VIN number on the truck found up on Green Mountain, but that seemed to be their only lead, and the case was as cold as a chrome bumper in January.

"I have an odd request," I said to an efficient-looking receptionist. "My brother, Joshua Standish, was a patient here between 2006 and 2009. I was wondering about his admission to the Blue House from here — how that happened, I guess. Is anyone here who would remember how that happened? Or if I could get a copy of his records?"

She frowned and shook her head sternly. "I'm afraid his records would only be available to his next of kin and his current attending physician, if he has one."

"I am his next of kin. Actually, I'm his only kin."

She shook her head, disapproving of people with so few kin. "I'm sorry, but we'd need to see some proof of that. An affidavit or ... perhaps your lawyer can help you, but we can't. I'm sorry." She clearly wasn't sorry and turned away to dismiss me.

"OK, well, is there anyone here who was here in 2006 or 7? Anyone I could talk with?"

"I can check, but they wouldn't be able to give you his confidential records either."

"I know, but could you check?" She turned to her computer with a frown. I suddenly realized I should have brought Marshall or Daniel with me. I had no idea if I was on any paperwork as Joshua's next of kin. I supposed I must be on the Blue House records — again, I should have gotten something from there —

"Dr. Blumfeld was here at that time. but I doubt if he'll have time to see you."

"Could you check anyway?"

She turned to her phone and spoke very softly into it.

It turned out Dr. Blumfeld *could* see me, but his office was in the sprawling Vineland Hospital complex, and I got lost twice among the multiple elevators and corridors. I found him at last sitting in a tiny office, cluttered with books, stacks of papers, bound reports, a computer, a flag I didn't recognize, hockey trophies, and a score of framed certificates and diplomas in several languages. He turned from his desk and held out a hand when I knocked on his door jamb.

"Miss Standish, I presume?" he smiled. "What a pleasure to see you again after all this time! How is your brother? Come in — just put that stuff on the floor." He pointed to a chair stacked with papers.

I didn't remember him, but then, I didn't remember much during that period of my life, addled as I'd been with grief, drugs and alcohol. He was perhaps in his late fifties with thick, crisply curling hair combed rigorously back from a high forehead, a Roman nose and large, close-set brown eyes. Far from handsome, there was something about his face that made you want to tell him all your secrets. Which I supposed was useful, since he was a psychiatrist.

"What has brought you here after all this time?" he asked, getting right to the point.

I suddenly thought how foolish I was about to sound. "I'm not sure," I said, truthfully. "But for some reason I feel I need to know how ... how Joshua got from here to the Blue House. There was no way my family could have afforded it, and it was such a lucky break that I — I'm sorry. I'm probably wasting your time. But do you have any idea how that happened?"

He folded his hands on his round paunch. "Yes, I remember quite clearly. But what I'm really asking is *why* do you need to know this? After all this time? What has changed in your life that this has become so important to you?"

"I — I'm not sure," I babbled. *Oh, yeah. A psychiatrist. Answer a question with a question.* But he was looking at me with such a guileless expression that I felt compelled to stumble on. "I've been helping the police with a murder inquiry recently, and some things have come up that have made me just — suddenly I'm just so angry at whoever did this to Joshua — and me." *Why didn't I prepare better for this?* "I realize that sounds like it has nothing to do with my question, but to me there seems to be some connection." I rubbed my forehead. "I'm not explaining myself very well." But now the anger began to swell again. Why couldn't he just tell me what I wanted to know or say that he couldn't? What was his problem?

He nodded. "We know that anger is a perfectly healthy response to both grief and injustice. I think the murder you're engaged with has belatedly sparked your anger at the injustice done to you and your family. You got involved in drugs after the accident, I believe?" I nodded, astounded that he remembered. "That will have interrupted your grieving process. May I ask what has been your dominant emotion since you got yourself clean?"

"Sadness. Depression, actually," I said without thinking. *WTF? Why was I telling him this? I'd kept it a secret for so long, and now it just came blurting out.*

He nodded and regarded me kindly. "Guilt? Suicidal thoughts?" I nodded, even though I was terrified he was going to lock me up. "Well, there you are then. You've just been a long time getting to this point. This murder ... Is it the murder of Dr. Pleasant?"

I nodded. *How did he know?*

"This new anger about Dr. Pleasant, and *her* unjust death, has pointed your anger at someone who has wronged *you*. At someone other than yourself, for a change. Once we move aside the survivor's guilt, we often find anger. So now you want to know the rest of the story of your parents' deaths — the part of the story that's not about you." He spread his hands. "This is a good thing. This is progress."

I stared at him. I probably looked like a landed carp. I could think of nothing to say.

He smiled. "So yes, I do remember quite a bit about your brother. He got to the Blue House through a recommendation from his physician here. The administration of the Blue House took a look at his case, and his terrible circumstances, and apparently decided to admit him at a — I think you'd call it a 'deep discount.'" He chuckled quietly. It was a comfortable sound. "They settled on an amount that was within the scope of the trust fund your grandmother had set up for his care. He — and you — are very lucky. I don't know of any other patients at the Blue House with that arrangement."

I thought back to the hospital records Daniel had read to me. "Wasn't it Dr. Pleasant who recommended Joshua to the Blue House?" For some reason my heart was pounding. I was still trying to process what he'd said about anger and ... all that.

"Yes." Dr. Blumfeld nodded. "For some reason Joshua was special to her. She was a young doctor at the time, and I think she may have found him ... attractive. Or needy. Probably both. I've seen it before. She visited him often, somehow arranged for his admission to the Blue House, and then she herself moved over there later, when there was an opening." He regarded me closely for several seconds. "Is that what you wanted to know?"

I nodded. I cleared my throat. "Was Dr. Pleasant here for long before Joshua arrived? I mean, she must have had other deserving patients. I wonder why Joshua was so special?"

He shook his head. "No, I think she came to us shortly *after* Joshua did. Highly recommended, I remember. From St. Anthony's."

I couldn't conceal my astonishment. Dr. Pleasant had been at St. Anthony's, then at Browning, then she had recommended Joshua to the Blue House, and then followed him there. Was she at St. Anthony's when my family was brought in after the crash? Was she their doctor? Impossible to know, since she was dead. But maybe someone was still at St. Anthony's who would remember. Now I was for sure going to go to St. Anthony's and try to find out if she'd been there that day.

I left Dr. Blumfeld's office and stepped out onto Old Hampden Avenue, taking a deep breath of the windy air. Where was I going, I wondered, disoriented by Dr. Blumfeld's analysis. Deciding to think about that later, I looked at my phone — it was nearly four-thirty, too late to go all the way out to St. Anthony's now. I'd call Mohammed to take me out to the wilds of Greenwood Village instead.

My phone buzzed in my hand. It was Marshall.

"Where are you right now?" It was the usual no-greeting call, but this time it sounded urgent.

"On Old Hampden a couple of blocks from Broadway. What's up?"

"Do you have your camera with you?"

"Of course," I said. "Never leave home without it. What's
—"

"OK, I'll pick you up on Broadway at the post office in
... five minutes. We've found Martinez." Belatedly I noticed a
kid in a black hoodie across the street, apparently texting. As
a precaution, I went back up the stairs to Anschutz Plaza and
ducked into one of the many parking garages.

"Wow!" I said. "What's he got to say?"

"Nothing. He's dead."

CHAPTER 19

M arshall drove with lights and siren full blast south on Santa Fe and turned east on County Line Road. We crossed the six lanes of Santa Fe, across the E-470 ramp against the lights, an experience I wasn't sure I wanted to get used to.

I was digging in my backpack, getting the Nikon set up for crime scene photos. I hadn't anticipated a crime scene when I'd packed that morning, but I knew the Nikon's brilliant 42 megapixels and the workhorse 24 to 70 mm lens would cover almost any situation. The light was fading fast as the mountains cast long shadows, and I didn't have the lens flash with me. So I dug out a flash that could be used remotely and stuck an LED flashlight in my back pocket. I didn't have my tripod, either. I'd have to hand-hold the camera. Not ideal.

We screeched around a corner onto County Line Road, then pulled into a cul-de-sac. There was a matching cul-de-sac on the other side of the road with matching tan stuccoed half-duplexes. Heavy traffic on County Line Road whizzed between them. There was a full-court press of Arapahoe County sheriffs, Douglas County sheriffs and Littleton cops. Police vehicles were parked helter-skelter all over the two cul-de-sacs, blue and red lights reflecting off the walls and windows of the surrounding duplexes. Two guys in paper coveralls were setting up lights on tall stands, and one cop was redirecting traffic at the entrance to the street.

The neighbors were out on their stoops, or behind front windows, but most were standing around on the sidewalks outside the police tape talking excitedly in several languages. Spanish and Russian predominated.

"What's Douglas County doing here?" I asked. "Isn't this Arapahoe County?"

"When the call came in it wasn't clear which side of County Line Road the crime scene was on. This place is right on the line between Arapahoe and Douglas County, so both sheriffs got the call. And I got it because it's my case," said Marshall around a recently lit cigar. "You go take pictures. I gotta discuss crime scene venue with these guys."

Even though the crime scene was on the south side of County Line Road, the Douglas County side, it was Arapahoe County's venue because it was related to the Pleasant case. The Douglas County ME, a Dr. Falstad, and the paper-suited CSIs were waiting around for me, but I didn't see Sheldon Davis, Douglas County's crime scene photographer, so I got to work. Martinez's body was lying face down to the right of his concrete steps in a pile of unmelted snow, leaves, dirt and sticks. His arms and legs were sprawled at abandoned angles. He was wearing a Rockies starter's jacket, jeans and black cop shoes. You could see his black tee shirt where the back of the jacket was scrunched up. No blood was visible, but the red plastic handle of what looked like a cheap paring knife was sticking out of his neck at the base of his skull.

After the first wide-angle establishing shots, stepping carefully, I hand-held the camera's flash in order to control the shadows. I placed numbered evidence markers and photo scales as I moved around the scene, recording each on my phone as I went. I placed my flashlight on the ground to bring up a footprint in the mud next to the broken sidewalk. My main concern was for perfect clarity and flawless focus, but I also tried to work quickly. Vaguely I heard the uniforms behind me asking the neighbors questions.

Marshall had marched over to where a group wearing more paper coveralls was standing behind the crime scene tape and appeared to be in a good-natured discussion with some laughter and back slapping going on. Then most of the Douglas County deputies left. One breathtakingly handsome guy wearing the Full Western — hat, shirt, cavalry twills and boots, all immaculately clean, pressed and shined — stuck around. He and Marshall talked for a short time, then they walked over to me. I heard the handsome guy say, "'Indeed, he is most grave.'"

Marshall laughed before saying, "This is Douglas County Sheriff's Deputy Duane Mangione," he said, introducing me. "He's wondering if it's OK for me to copy your photos over to him. His own photographer is on another job. I told him yours might be adequate."

Mangione smiled, dazzling me with his white teeth. "Glad to know you," he said. He made me a little breathless.

I nodded. "Same here. And sure, Marshall can send them over when we're done here. I wondered where Sheldon was."

"Hey!" said Marshall to Duane, "Maybe you'd like her to do your campaign shots. She took some of me that got me thinking." He turned to me. "Duane here is gonna make a run for Sheriff next year."

Lordy! With his looks, how could he lose?

"I'd be glad to," I smiled idiotically.

Mangione thanked me, and he and Marshall walked back to Mangione's cruiser. Pretty soon the whole circus was down to just some Arapahoe and Littleton uniforms and Marshall. Marshall came back over.

"OK," he said, "That's great, Clare. Let's get this guy where we can look at him. And gimme your phone for a sec." I handed it over as I lifted my camera for the wide-angle shots.

Dr. Falstad stepped aside to let Dr. Arthur Wallace, the Arapahoe county ME squat beside the body, but she stayed to watch. "Obviously, this is what killed him," he said, pointing to the knife handle. "He hasn't been dead long." He placed two fingers inside the collar of Martinez's jacket, "There's some residual warmth here, probably three hours or less. Rigor hasn't set in." Carefully, he turned the body over. Martinez's eyes and mouth were open, as if in surprise. The front of his jeans and zipped jacket were wet and muddy. His keys were in his right hand.

"Looks like somebody got him from behind while he was unlocking his door and then pushed him off the stoop. He would have been dead before he hit the ground. The knife appears to have severed the spine between the first cervical vertebra and the brain stem. Very neat job. This killer knew what he — or she — was doing. I'll have the full report for you tomorrow." He stood and motioned for the ambulance guys to bring over the gurney as the CSIs moved in. As Martinez was carefully lifted into a body bag, something inside the front of his jacket shifted. Marshall went over and unzipped the jacket. Inside was a wrinkled brown paper bag, the size that might contain three or four bottles of wine.

"Well I'll be damned," said Marshall, looking inside the bag. "Get a picture of this, Clare." I aimed my flash into the bag and snapped a shot of it and its contents, which I couldn't make out at first.

"OK, now these," said Marshall extracting a pair of men's shoes from the bag with two gloved fingers. "A pair of men's dress shoes. Size 10. Brown leather. Probably Italian. Expensive looking."

I felt my eyes get very wide.

"Not Martinez's, probably. His feet look bigger than that to me. And wider. People who are on their feet all day — cops, teachers, security guards, cooks etcetera — their feet get wider."

How the hell does he know all this stuff? I thought, not for the first time.

A CSI guy held out an open plastic evidence bag. Marshall replaced the shoes in the paper bag and dumped the whole thing into the evidence bag. The CSI sealed it and wrote on it with a Sharpie.

Marshall handed me back my phone as he steered me toward his car. "I've tracked your phone with mine. This is getting dangerous, and I want to know where you are at all times."

"OK," I said cautiously.

He nodded. "Let's go. I'll drop you at the Littleton light rail so you can go home. Get those pictures to me as soon as you can. I need to come back here, then go to the morgue for the postmortem."

I decided not to mention that I wasn't going home, but climbed into the cruiser and buckled up. Lights and sirens cleared the way as we sped back north. There was a train waiting as we pulled into the station.

"Mangione was impressed," he said. "I think he wondered if you could handle the whole dead body thing."

I shrugged. "It's easier to look at dead people through a lens."

Bradshaw was annoyed with me again by the time Mohammed dropped me off at Daniel's house, but I lay down on the floor, stretched my back, and pulled him onto my chest. "What's new with you, Buddy?" I asked him, pulling gently on his silky ears.

"Nothing much. How about you?" said a voice from the dining room doorway.

I jumped up. "Daniel! You're home!" and raced into his arms, nuzzling against his chest.

He laughed and petted my hair. "Hungry?" I nodded. "I brought you a cheesesteak from that Philla-Deli at the shopping center." He steered me into the kitchen and presented the paper-wrapped torpedo to me at the bar, then poured me a glass of the Malbec he'd been drinking.

"You want half?" I asked.

"I've already eaten. It's after eight. Where have you been?" I gave him the executive summary. "Martinez? That's the RTD guard on the train when Marla was killed, right?" I nodded, chewing. "Wow. Can I see the pictures?"

I shook my head, swallowing. The sandwich was good. "They're Littleton Police evidence." Daniel looked surprised. "I'm now officially the Littleton Police crime scene photographer. And I think I'll be subbing for Douglas County, too. I'm pretty excited."

Daniel nodded thoughtfully.

I handed a piece of sandwich to Bradshaw. "So I need to process these and send them off tonight."

"What about the ones from Dr. Pleasant's murder?"

"He already has all those. And all the interviews, people at the Blue House ... whatever."

Daniel poured me some more Malbec. I went on eating. Fresh air and dead bodies made me hungry.

"Speaking of that," I said, swallowing and taking a sip of the wine. It tasted good, too. Everything tastes good in the presence of death. "You never did tell me about your interview with Marshall, what? A week or so ago?"

Daniel nodded abstractedly but then squared his shoulders to attention. "No. I kept forgetting. Why weren't you there? You've been at all the other interviews, right?"

"I think so. But Marshall didn't want me at that one because of our ... relationship." I shrugged. "Maybe he thought you had some deep dark secret you wouldn't want to reveal with me there."

Daniel chuckled. "I guess you'll never know!" But seeing the look on my face, he continued. "Well, it wasn't that

interesting. He asked me where I was that day, so I told him
—"

"Weren't you at a conference?"

"— that I was at a conference at the Blue House. That
seemed to satisfy him, so he asked about my relationship
with Marla — Dr. Pleasant — which, as you know, was
pretty good with minor glitches here and there, as anyone
would expect. He asked me if I thought she had any enemies,
so I told him about the Demidovs and Dr. Kim and Dr.
Hussain ... Omar ... and even your friend Shiela ... and
explained that in Marla's role as chief physician, she probably
had several more.

"Then I remembered those two guys that kept showing
up who were chatting up the old ladies. Marshall found that
interesting and wanted to know if I knew who they were.
Remember I told you about the lawsuit the family of the
Golden patient was threatening?" I nodded. "It turns out
that Marla allowed those guys to have the run of the place.
Plus, they were pulling the same scam at several facilities
other than mine."

I looked at him, shocked. He held up his hands. "I know,
I know — I should have put a stop to it earlier. You're right,
she wasn't perfect."

"Far from it," I scoffed. Then I remembered the five
thousand dollars in the gym bag she'd been carrying on the
light rail. "So — were they paying her for access?"

He snapped his fingers. "Maybe! They could've put her
share in her locker at that Pilates place she went to, and she'd
pick it up."

"My God!" I said, thinking fast. "Maybe it was them who killed her. To get back their money!" Daniel shrugged. "Have you told Marshall about all this?"

"I will, I will." He smiled. "Gimme a minute, huh? And isn't it bedtime?"

I smiled happily. "It will be, after I get these photos done. And then, it'll definitely take more than a minute."

CHAPTER 20

Despite Daniel's best efforts, the black hole of depression and guilt threatened to pull me in when I woke the next morning. I contemplated just staying in bed. Rejected that. Over coffee, I contemplated going back to bed. Rejected that. Contemplated staying in my jammies all day. Rejected that.

Ultimately, I joylessly ate toast, fed Bradshaw, showered and dressed. I was not in my own home. I didn't have my precious clutter around me. I had no pressing assignments, and the one I did have I could cover with stock photos. There was no place interesting within walking distance, and I had no car. The cleaning lady would be here shortly, and I'd be in the way. Bradshaw was also depressed, lying on the kitchen floor with his head on his paws, though he brightened whenever I looked in the spotless and mostly empty refrigerator.

I looked aimlessly at my phone and scrolled through some photos. There was one of my family at Elitch Gardens in front of the carousel's brightly painted horses — Mom, Dad and Joshua smiling, me looking like the sulky teenager I was.

And just like that, the anger returned — white hot and so intense I had to steady myself against the kitchen island.

In an explosion of blinding light, it blew the black hole into outer space. Who stole my life? What sick, drunk or stoned bastard runs a red light on Santa Fe Drive, plows into a Camry, kills two people, destroys two others, and simply drives away? A murderer that's who. A murderer who escapes uncaught for 14 years. Just as much a murderer as whoever killed Dr. Pleasant and now poor Martin Martinez, RTD guard. A murderer who steals beloved lives away for no reason other than his own fears or his sick or drunk or stoned needs.

I am not at fault here, I told myself. *I wasn't with them. It was the driver of the truck that killed them. Not me. I survived because I was a sulky, selfish teenager, but that's all. Not a murderer. I was going to find the sonofabitch if it took me the rest of my life.*

I figured the first stop would have to be St. Anthony Hospital, so I stabbed Mohammed's number. While I waited for him to pick me up, I dug the hospital report out of my backpack and looked through it for any description of the anonymous guy who came into the ER the afternoon my family were admitted. There wasn't much — six-one, 152 pounds, age 24, medium blond hair, BP 125/88, blue eyes, broken nose, rib and wrist, a cut and contusion on forehead and chest.

In 2005, 14 years ago, St. Anthony Hospital had been in Denver on West Colfax Avenue in the heart of the culture wars between Hispanic and Jewish neighborhoods. It had now moved much farther west to Lakewood, on Alameda Parkway, at a point where the sprawling metro area gives way to white-fenced farms and ranchettes.

Mohammed dropped me at the hospital's palatial main entrance below seven stories of cream and ochre stucco. The reception area, wrapped around a cloister-like courtyard, looked like a cross between a first-class hotel and a cathedral. Crucifixes adorned nearly every wall, and tables full of flowers bloomed in the artistic lighting. To the right was a lounge with a baby grand piano, and to the left, another lounge. An enticing aroma of food drifted from the comfortable-looking cafeteria. Quite the contrast with the Browning Center I'd visited yesterday.

I stepped up to the semi-circular information desk, where a statue of St. Anthony stood guard. A man in his sixties — Fr. Bianchi according to his name tag — smiled up at me benignly. I explained that I was looking for anyone who would have been working in the ER in 2005 and why. Even I thought it was a pretty hopeless request. But he looked thoughtful rather than annoyed.

"I was here myself at that time," he murmured, "not in the ER, but in Patient Services. Do you have time for me to ask some questions? I might be able to find someone."

I was totally taken aback. What a different greeting from the one at the Browning Center! "Of course," I said. "Take your time — I know it's a weird request."

Instead of turning to his computer, Fr. Bianchi pulled open a drawer and extracted a large, heavily used book of bound computer printouts and began opening it to various tabbed sections while quietly chewing the eraser off a pencil. "I'm just trying to remember some names from that time," he explained. Just then a woman with very short, graying blonde hair sidled into the next chair. Fr. Bianchi turned to her, holding his place with a forefinger, and explained the problem. "Do you remember anyone from around then, Sister?" he asked.

Her name tag said Sr. Benita. She thought for a minute. "Morales? No, he was later. Dolan?" Bianchi looked through the book and shook his head. "Pleasant? Wasn't she in ER then?"

I gasped, and they both looked at me. "She was," I said, "but she went over to Browning a few years later." They looked at me expectantly. "And I'm afraid she's been murdered." They looked shocked.

Suddenly Bianchi snapped his fingers. "Monroe!" Sister Benita nodded enthusiastically. Father Bianchi turned to his computer and typed some commands. "She should be here. Hang on, would you? I'll try and give her a call, but if she's on rounds, she might not answer. Why don't you go on in the cafeteria and get yourself a coffee. I'll let you know if she's available, is that OK?"

I nodded, bemused by their helpfulness. Instead of going into the cafeteria though, I went outside and found Mohammed smoking a cigarette and chatting with one of the ambulance drivers, a sharp-faced guy, who looked about sixteen, with his Rockies hat on backwards. I explained the situation, and Mohammed said he'd wait.

Back in the cafeteria, I got myself a fancy coffee and a burger, fries and tea for Mohammed. His big smile was thanks enough when I handed it to him. I took my coffee back into the cafeteria and checked my phone. There was a text from Daniel.

Where R U

At St. Anthony's
checking to see if
anyone remembers the
guy who came in
after my parents accident.

Any luck

Not yet.
Waiting for somebody
named Monroe.
A doctor I think.

When will you be home
lets go to sushi den
for dinner.

Sounds great! 6?

Ok xo

There was also an email from Marshall.

"Are you home? I need you to come with me to the RTD Maintenance Facility to figure out this Martinez business. Your crime scene photos are not too bad. You're on the payroll."

I replied to Marshall telling him where I was and why and saying I'd meet him at the facility. But I was wondering. Did I actually want a real job? Last night's excitement had drained away along with the adrenaline — maybe the reason for my depression this morning. I still wanted to have time for my other photographic business. There might be problems if I, say, went to the ski races or to Europe or whatever. I needed to think. I needed to talk to Daniel. If we got married, how was that going to affect everything? What if I had a kid?

That last thought was one too many.

Luckily just then Dr. Monroe arrived. She was tall, hickory-stick thin, with fluffy iron-gray hair and sharp gray eyes behind half-moon glasses. I thought she was well over 60, probably past retirement age, but she walked like someone who has places to go and things to do. I figured a cozy chat was out, and I had better get to the point quickly. I stood, introduced myself and held out my hand, putting on my business voice. Dr. Monroe nodded, pulled out a chair and sat down, waving to one of the girls clearing tables. I launched into my story.

"In June of 2005, my parents and twin brother were in a hit-and-run car crash with a large black pickup truck. They were brought here, to the emergency room — well, not here, but to the Colfax Avenue location —"

Dr. Monroe nodded. "— where St. Anthony's was located at the time, yes." The girl delivered Dr. Monroe a cup of coffee, black. She blew on it and took a sip.

"Right," I said, taking a deep breath. "My father was DOA, and my mother died shortly afterwards. My brother, Joshua, was severely injured and was in the ICU for several months in a coma and treatment. Do you —"

"I remember that case," she interrupted me. "Why are you asking?"

"Well, the hospital records show that sometime that afternoon, a guy with several injuries walked into the ER, was treated, but gave a false name and paid in cash. I'm trying to figure out who that was because —"

"Because you think he might have been the driver of the truck." I nodded. "Well, that's a bit of a long shot, isn't it.

Especially now after all this time." She gave me a piercing look, a woman who was used to dealing with emergencies and got through everything else as quickly as possible. *She's not going to help,* I thought. *It's too long ago, and she's seen thousands of these things. I'm just too late.*

She fingered her cup, turning it on the table thoughtfully. "I *was* working the ER that day, though I didn't actually treat your family or the man you're asking about. But there was gossip — there's always gossip anywhere you work, and the ER is no exception." She looked up and smiled at me for the first time. "One of the other doctors, a Dr. Pleasant —"

My turn to interrupt. "Yes, I know — knew — her. She's been murdered."

Dr. Monroe looked at me sharply, whether in surprise or because I'd interrupted, I wasn't sure. "Dr. Pleasant was the one who treated the son, and she was convinced that the man who came in — John Smith, I think he said his name was, not terribly imaginative — was the driver of the truck. She got a little obsessed about it. She became attached to your brother — Joshua did you say?" I nodded. "This happens sometimes. We try very hard not to become emotionally involved, but sometimes a patient just — strikes a chord. And she was young at the time." I nodded again.

"Anyway, she tried hard to locate this John Smith, badgered the police, asked a lot of questions and so on. Then, some time after the crash, she just dropped it. The police questioned her and everyone else involved — the nurse, payment center people, me, the other doctors— but the result was nil. Dr. Pleasant remained close to your brother I think, but then, of course she went over to Browning and I had no further contact with her. Is there anything else?"

"I wondered if there are any notes anywhere — not the official hospital records, but maybe some personal notes? I mean —"

"I won't have anything, since I wasn't the one who saw your family. Now if that's all —" she stood.

"Thank you," I said, also standing. "I'd appreciate whatever help you can give me. I was only 14 at the time, and I've had ... challenges ... since then."

She nodded curtly, her gray eyes assessing. "Survivor's guilt and so forth. I understand." She held out her hand. "It was nice to meet you. Take care of yourself." She turned on her heel and left, carrying her coffee cup. She took a last swig and tossed the cup in a wastebasket as she passed the reception desk.

There was nothing to do but go find Mohammed and meet Marshall.

Marshall was standing on the corner of Yale Avenue and Elati Street smoking a cigar when Mohammed dropped me off. Located next to the light rail tracks, the Maintenance Facility is an enormous building on a huge chunk of Denver filled with rail cars, maintenance and security vehicles and a parking lot for personnel. All of that is behind an extremely sturdy locked steel fence. Outside the fence on Elati Street is a low-slung red brick building that is the administrative center.

Inside, Marshall waved to the receptionist and headed down a hallway to a small office that said "PERSONNEL" on the door.

"Bill," said Marshall, holding out his hand to the man behind the desk. He stood, a short, overweight guy in a white shirt and black slacks, his belly held up by a straining belt. He'd shaved his head to a shining dome, apparently an unsuccessful attempt to disguise a bad balding pattern.

"Detective," he said, shaking Marshall's hand. "Who's this?" Marshall introduced me as his assistant. "OK," said Bill — I never did find out his last name — "but this is all confidential personnel shit. I can't share it with a civilian." Marshall gave me a look, so I left, closing the door behind me. There was nowhere to sit, so I just loitered around in the hallway feeling like a naughty student waiting for the principal.

After about ten minutes, Marshall opened the door and motioned for me to come back in. "I need you to take a picture of this picture. Can you do that?"

I nodded, taking out my iPhone. This is where the iPhone beats a real camera. I pressed flat the 8x10 photo of a smiling Martinez and made sure there was no reflection. Then I centered and leveled the phone over it, so that the image exactly filled the screen, and touched the shutter. Then I emailed the image to Marshall.

"That's it?" he asked. "I need something I can run through the facial recognition thing."

"Yup." I said. "A miracle of modern technology."

"I hope you find the guy that offed him," said Bill. "We're short-handed as it is. Plus, he was a good worker, and real reliable, at least he was until he blew. I wonder what he was doing going back to his house? I can't understand where he's been — Will you let me know if you find out?" Marshall nodded. "Good. Anyway, some of the guys are having a little get-together in his honor this evening over at the White Horse bar. Feel free to drop in if you want. Maybe you'll find out something."

"I'll let you know," said Marshall, shook his hand, and we departed.

"Well, shit." said Marshall, lighting a cigar as soon as we were outside. "We definitely got a ringer here. It would have been nice if Bill'd told me all this a week ago. Would have saved us some time looking at pictures of shoes etcetera."

"What'd he say?"

"OK, so Martinez — his shift started at one o'clock the day of the murder. He clocked in, etcetera, and then boarded the C train. Apparently he got on the last car and worked his way forward and didn't get to the car you and Dr. Pleasant were on until the end of the line at Mineral. No other guards were scheduled to be on duty from Union Station to here. The killer was very, very careful about their timing."

"And knew exactly where to stab people with a minimum of mess."

Marshall nodded. "Sounds like a doctor, doesn't it?" I nodded. Marshall puffed on the cigar and looked at the sky. Cold clouds scudded across small patches of blue, opening and closing the sunlight like a child playing with a light switch.

"One other thing. When Martinez got back to the facility after Pleasant was killed, someone saw him looking at a pair of brown shoes in his locker—"

I goggled. "So they *were* his?"

Marshall shrugged. "— and then he invited everyone out for drinks etcetera at that bar they hang out at, the White Horse, and said he was buying."

"I thought the guy was broke?"

"Yeah. Well, anyways, a few of the guys went out with him, and he *did* buy a couple of rounds. Said he was coming into some money pretty soon."

"So do you think he's Pleasant's murderer after all?"

"Dunno. What do you think?"

I thought for a minute, comparing the two photos of the RTD guard on the train in my mind's eye. "I don't think so," I said, still thinking. "I think they're two different guys. The murderer didn't take the bag of money. And Martinez said he was coming into money *pretty soon.*"

Marshall sighed. "Yeah. All true. Anyways, whether he's the murderer or not, where is this money coming from if he didn't take the money in her bag? If somebody else killed her ... Maybe they bribed him to let them imitate him? Or maybe they paid him to keep quiet."

"That's blackmail," I said. "Does that sound like the guy Bill described to you?"

Marshall's cigar added some more air pollution to the Denver sky. "Well, like you said, he was broke." He threw the cigar on the ground in disgust. "Whatever. Occam's razor." I looked a question at him. "The simplest solution is probably the correct one. And the simplest solution here is that somebody was pretending to be Martinez, and he either did or didn't know about it. If he knew about it, maybe he got paid. If he didn't know about it, he found a pair of someone else's shoes in his locker and maybe he knew who they belonged to. And maybe that person killed *him*. Or not. But it's what we in the so-called Law Enforcement Community call a *Clue*."

"So now what?" I asked, chuckling. "Neither Omar nor Kim look anything like Martinez, though I suppose Omar could have disguised himself somehow ..." I was doubtful. Omar was maybe six-one and slender whereas Martinez had been shorter, but broader, with an incipient beer gut.

"Not that difficult. You said yourself that the other guy's face seemed thinner. Easy for Omar to wrap something around his middle to add some weight. Stoop. Put on some aviators and a little mustache. A Syrian and a Latino *could* look very similar. He's got no alibi to speak of — buying boots etcetera at REI." He scoffed. "I checked with them, and nobody remembers him."

"Kim's a little stockier and shorter, like Martinez," I said, thinking. "With aviators and a mustache, maybe a little makeup, that would hide him being Korean."

Marshall nodded. "Yeah, and his alibi is hardly iron clad. Shiela would vouch for him even if he was Jack the Ripper. And then there's —" He didn't finish.

We were thoughtful for a few minutes. "Well," Marshall said, stretching, "I need to go back to the office and start over. Go through those interviews, draw things on the white board, study the photos, do the facial recognition thing to make sure it *was* Martinez on the platform afterwards, etcetera. Then I'll have to show up at this memorial thing this evening. Maybe somebody there will know something. Listen, can you get home OK if I drop you at Oxford Avenue?"

"Sure," I lied. Marshall, of course, didn't know that I was not going home, but to Daniel's house in Greenwood Village. The trains didn't go that way, and it would take well over an hour by bus. I'd have to call Mohammed again — Jesus, this was getting expensive.

I pulled my parka around me more tightly. A tickling breeze had sprung up and the cloud cover was getting thicker. We were in for a March blizzard — you could smell the snow coming.

I made up my mind — I'd go home instead. That would give me a couple of hours there before meeting Daniel at Sushi Den, and then he could take me to his house. I called him after I got home.

"What were you doing with Marshall?" he asked after I'd told him where I was. "I thought he'd interviewed everybody already."

"We just went to get a photo and some information about Martin Martinez."

"The RTD guard? What did you find out?"

"*I* didn't find out anything. Marshall talked with the personnel director. It was all confidential. I just took a photo of the guy's photo so Marshall could do a face ID."

"Oh. Well, do you still want to go to Sushi Den?"

"Yup, sure. Do you?"

"I've ... um ... got some work I really need to finish up. Can we do a rain check? Meet me at home?"

Well, crap. I'd hoped to avoid another Uber trip. But then I remembered that I could get there pretty reasonably by bus from the Broadway terminal. "OK," I said. "I'll see you there—" I checked my watch, "—around 7:30, OK? I'll make you some dinner."

"Great!" I could hear his smile.

At home, I rummaged around in my freezer and cupboards and came up with two frozen chicken breasts, some cheese, some spaghetti and a can of local porcini marinara sauce. Bradshaw and I loved chicken spaghetti. I hoped Daniel would.

CHAPTER 21

"**S**o when would you like to tie the knot?" asked Daniel as he mopped up the last of his spaghetti sauce with a piece of bread. "That was delicious, by the way." It was now snowing fairly hard, big wet flakes dropping straight down from the clouds.

"Yeah, I slaved all day over a jar of hot pasta sauce," I said. "Daniel I — I'm not really ready to get married." I looked at him, silently begging him not to fight me too hard. I knew I'd cave if he did.

Daniel looked at me assessingly. "OK. Can you tell me why?"

I felt like a snake. "Well, I can't live out here, for one thing ..."

"I get that. I'll sell this place and buy a condo closer to downtown Denver."

"... And, there's my work ..."

"You can go on with that."

"... And I'm kind of in the middle of this murder investigation ..." Daniel started to say something, but I held up my hand to stop him. "And Marshall's given me the job. My photos of the Martinez crime scene came out OK —"

Daniel interrupted. "I'll be honest, Clare, I'm not happy about you trailing around after that detective — no let me finish — let alone working crime scenes regularly. I worry about you, my love. You might find ... You could attract the attention of some very dark characters. You already have! There's that kid in the hoodie following you around, attacking you —"

"That seems to have stopped," I mumbled.

"Whatever. What I'd *really* like is for you to quit this thing with Marshall and come away with me someplace — Taos maybe? Lake Tahoe? — and marry me and live with me for the rest of your life." I'm sure I looked unhappy. "Hey! Don't look like that! Isn't that a better offer than looking at dead bodies? I'd be very insulted if it's not."

I got up from my chair, walked around the table and climbed onto Daniel's lap, circling his neck with my arms. "Tell you what. I'll just finish up this investigation with Marshall — It shouldn't last much longer — and I'll turn down the crime scene photography job, and then —"

"I have a better idea," Daniel whispered. "You can continue the thing with Marshall, but we'll go to Lake Tahoe next weekend and get married. I'll move in with you, if that makes you happier, while I put the house on the market, and then we can look for a good condo near Downtown to buy. Come on, Love. Please?"

How could I say no? I nodded, and Daniel picked me up and carried me to bed, Bradshaw trotting behind.

The snow stopped around midnight, and Daniel and I lolled around in bed the next morning cruising the Internet for places to stay and marriage options in Nevada. Daniel also — to prove he was serious, I think — pulled up several real estate sites to get an idea of what he could get for his Hobbit-house and how much a house or condo on Capitol Hill was going to cost. The numbers made me fairly dizzy. House prices in Denver had certainly gone through the roof lately. But Daniel seemed to think it was all doable, and anyway, I thought, we'd still be living in my apartment for a while.

Meanwhile, my email carried a proposal from a local magazine for a photo essay on the "Plight of the Homeless" in Denver, and I thought the early-spring-snow cold and slushy conditions today would be perfect to illustrate the word "plight." So after Daniel left, Bradshaw and I rode around Denver on more busses than necessary until we got downtown. As I had hoped, the busses were about half full of street people escaping the streets, so we chatted with them, and I took some photos. Bradshaw was indispensable in these situations. Everybody wanted to pet him, and he endured it all with his usual good humor.

"I useta live in a shed out back of a farm in Greeley," said Ximena, wrapped up today in multiple layers of shawls and blankets. A Cleveland Browns knitted cap covered her tangle of dark hair. "But then they tore it down to make room for a trailer house, and I hadda come here. But the worst was I couldn't have my little poodle dog — Lola — in the shelter with me, so she ran off." Her eyes filled with tears as she patted Bradshaw. "I miss her so much ..."

Two fragrant guys in heavy overalls and tattered knitted caps told me they were riding around waiting to get back into one of the shelters. The shelters are emptied out in the mornings and reopen in the late afternoons. "Not Sally," said Bongo, the one with heavily stained teeth, meaning the Salvation Army shelter. "I hate that place, man. They make you pray all the damn time if you wanta eat."

The other guy, skinny Spider, nodded in agreement. "Nah. We gotta get into the Saint Chris. Blondie said she would stand in line for us." He looked at Bongo. "I hope she is anyways. We gotta get down there by four at the latest in case she gets wasted."

Bongo nodded. "Yeah. I hate that damn Sally. Nice dog you got here."

Bradshaw and I got off the 15 bus near the 16th Street Mall to meet Mohammed and to eat a hot dog with Alfred before heading west to the big homeless encampment by the South Platte River.

As Mohammed pulled the Crown Vic into a parking place by the bottling plant he said, "You sure not walking down there alone." I objected feebly and was overruled. So we walked to where smoke from small campfires climbed into the cold, damp air. The mostly male population was milling around among the tents, refrigerator boxes and shopping carts trying to keep warm. Almost everyone was addled in some way, either from drugs or alcohol or mental illness or all three, but there was a small group of young people standing around a fire smoking weed or meth, I wasn't sure which, until I got a whiff — meth.

After chatting with a toothless old guy with a long beard and taking his picture, I moved on to a man and woman sitting on their cardboard "porch" outside their tent, eating

MacDonald's hamburgers and fries. They had arrived by bus from someplace in Kansas, but would be heading south tomorrow, if she could get enough money by flying a sign at some intersection. She was hoping for Broadway and Speer Boulevard with its larger than average load of affluent cars.

"You really have to be fuckin' careful not to take somebody's corner without them telling you it's OK," said the woman, who had long stringy blond hair. "You can get really fuckin' beat up that way." Her cardboard sign said, "RECENT WIDOW ANYTHING HELPS." They let me photograph them, and I moved on to the group of young guys.

"Wait!" said Mohammed, who had insisted sticking to my elbow. "That girl — She is the one who attacked you, yes?"

He was pointing with his head at a girl in the young guys' group wearing a black hoodie and jeans. She watched us warily as we approached, her eyes outlined in thick black circles, her lips, nose and ears abundantly pierced. She looked like a poster child for meth with her cracked and bleeding lips, her deathly pale face with several scabs on her cheeks. Wisps of black hair stuck out from under her hoodie, and I could see that underneath the too-large clothes, she was as thin as cigarette paper.

As soon as she saw that Mohammed had recognized her, she turned from the group and started running north along the bike path that followed the river, her red Converses slapping the wet pavement. Bradshaw started barking as Mohammed broke away from me and ran after her. *Shit,* I thought. I had no choice but to follow, dropping Bradshaw's leash. Bradshaw's six-inch legs were not made for speed.

Pandemonium broke out in the encampment, people yelling curses and obscene suggestions, and even some offers to help.

Abruptly, the girl turned and ran back around Mohammed toward me. She held something in her left hand. Before I could react, she slammed into me, knocking me over. She was on top of me in a moment, and stabbed the box knife she was holding into my right chest. Then, kneeling astride me, she lifted herself up on her knees and slashed the knife down toward my face.

I turned my head quickly, the knife just catching my right ear. It hurt like hell, and I yelled at her to stop. But instead, she moved her right hand to my neck and started pressing down on it hard, the box knife now heading for my right eye. I hoisted my hips, hoping to buck her off me. It didn't work — she weighed almost nothing — but she was unnaturally strong and seemed determined to stay aboard. But my motion did manage to deflect her aim. The blow landed above my right eye. Immediately, I was half blinded by blood. Bradshaw was barking and growling, launching himself at her, trying to bite her leg, or her foot. I could hear footsteps running our way.

At last I managed to roll to my right and get a grip on my camera. But the hand with the box cutter was still swinging lethally toward my face. I felt a searing pain along my cheek just under my right eye this time, but I grabbed her wrist as she raised it to strike again.

And suddenly it was over.

Her slight weight lifted off my legs and her flailing arms flailed high above me. Mohammed had her around the waist. Bradshaw leaped up and yanked off one of her shoes.

"You fucking bitch!" she screamed, "It's all your fucking fault you fucking bitch!"

I felt muddled and couldn't understand. *What was my fault? Could I have harmed her somehow without knowing it?* I felt the ground next to me, cold, muddy and wet. Mohammed was squeezing her wrist with his long, strong fingers. The bloody box cutter dropped to the ground. The girl was still screaming and trying to kick Mohammed who held her above me. Bradshaw was barking and trying to bite her feet. A crowd had gathered around me, fragrant with smoke and body odor.

I decided my unscheduled nap on the ground should be over.

As I started to get up, blood now dripping on my hands, the cut on my chest screamed at me to stop. I tried to roll to my right to get my knees under me. Mohammed transferred the girl to the crook of his left arm and held my right arm to help me up. I leaned over thinking I might be sick, and the world whirled around me. The girl was still screaming at me, kicking at Mohammed, incoherent with rage.

I turned, and as I did, the girl broke free of Mohammed's arm and ran away down the bike path. Nobody followed her, especially not me.

"What the hell was that all about?" I asked the assembled spectators, trying to keep my balance and not be sick.

"Yo. Dude. That dude told her you were gonna turn her in."

I looked toward the voice, a skinny kid wearing basketball shorts and a too large sideways hat, but the world was still trying to pull me down. "Dude? What dude? This dude? Pointing at Mohammed. "Turn her in for what?"

"Nah. Tall dude, mustache, kinda heavy, like a beer gut, Dude. She's fuckin' DACA, and the dude told her you were gonna call the Migras to Trump her." He stopped for what almost looked like thought. "Dude," he added.

I thought maybe I'd dropped down through my black hole into some alternate universe. "Wha?" I was having trouble seeing the kid. I wiped blood from my eyes.

"Yeah, and she needed a tweak and you always had those Ali Baba cameras. So ..." said someone else.

"Yeah, and plus she's fuckin' batshit, yo," said someone else.

Mohammed caught me as I fell.

Sound came back first. Mohammed's voice. Bradshaw panting somewhere. Then motion. I was lying on something and moving. I felt sick and shaky and sweaty. The motion stopped. Something pressed hard on my chest.

"Ow!"

Strong hands pulled me up to sitting. "C'mon sweetheart. Stand up, OK? We've got you." Arms wrapped around me. Someone dabbed my face with something wet. It stung.

I opened my eyes. My arms were around the shoulders of two nurses in bloodstained scrubs who were walking me toward an open door with a sign that said, "EMERGENT CARE." They walked me into a small room and lifted me onto a table covered with white paper.

"That's it," said a black guy wearing a face mask and a doctor's outfit. "Let's cut this sweater off — hand me those bandage scissors, will you?" I couldn't see who he was talking to.

"It's Norwegian," I said as distinctly as I could. "You'll ruin it."

"Are you back with us? Already ruined, I'm afraid. Ripped and bloody. We need to stop the bleeding and get all those cuts stitched up. You're going to be pretty sore for a few days." He took my right hand and shook it. "I'm Dr. Washington. What's your name?"

Mohammed started to say something, but Dr. Washington shushed him.

"Clare. Clare Standish. And today is Wednesday. It's 2019 and Donald Trump is the President."

Dr. Washington laughed. "You'll be fine," he said.

Then like a light snapping out, I disappeared.

I had no sense of time passing or of being unconscious. It wasn't like sleep. It was as if I had ceased to be, had never been. And then, just as suddenly, I snapped back on, and I was fully conscious, feeling both rested and sleepy. Someone was holding my hand. I looked over the side of a bed that was bent in the middle and had a silver railing.

"Welcome back, my love," said Daniel. "Good sleep?"

"Yes, I — Was I asleep?"

"No, they gave you something to knock you out. Propofol, they said."

I tried to rub my eyes, but my left arm was attached to a bunch of tubes and wires. Something was beeping. Daniel let go of my hand and pressed a cool cloth against my eyes. It felt great. "Where am I?"

"Denver General. The clinic got you stabilized and trucked you over here in an ambulance. Dr. Washington called me. They've stitched you up and now you're getting pumped full of fluids and antibiotics and tetanus vaccine and some other stuff I can't remember. You're going to be fine, but you're here for a day or two."

Gingerly I touched my face. The two cuts felt like corrugated plastic and hurt like hell. "I must look like a zombie," I said.

Daniel cocked his head. "More like Frankenstein's monster, actually. You're going to have a couple of interesting scars. We'll have matching ones!" he pointed to the tiny scar on his nose. "But they'll only make *you* more beautiful."

I started to laugh, but that woke up the cut on my chest, so I stopped.

"Do you remember what happened?"

"Yes. Vividly. I need to talk to Marshall. Would you call him for me? And what happened to my camera?"

"Mohammed took care of that. He grabbed your camera — I have it here — and Marshall's been calling me about every hour." He held up the now very muddy Nikon. "And speaking of Marshall — I really, *really* wish you'd drop this investigation thing with him. This is getting more and more serious. What happens next? Somebody throws you off a roof? Please, Darling, quit now while you're in one piece. I'm having nightmares! Please — for me?"

I didn't correct Daniel that I'd been working a magazine photo shoot, not Marshall's investigation. Instead, in my mind's eye, I saw myself soaring outward from a roof, momentarily untethered from gravity, the wind caressing my face, the earth rising to embrace me. It was a dream I'd had often in the past. It was a dream of weightlessness, of unspeakable freedom, and I'd wake in tears of grief and joy.

Who had made my own leap to death feel like joyous flight? The anger rose again in my chest, and the beeping got faster. I closed my eyes and concentrated on pushing my heart rate down, and gradually the beeping returned to its regular two-step.

"Please, Daniel. Just call Marshall, would you?"

But he didn't need to. A soft knock on the door, and Marshall stepped in, closing it firmly behind him, a fat folder in one hand and an unlit cigar between his fingers. He nodded to Daniel and pulled a chair forward, so he was sitting next to the bottom corner of my bed. He twined his legs and put the folder on my foot. I moved my foot.

"So. I hear you had quite an adventure down at Little Del Rio." I nodded. It hurt. "Yeah, well, you should have called me."

"Mohammed was with me."

Marshall shrugged. "Looks like he wasn't all that much help." I started to speak, but Marshall waved the cigar. "Whatever. So what did you find out, if anything?"

I described what had happened. "One of the skaters said someone told the hoodie girl that I was going to turn her in to Immigration. They said she's here on DACA, so it was obviously a lie. They described the guy as tall-ish, with aviator shades, a beer gut and mustache."

Marshall raised his eyebrows. "Martinez?"

I shrugged. "Maybe. Or maybe it was bizarro-Martinez. Would you have described Martinez as tall?"

Marshall pulled his small notebook out of his breast pocket and wrote something in it. "No, but eyewitnesses are unreliable even when they're not spun out." Daniel got up to leave, but Marshall waved him back into his seat.

"Are you recording me?" I asked.

Marshall nodded. "OK, so can you describe this hoodie girl?"

I smiled. It hurt. "I can," I said. I reached out a hand to Daniel, who took it. "Would you hand me my camera, Daniel, please?"

Daniel brushed most of the mud off it and handed it to me. I turned it on and scrolled through the review screens. When I got to the one I wanted, I held out the camera to Marshall. "Her."

Under less ridiculous circumstances, the photo might have earned a Pulitzer. The girl's scabbed face — streaked with dirt, blackened teeth bared — was blazing with rage. Blurred by motion, her right hand holding the box cutter was raised above her head. There was no doubt about her intentions.

"Holy crap!" breathed Marshall, "That's Pain Jane!" and turned the camera so Daniel could see it. "I know that tweaker — She's got form as long as Santa's naughty list."

Daniel got up and began pacing circles around the room's small space, thinking hard. After several circles, he said, "I'm going to go get a Coke or something. Do you want anything?"

I shook my head.

"How the hell did you get this?" Marshall stuck the cigar between his teeth, and I thought he was going to light it, but he took it out again.

"She had me on the ground, but Mohammed had picked her up. I got my camera onto my chest and just started snapping. There are four or five more, but that's the only one that shows her clearly." Marshall looked down at the camera. "Go ahead and scroll backwards. There are also some pix of some of the homeless people and the skaters." Marshall stared at the back of the camera, looking frustrated. "Just push the left arrow button." He found it and looked surprised. I laughed. It hurt. "Let go of the button! Just press it quickly to see the photos one at a time."

Marshall looked happier and scrolled through all sixty-five photos making small noises in his throat. "These photos are going to help. Can you identify the person who described the Martinez-looking guy?"

I nodded. "Yes." I took the camera back from him. "He's this kid here," I pointed to a young white guy standing a little way back, a too large Raiders cap turned sideways, tattoos on his calves and a general suburban gang-banger air about him.

"Great! Can you email me those two photos?"

I nodded and used the wireless function to send them. "OK. You should have them now. But — Listen, Daniel doesn't want me to keep doing this with you. He's scared. He wants me to marry him and quit working with you."

Marshall nodded. "Mmm. I know. Well, marriage etcetera, that's a big step. But I suppose that's up to you, not Daniel. Right?"

I nodded, not really sure. Once again I thought, *He knows a lot more about me than I do about him.*

"OK, then just one more thing and I'll leave you to take a nap etcetera," he continued. "Denver PD says they have a partial on that VIN number from the burnt-out black truck that may or may not have killed your folks."

CHAPTER 22

I was suddenly wide awake and alert. "They have? What — Who — I mean —?"

Marshall lit his cigar, now that we were alone, and waved it at me. "Calm down. Jesus! Listen to you beeping! Calm down."

Indeed! The heart monitor had cranked up to about 120 bpm. I could feel the pulse in my neck throbbing, hear it in my ears, and my breath was coming pretty fast. "OK, OK, but spill the beans, Shamus."

"You've been watching too many noir movies. Unfortunately for us, the partial is *very* partial. VIN numbers are unique to every vehicle, so they're very long — 17 letters and numbers. It's a code that tells anyone who understands it where and when the car was built, the kind of fuel it uses, its brand and engine type, the model year and the car's own manufacturer's serial number which can be used to trace the car to a specific dealership, and with luck, to an owner."

I revolved my good hand in a "get on with it" motion.

"Right, but bear with me. What is important here is what it *doesn't* tell us. It doesn't tell us what color it is. It doesn't tell us how many miles it's been driven. And because the VIN on this truck is so partial, it doesn't tell us much about the manufacturer's serial number. So in other words, we can't use it to link it to a specific car bought by a specific person. Which is a damn shame, because we pretty much know all the rest of that stuff."

I nodded, understanding. "Yeah, we already know the make and model, Darth Vader black, probably 2005 or four."

"2005 Super duty. It was brand new. That part of the VIN came up OK. But keep in mind we don't have definitive proof that this is the truck that hit your folks. A very high probability, but no proof. For proof, we'd need DNA — not gonna happen because of the fire — or a paint chip matching your folks' Camry somewhere on the front end. Denver PD is looking, but not hopeful."

Marshall puffed on his cigar. "Now there is this, though," he continued. "We do have three of the six serial numbers. And there will have been a relatively small number of these types of trucks, black ones, sold in Colorado in 2005. So the cold case guys down at Denver PD said that maybe, if the list is short enough, they'd try to run down the buyer. But anything could happen after 14 years. The dealership could have gone out of business, records could have been destroyed, etcetera. And the driver could be dead. So don't get your hopes up."

"About what?" asked Daniel, coming in the door with hands full. "I got you a Seven-Up, Love. I thought you might be thirsty."

"Thanks!" I smiled. He was right. The fizzy drink's icy sweetness tasted delicious. "The DPD cold case guys have recovered some of the VIN numbers from the truck they think hit my folks."

Daniel turned a look like thunder on Marshall. "Are you responsible for this?" Marshall just gave him the cop stare. "Don't you understand that when you dig all this up you're just putting her through it all over again?"

I wanted him to stop. "Daniel, that's not —"

But he continued. "And — Listen, I'd appreciate it if you'd leave her out of all this in future. You're also putting her in danger. She almost got killed today. I'd like her around a little longer — at least till I can get us married." He turned to me, looking grim.

Marshall looked at me, eyebrows raised. I was getting tired. "Daniel, Pain Jane's attack had nothing to do with the murder of Dr. Pleasant or Martin Martinez or the truck's VIN. The visit to the homeless camp had been for my own work, and the attack was not about murder, but about Pain Jane's immigration status." I turned to Marshall. "I can take care of myself – I lived on the streets for five years; I learned a bunch of stuff about how to get out of trouble there. You both just need to back off."

Just shows how wrong you can be.

I was long overdue for a visit with Joshua, so three days later, when I'd been home for a day and was feeling quite a bit better, Mohammed Ubered Bradshaw and me to the Blue House. My face and chest were still sore, but Bradshaw was fastened to my hands-free contraption and wearing his vest, overloaded today with my camera, money and other junk I'd normally carry in my own backpack. He trotted along beside me, proudly smiling at the world as if to say, "Yup, I'm indispensable to her, that's me."

Shiela met me at the door and ushered me into the day room where Joshua, Roger and several other guys were playing a noisy game of wheelchair Blind Man's Bluff, with Roger as the blind man, of course. Some others, working quietly on various projects or playing cards, were watching them with disfavor.

"You're lucky today," said Shiela, "Whatever was bothering him seems to have gone away. He seems fine."

"C'are!" Joshua called, and was immediately "bluffed" by Roger, who was playing by ear.

"Did you bring the detective?" called Roger. The game began to break up.

I laughed. "Not today! Maybe next time." Roger shrugged and wheeled over to the other guys, high-fiving them before retiring to the vending machine in the corner.

"W'as up?" asked Joshua, leaning forward for a hug. I detached Bradshaw, who leaped into his lap. As always, I unconsciously translated. "You hurt something?"

"A little," I said. "Somebody hurt me with a box cutter."

Joshua wheeled over to an empty table where I sat down gratefully. "Wow! Who?"

I laughed again. "Nobody you know. Somebody who didn't want her picture taken."

Joshua nodded. "You should be more careful."

Shiela came over to sit with us, bringing a Coke for Joshua. "He's right," she said. "Can I see the wounds? Purely a professional request, of course."

I pulled aside my shirt and showed her the pile of bandages covering the many stitches that were starting to itch maddeningly. "I'll give you some cream that will help with that," she said, gently pulling away the gauze and taking a look at the red and swollen slice with the stitches running up it like train tracks. "Wow. You were lucky it hit your breastbone."

Lucky wasn't exactly how I'd have put it. Maybe if nobody had tried to kill me I'd have thought it lucky. However ... Time to move on.

"Joshua, I need to ask you something, and I don't want you to get upset. It's about Dr. Pleasant —"

"Marla, yeah." He sighed, and considered me sadly, but calmly. "I miss her."

"I'm sorry," I said, taking his hand. "But I need to know why you liked her so much. She had lots of enemies, seems like everyone but you."

He nodded again, sadly. "Yup. But she was special to me." I saw we were in for a long chat, so I sat back, but kept hold of his hand. "I didn't just like her. I loved her, and she loved me." Shiela gasped. Joshua took a swig of Coke and wiped a tear off his cheek.

After a minute, he continued. "We started getting serious when I went to Browning. She visited me, then she came there too and started looking after me, like special. We talked a lot. She could understand me when nobody else could. And I made her laugh. So I told her about mom and dad and the accident ..." He wiped another tear, and Shiela handed him a tissue. "She already knew, of course. And then, it just went on from there. Sometimes she would visit me at

night ... you know? I mean, I'm not *completely* paralyzed."
He looked at me meaningfully.

I was shocked. "She raped you?"

"Shit no! I told you! We loved each other! You know
how I am! I have these fucking legs that don't work too good,
but I still need love! To be warm and sweet and happy with
someone, and Marla was ... all those things."

Shiela got up and brought each of us another Coke.
"OK, I get it," she said.

I thought about my own few years after the accident
— the drugs, the alcohol and the boys in filthy squats, on
rooftops, on the streets. I had been looking for comfort, or
maybe love, through the terrible pain, a pain that no amount
or kind of comfort could wash away. Ironically, Joshua had
been luckier in a weird way — he'd had love — and maybe
that's why the black hole had never opened up and pulled
him into the next world, even though he'd been far more
physically damaged than I had. He'd had Marla Pleasant,
kind, caring, loving him. The woman everyone else hated.
Maybe she'd needed his love, too.

"But ... Wasn't she a lot older than you?"

Joshua shrugged. "Yeah, ten or twelve years. Didn't
matter to either of us. About the same as you and Daniel.
Doesn't seem that important to *you*." I had to admit he had a
point. "Anyway, she pulled some strings with somebody and
got me in here, and then she came over too, and ... we just
went on. Until ..." He looked down at Bradshaw, stroking his
soft back.

Shiela was shocked. "She slept with you *here*?"

Joshua laughed — the first really happy laugh in a while. "Nah! Not *sleeping* exactly!" Shiela and I must have looked *really* shocked then. "More like what *you* do with Dr. Kim on his afternoons off," he smirked.

Shiela blushed and rearranged her scrunchy. "How do you know about that?"

"You'd be surprised what we know. We're all fucked up, but we're not stupid. Well, most of us anyway." He smirked over at Roger who was listening to something on his AirPods with his eyes closed.

Shiela looked ashamed.

"Anyway, yeah, she'd come into my room and we'd ... you know ... and we'd laugh and talk and cuddle for a while and then she'd go finish her shift, or go home, or whatever."

I was trying to figure out what to think about all this. Shiela and I looked at each other, and suddenly we began to giggle. Then laugh. Then really laugh until we were breathless and wiping tears away. Joshua looked relieved, then laughed politely along with us until, exhausted, Shiela and I began to quiet down. But then, I felt the loss and grief and anger welling up inside me and began to sob uncontrollably.

Shiela rubbed my back, then scooted her chair close to mine and put her arms around me. Joshua embraced me on the other side.

"Whatcha cryin' about Sissy?" he asked. "You don't think it's sad, do you?"

I was hiccupping now. "Fuck no, bro. I'm just ... I can't believe I wasted all that misery on getting high and worthless boys while you ... You found what we both needed, someone to love and be loved by." Shiela cooed and stroked my back some more.

"And ... and I'm just SO FUCKING ANGRY!!" I couldn't control my voice. I was shouting. I took a breath. "Somebody did this to us and got away with it and ..." I waved my hands helplessly, taking in the whole miserable situation. Then I was overcome with fresh sobs.

"But you've got Daniel now," whispered Shiela. I saw Joshua nodding out of the corner of my eye.

"Daniel is good, Sissy. You can be happy with him, right?"

I wiped my eyes and looked at them both, so thankful for my two best friends. "Well, yes, I have Daniel to love, and he is very, very good to me. But I just ..." I stammered to a stop.

"Go on, tell your auntie Shiela."

"Oh, he keeps pushing me to go to Vegas or somewhere and get married, like right away. In fact, he seemed angry that I got myself cut up so I couldn't go this weekend."

"And ...?" said Shiela.

"And ... I don't WANT to get married! There! I've said it! I want us to go on as we are, at least for a while longer." Bradshaw looked over the top of the table, concerned about my tone of voice. "But, I mean, check out this ring!" I held up my left hand to show them the gorgeous diamond and sapphire ring. "Oh, Shiela ... I just don't know what to do!"

"Well, that's easy," said Shiela, smoothing her braids. "Just take a page from Nancy Regan's book and *Just Say No*. It's a beautiful ring, but is it really worth it? To be pushed into something like marriage when you don't want to be?

And what's the hurry anyway? Or you could just give me the ring, and I'll ask Kim to marry *me*."

I shrugged and tried to smile. Joshua nodded. Roger tapped over and reached blindly out to Bradshaw on Joshua's lap, feeding him half a moon pie. "Let's sing," he announced. Roger has a lovely tenor voice which he used to launch us into our year-round favorite, "All I Want for Christmas is You." Bradshaw went back to sleep.

Daniel stared at me in disbelief. "You *what*?"

We were back at my apartment, doing dishes. "Daniel, I'm so, so sorry, but I just really don't want to get married right now." How's that for weasel words? "Can't we just go on like we are? I mean, of course you can move in here with me — I'd love that, I would. But ... I really, really don't want to get married. Not yet anyway. I mean, someday, sure. Maybe sooner than ... Maybe not too long, but just ..."

Daniel held up his hand, and for just the tiniest fraction of a second I thought he was going to slap me. His eyes were like the sky full of summer lightening, dark blue and gray and flashing. I'd never seen him really angry before. But of course he didn't slap me. He just wanted me to shut up, so I did.

"I don't get it," he said. His voice was straining to remain controlled. "You were OK with it when I gave you that ring. You should have said no then if you didn't want me to come with it. What's changed? Are you ... I don't know ... wanting somebody else? That detective?"

"*NO!*" I almost shouted. "No no no! I'm crazy about you, I am! I don't want anyone else but you. But you surprised me so much with the ring and your lovely speech, and I ... I didn't think, I didn't know what to say. I mean, yes seemed the right answer, right? But I didn't realize you wanted to get married, like, *instantly!*" Daniel started to say something, but this time I raised *my* hand. "And what's the big rush anyway? Why can't we just go on?"

"Well, why *not* now? Huh? What is it that's holding you back? I've said I'd move in here. I've said I'll sell the house and find someplace around here for us. I've said you're welcome to go on with your photography business —"

"But not with Marshall. Not crime scene photography, right? Isn't that the issue, really? You don't like Marshall, or you don't want me around him or —"

"I just don't want you in danger! Is that so crazy? I want you to be safe, not trucking all over *homeless* camps and getting stabbed or knocked down in the street or —"

"None of that has anything to do with Marshall! The homeless camp was for *Denver Uptown* magazine! And I don't know what all that crap with the hoodie kid — Pain Jane? — was all about, but whatever, she seems to be neutralized now, thanks mostly to *Marshall!*"

"*She was after you because of something to do with Dr. Pleasant's murder,*" Daniel hissed. "Which, I'd like to point out, thanks to *Marshall* is still not solved. There's a murderer out there, Clare. And you've got yourself tangled up in it somehow. And *that's* Marshall's fault."

He wasn't wrong. But I was damned if I was going to admit it.

Daniel stalked toward me and took both my hands in his. "Don't fight me on this, please, Clare." His voice was gentle, and his eyes had gone back to their sweet clear blue. "Did you know, the hospital wouldn't tell me anything about your condition or let me see you unless I'm your next of kin? I had to lie and say I was your brother. Do you have any idea how frightened I was? If we'd gotten married just a few days before, they wouldn't have tried to keep me away."

I looked up at him, completely disarmed.

He bent down and kissed me tenderly. "I love you, Clare. If you don't want to marry me, then please, stop putting yourself in danger. But I'd really prefer you married me. As soon as possible."

Well, of course, it ended up the way it always ended up — in bed. Happily so. But in the back of my mind — when I had a mind, that is — I knew that if I married him, he'd keep pressuring me to quit working with Marshall. And I wasn't sure when it had happened, but somehow, working with Marshall had become more important to me than all the ski and bike and magazine and tourist board and greeting card and website business in the world.

CHAPTER 23

With the whole marriage/Daniel/Marshall thing still unresolved, I met Marshall the next day at the Littleton police complex. "I had the Rio Blanco County Sheriff pick up our Dr. Omar Hussain this morning. They'll be questioning him shortly, and I'll be watching on our CCTV link, so I can feed them questions etcetera. I thought you might want to watch."

"So he's our suspect now?"

Marshall nodded. "Yup, as long as Doctor Kim's alibi holds. The Demidovs are out of the picture, Dylan the bike messenger's alibi is weak, but I checked with the judge in his case, and it seems legit. Also there's no motive there, so I've ruled him out. Daniel —"

"— was at a conference at the Blue House."

"Mmm. So Omar is our best bet at the moment. Weak alibi, strong motive, etcetera. But of course we have to consider Martinez's murder, too, which makes Kim the better suspect, since he's here in town. It's quite a long hike from Rio Blanco." Marshall sighed. "But what I really want to do is tell you about Pain Jane." He pointed me to a chair in his office, and I hoped I looked receptive instead of terrified.

"We interviewed her yesterday —"

"You didn't want me there?"

Marshall shook his head. "Nope. She goes ballistic if we even mention your name. Too much emotion, and frankly, too much bat-shit craziness —" He checked to see if I was still paying attention. I was. "— but I did want to tell you what we found out. She was approached about a month ago by a fairly tall man with sunglasses and a mustache and a beer gut —"

"Martinez?"

"Hang on. This guy told her that the cops were after her and the border patrol and maybe Space Force for all I know, and they were going to arrest her because *you* had turned her in."

"That's ridiculous! I didn't even know who she was till she stabbed me with a box cutter."

"I know, I know. Just listen, will you? I told you, she's crazy. And she was crashing out of a meth high, so she was even crazier — paranoid." I nodded. Marshall sighed and got out a cigar. "*Anyway* about the same time Pleasant was killed — she didn't know if it was before or after — this guy said he'd supply her with meth etcetera if she'd follow you around and report back to him about what you were up to."

"I wasn't up to anything! I was making photographs and … then I guess I was hanging out with you!"

Marshall nodded impatiently. "Right. But the guy also told her to steal your cameras and destroy your computers. He told her how to break in through that back window. So you know how these tweakers are — she had some parkour experience, and the meth makes you strong and agile, so …" I nodded, resigned. What an idiot I'd been not to put bars on that window. "Then I guess the guy didn't get what he wanted, so he told her to grab your computer."

I nodded. "So why did she attack me again and steal *another* camera?"

"Well, this guy told her to follow you and attack you as soon as she got the chance. Stealing the second camera was her own idea. So she followed you around." Marshall shrugged. "And then you showed up at the homeless camp, and she went ballistic."

"I don't get it. What was the point of following me around?"

Marshall shrugged again. "No idea. *She* thought it was maybe to scare you. The guy told her not to bother trying to be covert. She didn't put it like that, of course. She said it was a secret between her and the guy, not you."

"OK, but wait," I said, struggling out of my coat. The office was hot. "There was a second break-in at my apartment by somebody much more careful. They seem to have searched for something, but they only disturbed a couple of things around my desk. I didn't report it."

Marshall looked resigned. "She didn't say anything about that. I'll check with her again. How'd they get in?"

I shook my head. "I don't know. Somebody must have let them into the building and then maybe they picked the lock on my door."

Marshall shook his head disgustedly. "That doesn't sound drug related. But Colorado is one of the few states where there's no background check on locksmiths. Could have been somebody with lock-picking tools. That door of yours isn't any Fort Knox. Who else has a key?"

"Building manager. Daniel. Shiela. Marlon, my downstairs neighbor. That's all, I think."

"That's plenty. You need to be more careful." Marshall checked his watch. I guess he wanted to finish the story before we went into the video room. He sighed and twirled the still unlit cigar through his fingers. I realized suddenly the cigar was a kind of comforting fidget for him. Like prayer beads, or a key chain. I snapped a shot of him. He didn't notice, deep in thought.

"So what about Martinez?" I reminded him. "Do you think this guy Pain Jane was describing was Martinez?"

He shook his head slowly. "I don't know. When I showed her the photo line-up with Martinez and our UNSUB in it, she didn't ID either of *them,* but inconveniently, she did pick out Dr. Hussain. She's too addled for that to be reliable, but that's why we have to interview Hussain again."

I noticed he was not Dr. Omar anymore, but scary Dr. Hussain. "OK, but back to who killed Dr. Pleasant, what about those two guys who were running the scam at the nursing homes?" I didn't want it to be Dr. Omar. I liked him. "Maybe one of them killed Pleasant so they wouldn't have to share the money."

"Yeah, I thought of that, too. I've been trying to find them, but no luck. They've disappeared. Which in itself is suspicious. So you could be right."

He checked his watch again. Let's go watch Rio Blanco talk to the doc. You don't say anything, OK?"

"OK," I said, following him through the door. "Did anyone see see Daniel at the conference that day?"

Marshall nodded. "Yes, a couple of orderlies saw him. Around eleven-thirty. He said he was going out for a run during the lunch break. They remembered because he checked his watch and said he'd be back by one."

"Great!" I said. They'd just corroborated his alibi.

Marshall led me into a small, dark room with a big TV screen above a desk. On the screen, Dr. Omar Hussain was sitting at a table in a room with cinderblock walls. The screen was divided into three pictures, showing Dr. Hussain from above, wide angle from the side, and straight on. He was fiddling with an empty Styrofoam coffee cup. He looked exhausted, carelessly dressed, his hair was messed up, and he hadn't shaved. Apparently the Rio Blanco Sheriff had gotten him out of bed. Or maybe he'd been up all night.

I had to admit that it would have been very easy for him to disguise himself as Martinez. His Middle Eastern coloring could read as Hispanic, his overnight stubble showed he could have grown a mustache very quickly. He was taller and slimmer than Martinez, but some padding and a slight stoop would have fixed that well enough for people who were pre-disposed to see Martinez himself, not an imposter. People do see what they expect to see.

Marshall dug out his RAZR and dialed. "We're all set here. Ready when you are." He listened for a minute and then flipped the phone shut. In a few minutes, two people in sheriff's uniforms entered the room. Both took off their white cowboy hats and set them brim up on the table. The

Sheriff himself was maybe late forties, lanky and weather-beaten, a man who spent a lot of time outdoors. The other was much younger, early twenties, with pink baby skin and a sun-bleached crew cut.

"That's Sheriff MacRae and his deputy — Jonah I think." whispered Marshall. The screen said he was muted. We could hear Sheriff MacRae and the deputy clearly.

After the usual preliminaries, Sheriff MacRae asked Omar about his whereabouts on February 9th, 2019. "I've already answered that question many times," said Omar tiredly.

"We'd like you to answer it again."

Omar sighed. "I've said I was at a conference —"

"But you left —"

"YES! OK! I've already said I left the conference after the lunch break and took an Uber over to REI to buy a pair of hiking boots. I do a lot of hiking out here. I gave the police a receipt for the boots."

"Who was the Uber driver?"

"I don't know. He was Somali, that's all I know."

"How did you know he was Somali?"

"He told me."

"But you didn't see his name on the required documentation placed in the car?"

"No. I was thinking of other things. My wife left me recently. And she took the kids."

"How long were you at REI?"

"Don't you have CCTV from the store?"

MacRae sighed. "Quite a few of the cameras weren't working. Often happens."

"I was there all afternoon."

"Really? It takes all afternoon to buy hiking boots?"

"Of course not. I was bored and missing my family. I wandered around the store looking at stuff. Things for the kids —"

"You weren't on the light rail train from Union Station? I understand it's a short walk from REI to the station?"

"Absolutely not. I was at REI and then I went back to the hotel for socializing and drinks and dinner. To me, that was the most useful part of the conference. Then the next day I came back home, here. I've been here ever since, except for meeting Detective Marshall at Glenwood Springs. That's it. Can I go now? I've been up all night with a patient."

"How did you get back to the hotel?"

"I walked. It's quite a pleasant walk from Confluence Park to downtown. It took me about half an hour."

"Why didn't you walk *to* REI, then?"

Omar shrugged. "I didn't feel like it."

"Not because you wanted to establish an alibi?"

"Obviously not, since I didn't bother to get the driver's name."

"Are you willing to take a polygraph?"

"Not at the moment, no. As I just said, I've been up all night. And those tests are notoriously inaccurate, especially for people under stress."

"*Are* you under stress?"

"Of course I'm under stress."

"Why?"

Omar began to stand up, but the deputy said sharply. "Sit down, Dr. Hussain."

Omar sat down. "Because I'm here answering all these questions *again.*" He was silent for a few minutes. The two sheriffs watched him silently. Suddenly Omar slapped the table — hard. I jumped. "Am I under arrest?"

"Not at this time. We hoped you'd cooperate in this murder investigation. Your refusal to take a polygraph test tells us you have something to hide."

"I *did not* refuse to take a polygraph! I just don't want to do it now, when I'm tired and upset!"

The Sheriff didn't respond to this. "You admit you hated the victim, Dr. Marla Pleasant, and your alibi is uncorroborated, so you have both motive and opportunity. Would you be surprised to know that a witness has identified you as one of the two RTD guards on the train that day?"

"Very much so, as I wasn't *on* that train."

"As for the means, a cheap boning knife would have been available anywhere, including REI."

"Oops," said Marshall quietly.

"So you believe I did go to REI." said Omar. The two sheriffs were silent. "Well, either I was at REI not killing the doctor, or I was on the train not buying a boning knife. Which is it?"

"You could have bought the boning knife at any time, anywhere. You went to REI, bought a pair of boots, kept the receipt to establish your alibi, then got on the train at Union Station."

"OK, that's it. I want to call my solicitor ... um ... lawyer. You haven't got a thing to hold me on. How could I know Marla Pleasant was going to be on that train? Why would I just happen to have a sodding boning knife at a geriatric medicine conference?" He looked from one of them to the other. "Do you hear me? *I want a lawyer!*" He was shouting now.

"Shit," said Marshall.

"Interview terminated 10:25 a.m." said the deputy and shut off the recording. The two left the room, but the cameras stayed on.

"Hang on," whispered Marshall, a hand on my arm. "Sometimes this is the best part."

We watched Omar get up and walk around the room, clearly talking to himself, though we couldn't hear what he was saying. He stood by the cinderblock wall and banged his forehead against it gently. He returned to the table and sat down. He put his head down on his crossed arms and was still for several minutes. I thought he might have gone to sleep. But suddenly he got up and banged his fist on the door, "shouting, "Lawyer, lawyer, lawyer!" He kept on shouting until the door opened, and the baby-faced deputy escorted him out, holding his right arm tightly above the elbow.

"Too many questions and not enough answers," said Marshall. He sighed and stretched. "I need a smoke."

Instead of going out front as I'd expected, Marshall led me up a series of stairs to the flat roof of the complex. It was a gorgeous day. The sun, still low enough to get in your eyes, shone blindingly on perfectly white Mount Evans, standing like an ice cream cone against a child's blue dress. The air was so clear you could see all the way from Longs Peak, 40 miles to the north, to Pikes Peak, 60 miles to the south. There were tiny buds on the ends of the maple tree branches. I turned my face to the sun and basked in the soft, sixty-degree weather. Marshall was looking at the view through blue cigar smoke.

"Do you think he did it?" I asked.

"Dunno," said Marshall. "Suspects have a lot of different responses to being questioned — anger, nerves, fear, tears, yelling, etcetera — but guilty ones also evade, or try to explain away whatever evidence you have or blame someone else. He didn't do that, but he's a smart guy, so maybe he decided that making fun of the evidence was his best shot. No question he's depressed about his wife and kids leaving him. And mad as hell at Pleasant. I've seen weaker motives for whacking somebody." He thought for a minute. "I gotta say, he's still a real strong suspect. I gotta go talk to that Pain Jane again. There's something about her story that's bothering me."

I kept quiet while he smoked and thought. "So so far we got a very unpopular dead doctor on a train carrying five-thousand bucks, two more doctors and a nurse who admit they don't mind that she's dead, two missing con artists connected somehow, maybe to the five-thousand bucks, a bat-shit tweaker attempting to steal your cameras and computers, which had pictures of the crime scene on them —"

"Maybe she just wanted whatever money she could get for them."

"Nope. The guy, pseudo-Martinez or whoever it was, told her to follow you around and steal them, remember? So maybe the murderer was in those pictures — I mean, it's pretty certain he was in those pictures —" He stopped and stared at the mountains. "But why follow you around? And then we got a dead RTD guard, maybe because ... maybe because he knew who the murderer was. But we never found any unexplained cash in his bank account or anywhere."

"So what?"

"Well, if he knew who the murderer was you'd expect to find some hush money somewhere. He said he'd be coming into money soon. But nada. And then those damn shoes ..."

"The shoes definitely weren't his?" Marshall shook his head and went on staring at the mountains. His cigar had gone out between his fingers from lack of attention. "So anyways, Dr. Pleasant and the con artists were connected. And Pseudo-Martinez and Pain Jane were probably connected. And the murderer and Martinez were probably connected. Blackmail? But where's the money?" Marshall threw his cigar down in disgust, then picked it up again, blew the dust off it and put it in his pocket. "Anyways, I gotta keep digging. You probably have better things to do." He turned and headed for the stairs.

Did I? I wondered. But I called after him. "Did you ever get any word from Denver PD about that VIN number?" But he hadn't heard me. He'd disappeared down the stairwell.

CHAPTER 24

F or the next few days, I was much busier than usual for
some reason. Perhaps the spring weather had inspired
my clients, but I doubted it. Spring in Denver is always four
seasons per day — wind, melting, cold, warm, repeat. But the
crocuses and hyacinths were poking up through the thin
layer of crystalized snow, some of the buds on the maple trees
had split to reveal light pink baby flowers curled inside, the
lawns were turning green, and the chickadees were
dee-deeing their mating calls. On the wet sandstone
sidewalk I found two shattered whisper-white pigeon eggs.

A local discount shoe chain wanted pictures of African
American runners. The probably last remaining fur retailer
wanted gorgeous, "diverse" straight-looking women and
gay-looking men wrapped in fur hats and coats in snowy
scenes, which meant a trip to Eldora ski area above Boulder
where it was still mid-winter. Denver Parks and Recreation
wanted my stock shots of Denver's parks in each month
of the year for its next year's calendar. And during one
particularly fierce hailstorm, I shot a truly gargantuan traffic
crash — twenty-three cars and trucks scattered all over I-25
— that was picked up by local and national news.

One day toward the end of March, Bradshaw and I were
shooting cross-country skiers in City Park after another

spring blizzard had dumped six inches of snow. I'd let Bradshaw have a good run in the off-leash area, nuzzling snow, rolling, and playing tag with other, much taller, dogs. So he was now lying sleepily at my feet, enjoying the sun.

I was anxious to get the photos, because in this warm, sunny weather, the snow would be gone by tomorrow, and I needed to replenish my now depleted stock shots of Denver's parks. The day was brilliantly clear. Downtown's skyscrapers shimmered between the whiteness of the mountains and the park's Spanish revival pavilion. As I was resetting the tripod for a different angle, to my surprise, Duane Mangione, the handsome Douglas County Sheriff's deputy, appeared beside me. He leaned down and scratched behind Bradshaw's ears. Bradshaw looked up at him and fell in love.

"Hi," I said. Mangione looked at the view, then at my camera.

"Hi," he said, smiling. He had a beautiful smile. *Stop it,* I thought.

"Are you here about the photos? Were they any good?"

"Pretty good, yeah. We might be able to use you when our regular photographer, Sheldon Davis, isn't available. Strictly on call, of course."

"I've met Sheldon," I said. "He was at Dr. Pleasant's murder scene. I'd be happy to sub," and I meant it. I could always use more work. But then I thought of what Daniel would say. He wasn't happy about my working with Marshall. If he was jealous, what would he think about my working with much handsomer Deputy Mangione?

"So what brings you to Denver?" I asked, making small talk. I wasn't quite finished with the skiers, but I wanted to get acquainted with this guy. To network, as the jargon goes.

Mangione looked around at the skiers and up toward the glass wall of the museum. Three skiers were mostly falling down the small hill on which it sat. Their laughter reached us on the still, warm air. "I was just up for the day," he continued, "I've been meeting with the Denver PD cold case guys about a case I've got down south that involves an old rifle we found in Plum Creek. The lab guys were showing me how they lift a serial number with acid. They had a truck part there that they had worked on. Apparently connected to an old vehicular homicide case."

I was so astonished that I knocked the Nikon on its tripod sideways. Mangione caught it one-handed before it hit the snow.

"That's —" *What? Amazing? Coincidental? Interesting? Suspicious?*

"Yeah, amazing," supplied Mangione.

I'm sure my mouth was open, and I was doing a good imitation of a landed bass. "I —" I didn't know what to say. But Mangione was looking at me with what I would call a tight focus.

"You know something about this, I think," he said. It wasn't a question. I didn't answer it. "The victims' name was Standish. Like yours." I didn't say anything.

Mangione waited, watching my face. Not the skiers, not the view, not the camera. My face. He looked at me the same way Marshall did, his one-way cop's eyes revealing nothing and pulling out whatever truth there was to be had.

How did he get here, to me? The Douglas County sheriff's office is over 25 miles south of City Park. The county itself is huge — about 850 square miles of rolling prairie rapidly disappearing under battalions of tract homes, some of the largest McMansions in the U.S., working ranches, an exclusive golf course, the large town of Castle Rock, several tiny villages and two state parks.

Then I remembered that this park was not far from the downtown police forensic lab.

"Yes," I said at last. "They were my parents. And my brother." My new best friend —anger — was beginning to move in again.

Mangione nodded. "Are you finished here? Can we go someplace to talk?"

"Um ..." *Was* I finished here? I supposed I'd better be. "Yes. Sure. I just —" I started telescoping the tripod. Bradshaw and Mangione waited.

Because it was convenient, we adjourned to the coffee shop at the Museum of Nature and Science a short uphill walk away.

"How did you know I was in the park?" I asked when we were seated with our coffees under the gigantic Plesiosaur skeleton suspended from the ceiling. "You didn't just happen to see me, did you?"

Mangione didn't look even faintly embarrassed. His aviator sunglasses were hanging from the second button of his Rockmount shirt. His eyes were a soft brown with laugh lines around them, but there was no mistaking the cop look in them, sharp and searching.

"Nope," he said. "I ran into Detective Marshall at the forensic lab, and he told me where to find you. He saw you as he was on his way down 17th Ave. And the camera and the Corgi were kind of a giveaway."

Jeez, they miss nothing, I thought. "OK, so what do you want to talk about?"

"Well, Marshall thought you should know how Denver PD is proceeding. I guess he told you that DPD had raised a few of the numbers off that truck part?" I nodded. "Well, we thought you should be brought up to date. So I volunteered to come talk to you because Marshall had to get back to Littleton, and I wanted to ask you about covering for Sheldon anyway."

"OK," I said, warily.

Mangione took a big sip of his scalding black coffee. "They've got several numbers from the VIN that might lead to a suspect." I nodded. "But they're swamped. The cold case unit is very small, just three on staff, and they've got like 700 and some cold cases." This surprised me. Mangione tilted his head back and forth a couple of times, not actually shaking it, but expressing frustration with the way the world worked. "See, DNA analysis came along and offered a real chance of closing some of these old cases. And now genetic genealogy can trace some Unsubs even if they're not in CODIS."

"You've lost me."

"Well, detectives in California solved a case recently when unidentified DNA evidence was traced through a public ancestry data base. They were able to identify a common ancestor and then work forward to identify younger members of the family that might be suspects."

"Wow," I said.

He nodded. "Well, unfortunately that means that a case like yours — no DNA, no trace evidence — gets shoved down to the bottom of the pile in favor of cases with a real chance being solved. Your case is going to require running the VIN through CBI's database. Because it's a partial, and not a very good one at that, the database is going to throw up quite a few hits. Then those will have to be checked against the known make, model, year and color of the suspect vehicle. Probably several of those will show up, and they'll run them through DMV to find the owners' names. After that, they'll need to conduct interviews, and well, you can see that's all going to take some time. These cold case guys have to triage these cases, solve the ones that look solvable first. So —"

I stood up. Fury had rushed me from behind and had me around the throat. I was ready to either throw something or start yelling. I started yelling. "So *still* nobody cares enough to find the sonofabitch who killed my parents and left my brother helpless, is that right?" Several people looked around for the commotion. I didn't care. "A double murder and grievous bodily harm don't count once the clock ticks past some arbitrary amount of time? What is it? 48 hours? Six months? I've been grieving for *fourteen years* and you're telling me that DPD is too busy playing techno-wizard to do anything about it?" My face and body were hot and sweaty. Shakily, I reached out for my camera and tripod, ready to stomp the hell out of there and get back to work. Bradshaw stood up too and yawned.

"Hold on," said Mangione sharply, grabbing my free arm. "I'm not finished."

I stood there, undecided for maybe fifteen seconds. Mangione's eyes never left my face.

"What." I said, finally.

"Sit down." I did, probably with bad grace. Bradshaw lay back down, adopting a Lion Pose. "DPD really *can't* give your case the attention it deserves. It's not that they don't care, it's that they just don't have the resources. Lifting obscured ID numbers from metal is a fairly new technology. It was Marshall who thought it might work. It was Marshall that got the Denver guys to give it a try. AND it's Marshall who'll try to talk the DPD chief into doing the database search and all the rest of it. So cool it."

"OK," I held up my hand in surrender. "I get the picture, but still —."

"I doubt you do," he said. "You have no idea how time-consuming and miserable this work is. And it's going to require constant lobbying on your part to get it done. DMV is under-staffed, and your case is probably going to go to the bottom of somebody's in-basket more than once. Getting the info from CBI's database is also going to take time — It's not like CSI Miami where the information just magically appears on a giant screen." I laughed. "And of course the follow-up — phone calls and porch stepping — is going to take time, too. So you'll need to be patient. Marshall just wanted you to know that it's *in progress.* That's all."

And just like that, my anger disappeared and was replaced by a sense of profound relief. "Thank you," I said. I didn't cry. I *did not*. But there was pressure behind my eyes.

"You bet. You're welcome. It's been a long wait, I know." He unsnapped his shirt pocket, two-fingered out a piece of notebook paper, and handed it to me. On it were several numbers written in what I recognized as Marshall's printing:

1 F? 7??BT ? F ? ??63?5

"So it's the last six characters that identify the specific vehicle, right?" I asked, trying to remember what Marshall had told me about VIN numbers.

"Right. But it's the first five or six characters that the database prioritizes. Denver will do the database search and send the results to DMV to get possible vehicles."

"What can I do to help?"

"Probably nothing at this stage. Maybe later. Marshall will keep you posted."

"I will do anything, *anything,* to help find this guy," I said. I realized I was grinning like Jack Nicholson.

Mangione regarded me steadily. "'to take arms against a sea of troubles and by opposing end them'?" He saw I was puzzled. "*Hamlet,*" he said.

If I remembered correctly, it hadn't ended that well for him.

CHAPTER 25

At home, I processed and filed the photos of City Park, then I couldn't resist seeing if I could find out anything about the VIN number Mangione had given me. Google suggested the NHTSA site that claimed to be able to use partial numbers. But either it couldn't, or I didn't know how. I realized I was just going to have to leave the database search to Denver.

I consulted with Bradshaw. He yawned and suggested that the truck had probably been bought somewhere other than in Denver because the sales tax in Denver was quite a bit higher than in the surrounding counties. Also, that pickup was advertised as capable of hauling over five tons — more than you'd typically require for groceries from Safeway. So if I were going to buy a BFT [Big Fucking Truck] I'd buy it in Douglas, Adams, or another rural county where the sales tax is lower and the demand — given the populations of ranchers and pseudo-ranchers — was larger.

So I started by looking for current dealerships. But even that was a challenge because several states have Douglas, Jefferson and Adams counties. I finally put together a partial list. I looked at their Websites to see if I could find out if any had been in business in 2005. Only four had been. By then Bradshaw insisted that it really was time for a walk.

By the time we got back from our walk and had decided on a delivery pizza — Bradshaw likes sausage, but not pepperoni — it was too late to start calling, so I called Daniel instead.

"Hey!" he said, "What are you doing?"

"Thinking about you. Do you want to come over?"

Daniel laughed. "Oh, OK, if you insist. Half an hour?"

And half an hour later, there he was, dressed in his cream Aran sweater and some jeans that fitted him in a way that made my heart beat faster. He had a big suitcase and a grocery bag full of eggs, milk, bread, cheese and meatballs. "I thought I might start to move in, if that's OK. Can I stay for a few days?" I think my grin gave him an affirmative.

"Should I carry you over the threshold?" I asked. For answer, he scooped me up in his arms and carried me to bed.

"What are you doing?" he asked the next morning, munching toast and drinking coffee.

I was still in jammies, in the early stages of caffeination. "These are print outs of some Darth Vader truck dealers' Websites. I thought I'd try contacting the dealers on the off chance they'd help. These," I pointed to the four printouts I'd made, "are dealers in the nearby cowboy counties that were in business in 2005. I'll start with those and work outward."

"OK, but what if he lived in Kansas? Or Wyoming? Lots of trucks out there."

I shrugged. "I'm just starting with the most likely scenario. It's going to take time." I smiled up at him.

"Between me and Marshall, we're going to find this bastard. You can bet your life on it."

He looked thoughtful. "I don't think I'll take that bet," he said, leaning down and kissing me quickly. "Gotta go, Love. Off to the sweat shop."

I followed him to the door. "Are you coming back here tonight?" He nodded and kissed me again, then took the stairs down.

I called a couple of dealerships that were in business in 2005 according to their websites. No dice. To check 14-year-old records was too time-consuming and too big an ask. So after lunch, I got Bradshaw's leash, shrugged into my heavier weight fleece — it was chilly and damp outside with a light, annoying breeze — and Bradshaw and I stepped out smartly to walk the mile or so to Cheesman Park.

By the time we got home, we felt much too refreshed from our walk. We had just decided on a snack when my phone buzzed in my pocket.

"What are you doing?" asked Marshall, blunt as ever.

"Just got back from a walk —"

"Yeah, well, Pain Jane made bail this morning. Not sure how or who. Denver only just called me."

"Should I —?"

"But that's not the worst of it. Apparently she's stolen a car."

"Wh —?"

"Yeah. So pay attention. She's out there someplace with a vehicle, so she could be going anywhere. I think she has people someplace out in the eastern part of the state, Fort Morgan or someplace, an aunt maybe. But she could also be around Denver looking to score some meth etcetera —"

My turn to interrupt. "Or she could be coming my way, right? Isn't that why you called?"

The zippo clinked in the short silence. "Yeah. Anyways, I thought you should know."

There was something else on his mind, I could tell. I was getting good at interpreting his silences. I waited.

"So maybe you should let Mohammed know. And, I don't know, how would you feel about staying someplace else? Like Outer Mongolia."

I laughed. "I will call Mohammed, but I'm staying here. Daniel just started moving in with *me* because I won't move in with *him*. So he'll be around. I'll be safe."

Marshall hmphed and coughed. "OK, maybe, but you be careful. I wouldn't want Bradshaw to get hurt." He hung up.

I was chuckling to myself, thinking about how entertaining I found him despite all his quirks and annoying habits when my phone buzzed again. Shiela.

"Hey," I said.

"Oh, Cas ...!" Was she crying? "Cas, you've got to get down here right away! It's Joshua!"

"What?"

"Joshua! He's hurt! Oh, Clare, he's in an ambulance. Going to Vineland Hospital. You need to go there! Now! Oh, *God* ..."

"Shiela, please ... tell me what happened?"

Shiela took a deep, shuddering breath. "No, I ... He's ....
They wouldn't let me go with him because I'm not ... um ...
next of kin or something. But I'll get there as soon as I can.
But you should go ..."

"OK, but what happened?"

"They'll explain it to you. You need to go. NOW! Hurry,
please. He's ... Clare, I'm afraid it's bad ..." She was sobbing
uncontrollably now.

"OK," I said. Abruptly Shiela clicked off. I stabbed
Mohammed's number.

"Are you OK?" I asked when he answered.

"Sure you betcha," he said. I heard his turn signal
clicking. So he was driving. "What's up, doc?"

"How soon can you get here? And get me down to
Vineland Hospital?"

"Where you at?"

"Home."

"Ten to you and twenty to Vineland. You got trouble?
You need ambulance?"

"No, no. I'll explain when you get here. But hurry,
please."

I dialed Daniel. It went straight to voicemail. Where was
he? He must know about whatever it was that had happened
at the Blue House, even if he wasn't there. They would have
notified him, wouldn't they? Him being the owner? But
obviously he had his phone off or was out of cell coverage.
That wouldn't be too unusual. Lots of places in Colorado,
even here on the Front Range, had little or no cell coverage.
Or maybe he was in the middle of the crisis, whatever it was,

and couldn't answer. I left him a message telling him where I was going and why, and asked him to take care of Bradshaw.

Mohammed pulled up to the curb where I was waiting for him after about two hours. OK, so it was only eleven and a half minutes. He was heading down the street before I got my door shut.

"Why you ask me if I am OK?" he asked, as I struggled to right myself in the marshmallow-y seats.

"Because Marshall called me to tell me that Pain Jane was out on bail. He was concerned she might come after you. Because of what happened at the homeless camp."

"How she can come for me?"

"She stole a car."

Mohammed nodded in an "it figures" kind of way. "OK, so what's up with the hospital and all the hurry up stuff?"

"Something to do with my brother. Somebody from the Blue House called me ... It sounded pretty serious."

"OK, then I will hurry up." And he put his foot down to prove it.

Vineland Hospital is enormous, covering four or five city blocks and who knows how many stories. Mohammed pulled into the semi-circular drive off Old Hampden Avenue in front of the main entrance. I had my door open before he came to a complete stop.

"I am gonna wait out here on the street someplace. You need me, you call, OK?"

"OK," I said through his driver's side window. "But look out for that crazy Jane. Marshall thinks she might be after one or both of us."

Mohammed nodded impatiently and leaned over to open the glove box. "Yeah, yeah. You forget that I am real American guy," he emerged with an automatic pistol in his right hand. "Also I am real Iraqi guy. Trained with Americans" He held up a rifle with a scope. *Where did that come from?* "Lotta crazy people Ubering around these days."

Jesus! Was everyone in Denver armed to the teeth? "OK, but be careful. I'll call you" — I waggled the sign of the phone with my fingers — "once I know what's up.".

Once inside, I found the information desk. The lobby was much more crowded than the lobby-dash-cathedral at St. Anthony's, and more utilitarian, but still not bad looking. The lighting was pleasant, and the mostly stone surfaces gleamed softly. The woman at the desk directed me down a hallway to the right to the emergency room. Here things weren't so pleasant. Bright white and stainless steel everything bounced fluorescent lights everywhere leaving no shadows and no comforting textures. A line of uninviting plastic chairs said, "Don't stay long."

"They're operating on him right now," said a hurrying nurse when I'd stepped in front of her to ask about Joshua.

"What *for*?" I asked. Christ! Would nobody tell me what had happened?

"Multiple gunshot wounds. The doctor will explain."

"*WHAT*?? Is he going to live?"

"The doctor will be with you as soon as she can," she said, and dodged around me to be on her way. "You'd be more comfortable in the waiting room," she added, over her shoulder.

The waiting room, when I found it, was a slightly less well-lit box with a "calming" color scheme of grays, creams, and rust on the walls and carpet. Gray armchairs were scattered around in small groups separated by a few gray Formica-topped tables. Over in one corner, a middle-aged couple sat close together, he holding her hand, she trying to control her tears. I heard her say "mom" a couple of times, so I assumed that's why they were here. Dying parents — I felt their anguish even though my parents had died long ago and far too young. All of us had been too young.

I sat in one of the chairs facing away from them to try to give them what privacy was possible and thought hard about Joshua. My twin. When we were little kids, we'd often known what each other was thinking. Later we often picked up the phone to call each other at the same moment. We'd had the same teeth pulled, worn each other's clothes, and had a kind of coded language we'd shared. We often slept in the same bed, drank from the same cups, used the same toothbrush. The smell of asparagus made us both feel sick. We were only fraternal twins, of course, and as we grew up, differences emerged. But still, we were much closer than ordinary siblings.

So now I sent him urgent messages not to die. I hoped the lines between us were still open. If he died, I would be absolutely alone, not only an orphan, but an incomplete person, a person with a big Joshua-shaped hole in my soul.

What in the hell had happened? Why would nobody tell me?

I pulled out my phone and called Mohammed, telling him not to wait, I was going to be here for a long time.

CHAPTER 26

A doctor came in and spoke apologetically to the couple across the room. The woman turned her face into the man's shoulder and sobbed. I heard the doctor say, "I'm so sorry."

After a while, another doctor — Dr. Jones it said on her name tag — came in and sat down next to me. She was wearing light blue scrubs, and a pillbox hat covered her very short hair. Her aging skin looked scrubbed and faintly masculine around her nose and mouth, but she had large, darkly lashed blue eyes.

"We're doing all we can for your brother," she said. "But he's in very serious condition, so it's touch and go. He has two penetrating gunshot wounds to the upper left quadrant of his abdomen. One clipped the upper left pole of his left kidney. The other broke a rib that injured his lung. He's in reasonably good health otherwise, so that helps, but we're concerned that there's another injury we haven't found yet. We'll keep you updated on his condition as often as we can."

Well, what did all that mean? Either he'll get better, or he won't? We'll tell you something sometime, or if he dies?

"But what happened?" I asked after a longish pause.

"I'm sorry, I don't actually know. But there's a police officer here who wants to talk to you when he gets finished questioning some people. I'm sure he can tell you." She rose, off to the next misery.

Time went on. I kept sending the don't-die messages to Joshua.

It was starting to get dark outside when Shiela rushed in and smothered me in a bent-over hug around my shoulders, re-smoothed her braids into their scrunchy, then sat down next to me in the chair Dr. Jones had vacated.

"Oh, Cas I'm so, so sorry I just can't believe this has happened and at the Blue House of all places you'd think it would be safe as safe can be there I can't believe Joshua — can't believe she shot him just like — just like he was a rat on the floor or something it was so awful you can't believe how awful it was —"

I grabbed her hand. "Hush! Stop! It's OK. Not your fault. Just please tell me what happened."

"She just walked in and shot him!" said Shiela, as if to a child. And I realized she thought I would have been told all about it.

"That crazy Pain Jane," said Marshall's voice behind me. He paced around to the chair opposite mine and Shiela's, and sat down tiredly, and tiredly pressed thumb and forefinger to his eyes. The chair was too low for him, and his knees stuck up. Shiela again smoothed her braids back and re-scrunchied them. He double crossed his legs. I waited.

"Jane somehow stole a car, and even more surprisingly managed to drive it to the Blue House. She entered and forced one of the orderlies to take her to Joshua's room, threatening him with a revolver she had acquired, apparently from one of her buddies down at the camp by the river.

No one knows how she knew Joshua is your brother, that he was at the Blue House, or where the Blue House is. She was screaming about how you got her busted and sent the Migras after her, waving the weapon around, and at one point firing it into the ceiling when she thought the orderly wasn't moving fast enough.

"When she got to Joshua's room, she yelled at him something about getting even with you and shot five times, hitting him twice and other items in the room and the wall the other three times. The orderly she'd threatened tackled her, got her on the floor, and somebody else subdued her and took the weapon from her. Someone else called the Greenwood Village police department, and the dispatcher there called me and an ambulance. Very quick thinking on their part, I'd like to say."

By this time I could feel my eyeballs trying to leave my head, and I'd stopped breathing. Shieeila was squeezing my hand, and suddenly I realized it hurt.

"My God!" I finally managed to croak. "Where is she now? How the hell did she get out of jail? Where ... How could she get a weapon and a car and find Joshua? Why didn't she just come and kill me?"

Marshall spread his hands and shrugged. "God only knows. And Jane, of course, but I doubt we'll get any sense out of her. The EMTs say she went into some kind of fit or fugue state right after she was subdued. They had to call another ambulance to bring her here."

"*SHE'S HERE??*" I was close to going into some kind of fit or fugue state myself at this news. "WHY IS SHE

HERE?? Joshua is still in the operating room, for Chrissake! She could ..." Words failed me.

"No she can't," said Marshall calmly. "She's restrained and sedated. Handcuffed to her bed. Once she's stabilized, she'll be back in custody, and this time I doubt bail will be an option. Although, you never know ..." He stood up and stretched his back. "I'm gonna use one of the offices here to get started on the paperwork, etcetera." He looked tired and not very happy. "Shiela — Stick around, OK? I'll need to interview you later after I find Daniel."

Shiela nodded, her whiskey-brown eyes huge. Her grip on my hand had loosened slightly, but I wasn't sure my manual dexterity would recover. That said, I was thankful she was there.

After Marshall left, we sat in silence for a while. I was trying to make sense of it all. But suddenly something occurred to me. "Wait! Wasn't Daniel at the Blue House when all this happened?"

Shiela shook her head. "No, he was in Golden — Thank God he wasn't in Steamboat! He got to the Blue House just as the EMTs were taking Jane out. And of course, he's been overwhelmed ever since — answering questions, calming everyone down, reorganizing — all that stuff. I told him I was coming here, and he said, 'Great. Thanks.' and that he'd be along as soon as he could. He was really shaken. I've never seen him so ... so kinda *lost*, you know?"

I tried to picture Daniel shaken and lost and failed. He was always so competent, so in control. I'd never even seen him drunk! Only once seen him lose his temper. But I guessed that because this had happened under his roof, and to Joshua, my brother, it was just too close to home.

I wished very fiercely he were here. I texted him,

I wish you were here. 🐱

He answered almost immediately, and just because he did, I felt better.

I do too Ill be there asap

Just then Dr. Jones, whom I'd spoken to earlier, came in. Now her blue scrubs were stained and wrinkled, her hat gone from her short graying red hair. Her eyes looked very tired, and she sighed as she sat down in the chair vacated by Marshall. Shiela took my hand again.

"Good news and bad news, I'm afraid," said Dr. Jones, and yawned convulsively. "Oh, excuse me. It's been a 70-hour day today. Can you listen for a bit? I'd like to start from the beginning." I nodded. "Your brother Jason —"

"Joshua," I said.

"Joshua, I'm sorry. Joshua had two penetrating abdominal wounds from a .22 caliber firearm — a revolver, I'm told. Now the injuries could have been much worse, if, say, the caliber had been larger, or the bullets had penetrated one or more vital organs. As it was, one bullet penetrated his upper left quadrant and clipped his left kidney — generally a serious but not a life-threatening injury. Much more seriously, the other bullet passed through his descending colon, opening that to the perineal cavity, causing a life-threatening condition, peritonitis. That's an infection of the gut cavity caused by leakage from the colon and bowel. The bullet had an upward trajectory, so it broke a rib, which then punctured his lung." She glanced with her tired eyes at

Shiela and me to see if we were following. We were, Shiela better than I was, probably.

"We didn't catch the peritonitis at first, but after we'd stabilized him — his breathing, heart rate, blood loss and so on, we noted the two entry and one exit wounds. He was in terrible pain — characteristic of gut injuries. So we skipped the normal CT scan in favor of immediate surgery. Once we got him opened up, we found the injury to the kidney, and also that the bullet had both entered and exited the colon, causing great damage. This meant resecting that part of the colon and suturing the two ends together." She paused again, and Shiela and I nodded.

"We had trouble locating the second bullet, which we knew, absent a second exit wound, was still inside his abdomen. If we'd had time to do an X-ray, we would have known where to look. But as it happened, we found the bullet lodged against the rib it had broken. So in addition to the gut wound, there was more damage to the kidney, rib and lung than we'd hoped."

"But he's OK ...?" I halfway asked. "I mean, he's not ...?"

"He's in very serious condition. We have him heavily sedated with a strong opiate — he's not conscious at this time — and will keep him sedated for the next few days, perhaps even a week, though we have to be careful about the addiction factor. Unfortunately, he won't be able to talk with you — or the police — "

"What about food? And water? I'd like to bring him some treats —"

Dr. Jones shook her head. "No, no food. His colon needs complete rest — the opiates will help with that. They depress the gastrointestinal motility. He'll receive parenteral nutrition through an IV, along with IV antibiotics and hydration and anything else he needs, but nothing by mouth until we're sure the partial colectomy is fully healed. After that we'll start him on clear liquids for a couple of days, then gradually add more semi-liquids and soft solids as we see how his gut is responding."

"And the kidney?" I asked.

"What kidney?" asked Daniel's voice behind me.

I jumped up and wrapped him in my arms. "Oh, thank God you're here." I was muffled by his shirt, comforted by the starch and ironed smell of it.

Dr. Jones looked up. Daniel reached around me to extend a hand to her. "Daniel Coldwell. I own the nursing facility where Joshua lives. And Clare is my fiancé. So ..."

"I see," said Dr. Jones, but she pressed her lips into a thin line. "I'd like to speak with you about your security arrangements when we finish here." Daniel nodded. We all sat down again, Shiela now moving into the chair next to Dr. Jones to give Daniel the seat next to me.

"Um ... Yes, the kidney," resumed Dr. Jones. "We'll know in time if the damage was severe enough that it will have to be removed. But that's a ways down the line. For now, I think you should expect Joshua to be here for at least ten days, or possibly two weeks, barring complications."

"What kind of complications?" I asked.

"An infection that can't be controlled with antibiotics would be the most likely." She cocked her head. "I think that's all I can tell you at the moment. Joshua is in intensive care, and you can see him if you wish, but again, he won't be conscious or responsive." I nodded and thanked her as she stood to leave. Her shoulders drooped and she looked dehydrated, almost desiccated, by exhaustion.

Shiela and I began to move in the direction of the intensive care unit while Daniel followed Dr. Jones out the other door toward the emergency room hallway..

The lighting in the ICU was soft and unobtrusive, and there was virtually no noise except the soft beeping of equipment and the low murmurs of the staff. Like all the other patients, Joshua was in a wedge-shaped room fronted with a glass sliding door. The room's shape was dictated by the semi-circular plan of the ICU, with the nurses' station centrally located and enjoying a view of all eleven of the rooms. A monitor for each room was ranged around the nurses' station, so one attendant could keep an eye on all of them while the rest of the staff tended to the individual patients.

Joshua was in room seven. His glass door was closed, but the inner privacy curtain was only pulled halfway across. Shiela had to hold me tightly at the first sight of him. He was the color of oatmeal and seemed to have shrunk to about half his size into the bed. A sheet covered him loosely from the chest down. There were tubes going into his left arm, a bigger tube snaking under the sheet, and another tube emerging into a bag hanging from the lower side rail of the bed frame. A clip on his index finger relayed his pulse to the monitor above his bed; a cuff on his upper arm relayed his blood pressure and made soft puffing noises as it inflated and deflated. His temperature was 39.2° C. I didn't know what that meant.

I stood next to the bed, unsure what to do. At last I took his right hand — it was lying loosely on top of the sheet. It was warm and dry, the nails pink and shinier than normal. I lifted it to my lips and kissed it gently. "You're going to be fine," I whispered. "You're going to come back to me, and you'll be fine. We'll race Roger in your wheelchair, and you'll learn to walk someday. We'll go for walks along the river and look at the ducks." Tears were pouring down my cheeks and landing on his hand.

Shiela was at the end of the bed reading his chart. Written in large red letters on a whiteboard on the wall behind her was "NOTHING BY MOUTH."

"It looks good," she said. "His fever's stable at about 102, but his blood pressure and heart rate's up. That's all pretty normal."

I sniffled and replaced Joshua's hand on the sheet, giving it a pat. "I'll be back, Buddy. You just work on getting well." And I kissed his too-warm forehead. "Let's go before I completely lose it," I said to Shiela.

CHAPTER 27

When we returned to the lobby, Daniel was waiting for us looking cool and elegant sitting in one of the blue armchairs. His legs were crossed, and his silver-gray slacks somehow remained uncreased. He stood and joined us, taking my hand and kissing me lightly on the cheek.

"OK?" he asked. I nodded. "Good. Let's get everyone home."

"I'm going to Kim's," said Shiela.

"OK," Daniel nodded.

"What did Dr. Jones want?" I asked.

Daniel shook his head. "She just wanted to know about our security arrangements."

It was dark as we all left the building together carrying our own and Joshua's stuff, but we found Marshall smoking a cigar on a bench beside the doors, legs entwined. He stood and stopped us with a gentle hand on my arm.

"I need to get these people home," said Daniel, maybe a little too sharply.

"Yeah, well. Turns out I need to talk to Shiela, here." He rubbed the ash off his cigar on the pavement.

Shiela's whiskey-brown eyes sharpened as she regarded him. "What about?" she snapped. "We're all tired, and I told that officer everything I knew at the Blue House."

"This is about something else." said Marshall in his rough voice.

Shiela paused, regarding him sharply. "OK. But Clare comes with me."

"What?" I said.

"OK," said Marshall, unsurprised, and turned to re-enter the hospital. I turned to Daniel, who shrugged and pointed to the lobby, saying he'd wait for us there. I trailed after Shiela and Marshall.

He led us into a small empty office at the back of the lobby, to one side of the cashier's cage, and pointed to the two guest chairs as he sat tiredly on the front of the desk. He dug out his tiny digital recorder and set it on the desk next to his leg.

"Am I under arrest or something?" Shiela asked, smoothing back her braids and re-winding them into their scrunchy.

Marshall chuckled, then coughed. "This is just an interview. If you were under arrest, I'd have Mirandized you, etcetera. I just have some questions. Are you two OK? Do you need some water or something?" We both shook our heads, although I was so exhausted I could have murdered a Coke. But I just wanted to get this over with as soon as possible and climb into bed with Daniel and Bradshaw. I didn't think I was finished crying yet.

"How well did you know Martin Martinez?" asked Marshall, as if asking about the weather.

"*What?*" squawked Shiela. "What are you talking about? I didn't know him at all!"

Marshall settled himself more comfortably on the desk and let the silence grow tentacles. Shiela stared at him, and her eyes, usually the color of good whiskey, got darker. Anger? Fear? I didn't know. I reached over and took *her* hand for a change.

"See, here's the problem," said Marshall, conversationally. "You did know him, though maybe only slightly. You were his mother's nurse. I think you must have spoken with him at some point."

Shiela's eyes got very wide. She didn't seem to know what to say.

"So let's try this again. How well did you know Martin Martinez? On a scale of one to ten, one being just to say hello, and ten being, I don't know, sleeping with him, I guess."

"One," whispered Shiela.

"So. You never discussed his mother with him?" Shiela shook her head. "I think you did." Marshall continued, unconcerned. "His mother was very ill, wasn't she?" Shiela nodded. "She had pancreatic cancer, is that right?" Shiela nodded. "And pancreatic cancer is very painful?"

"Yes, it is," said Shiela, on firmer, professional ground now. "And Mrs. Martinez's was terminal. She was receiving only palliative care. We were keeping her as comfortable as possible."

"Not on chemo?"

Shiela shook her head. "We'd discontinued that at her request about two weeks before. The Blue House has an agreement with the local hospice, so we didn't have to move her. She stayed with us, and the hospice nurses and doctors came in every day to bathe her and do other things you probably don't want to know about. They're saints, those people. The docs are specially trained in pain management, so they'd leave orders for us, and we'd just carry them out. At the time, Omar was the physician in charge of her case — he's trained big time in geriatric pain management, among other things."

"And then she died," said Marshall.

"Right," said Shiela.

"What medications was she on?"

Shiela thought briefly. "The usual. Not much. an anti-nausea THC derivative, a laxative, a liquid nutritional supplement — Boost or something like that. Usually we blended it up with a little ice cream to make it taste better. She liked chocolate with a little raspberry syrup in it." Shiela smiled at the memory.

"What about the pain meds?" Marshall was acting like someone who was merely curious about the care of terminal cancer patients. I realized he was lulling Shiela into her professional role, a consultant, a helper. It scared me.

"Liquid morphine," said Shiela succinctly. "on demand, drops under the tongue."

Marshall let the silence lengthen again. Shiela began to fidget and run her fingers over her braids.

"And then ...?" asked Marshall. He leaned over and turned off the recorder. "Look. I'm not going to let you incriminate yourself. That's not what we're here for."

"And then *what*?" Shiela was on guard.

"And then Martinez asked you for some help. Some help for his mother?"

Shiela sighed, let go of my hand, and rubbed her face. "Oh, shit. Yes," she whispered.

"And you provided that help?" Shiela nodded miserably. "I put morphine —"

Marshall interrupted her. "Stop. I'm not interested in that other than what happened afterwards. I doubt you're the only nurse who's provided help to a dying patient."

Shiela looked up at him. There were tears swimming in her eyes. "Thank you," she whispered.

"Don't thank me yet," Marshall was still all business. He turned the recorder back on.

"And then she died," continued Marshall matter-of-factly. "But unfortunately, Martinez blabbed to Dr. Pleasant, and then they both started blackmailing you, separately. Didn't they?"

Shiela nodded miserably. I looked at her in surprise. Why hadn't she told me? I would have done anything to protect her. OK, I couldn't have done much. But maybe I could have gotten Daniel to stop Pleasant. And then maybe ... Oh, hell. No point thinking about what might not have happened. About trying to change the past.

Shiela took my hand again. Maybe she knew what I was thinking. She sighed. "I think Martin needed the money and just saw an opportunity. Just little things at first — Pleasant would request an extra shift here, Martinez, fifty bucks there. Nothing I couldn't handle. But then ..."

"But then Pleasant found out about you and Dr. Kim and things got really ugly. She threatened to get you both fired for violating the non-fraternization policy, and the real harassment began. Kim pulling double shifts, early shifts, late

shifts, a Rota designed to exhaust him and drive him out.
And she watched you like a hawk. One little error, one day
back late from lunch or an unaccounted-for Percocet and ...
pfffft!" Marshall waved his hand. "You're both out on the
street and forget the recommendations."

Shiela put her hand over her eyes. Her fingers were
shaking.

"How do you know about all this?" I asked Marshall,
even though I knew it was against the rules.

He didn't answer but just watched Shiela. Torturing her.

"She said she'd make sure we'd never work in medicine
again. So ... so we just did our best and tried to think of
something we could do. I tried reporting the harassment
to HR, but nothing happened. I even talked to Daniel" —
she glanced at me — "but he just said she was a tough
taskmaster, and he couldn't or wouldn't rein her in. I
couldn't tell *him* about Mrs. Martinez or Kim and I, of
course. We'd just about decided to quit and look for another
hospital. We'd thought we'd found one in Wyoming, and
we were trying to figure out how to get on there without
Pleasant finding out. She would have done something ...
something to obstructicate it. But then she was killed ..."

Marshall kept still and silent.

Shiela rushed on. "I didn't want to leave Joshua and
Clare, and Kim didn't really want to move to Wyoming, so
we were so relieved. We just ... we just went on. Kim was
looking around for a job in the Denver area so we could
get married, and I could stay at the Blue House. Martinez
was still a problem, but I figured that without Pleasant he

couldn't do much. His word against mine, right? And then somebody killed *him*, and ..."

"And it was all very convenient, wasn't it? Is that why you weren't worried that afternoon when you came back late from lunch?"

Shiela looked up at him in surprise. "Are you saying Kim or I killed those two?"

"Did you?" asked Marshall.

"Jesus! *No*! No! We were at Kim's place! I swear! We would *never* do anything like that! I was scared to death — We'd just lost track of the time, that's all! Jesus!"

Marshall slid down off the desk and stood up. "Maybe," he said. "*Maybe* you were together at Kim's. You only have each other's word for that. And neither of you has any alibi for Martinez's murder." Shiela started to protest. Marshall held up his hand. "I can't charge you without further evidence. But I'm warning you, if we find that evidence, you'll be charged with two homicides, whether as the perpetrator or as an accessory. Things will go easier for you if you tell me the truth, though. Maybe you're protecting Kim? Maybe Kim killed them?"

Shiela took a deep breath. "I *have* told you the truth. What I just told you, that's what happened. I didn't kill Pleasant — though I admit I wanted to — and I didn't kill Martinez, and neither did Kim. That's it."

We all did get home at last. Daniel dropped Shiela off at Kim's condo down by South Platte Park and then took us

home to my apartment on Capitol Hill. It took forever —
driving way south, then way back north with the usual traffic
snarls on Santa Fe Drive. Bradshaw needed a walk and some
dinner, then another walk. Daniel did that and picked up
some spicy Middle Eastern grub for us. While he was gone, I
mostly sat on my sofa and stared out the window at the lights
gleaming on the gold Capitol dome. Something was wrong,
something wasn't working, something didn't make sense, but
I couldn't put my finger on it.

Maybe it's this everybody blackmailing everybody, I
thought. *I must be the only person in Denver not being
blackmailed.* On that thought, I fell asleep.

I woke suddenly at 3:22. I was spooning with Daniel,
my fists balled between my chest and his back. I felt him
breathing softly. Bradshaw was curled up against the backs of
my bent knees. The something that was wrong crystallized
suddenly in the dark.

How did Pain Jane know where to find Joshua?

I mentally flipped through everyone who knew us. We
had lots of friends. Jane could have found out from any of
them. But how would she know them? I didn't think any of
our friends were in the meth scene. Maybe she Googled him.
Was he on Google?

I reached over to get my phone from the bedside table,
trying not to disturb Daniel or Bradshaw. Daniel rolled onto
his other side, facing me, and Bradshaw grunted, annoyed. I
Googled Joshua.

Yup, there he was in a post about *me,* for Chrissakes. "...
*currently in treatment at Greenwood Village's Blue House for
injuries sustained in a tragic 2005 auto accident.*" The post

was dated two years ago and was from a bio published in a local Crested Butte promotional magazine along with some photos I'd taken for a big summer event there. I remembered telling them about Joshua during the interview. But on second thought, I didn't think of Jane as a voracious reader of vacation literature.

Daniel shifted again and wrapped his arm around my waist, now spooning with me. Bradshaw stood up, turned three times in a circle and resettled against my shins.

"What are you looking at?" Daniel mumbled against my hair.

"Just trying to figure out how Pain Jane found Joshua," I whispered.

But he'd already fallen back to sleep.

When we all woke up the next morning, I stretched out luxuriously, enjoying Daniel's warmth under my duvet, but Bradshaw jumped onto the floor and headed for his bowl in the kitchen. Of all the things I didn't want to do, getting out of bed was at the top of the list, and that made it imperative that I do just that. If I stayed in bed, I'd end up staring at the ceiling with tears in my ears. Daniel made it easier.

"Well, back to work," he said, swinging his legs over the side of the bed. "C'mon, woman. Make me some coffee." He kissed my forehead.

"So what are you doing today?" he asked around a piece of toast. We were showered, he was dressed, and my hair was dampening the collar of my bathrobe.

I had several things in mind. Number one was, of course, going to see Joshua. Then there was always email and responding to requests for photos. Maybe Marshall would need me. Maybe I'd work some more on the VIN numbers. I sighed in frustration at that thought.

"I have a better idea," said Daniel when I'd told him all this. It seemed Daniel always had a better idea. "You should take a day off. You've had a rough ... time of it lately. How is the wound on your shoulder, for instance? Try to take it easy, darling. Also, I'm not kicked in the head with the idea of you doing anything with Marshall. It's dangerous. Also, can we get married pretty soon?"

"Daniel, I —"

He held up his hands. "OK, OK. Never mind. I'll see you tonight." And he was out the door.

I put my plan into action. There wasn't anything urgent in my email, so Bradshaw and I walked down to Broadway and took the number zero bus to Vineland Hospital. Joshua was much the same, but I held his hand and talked to him about my concerns about Pain Jane, then read to him from a copy of the *Denver Post* that was drifting around the waiting room. He always liked to know how the Avalanche were doing, and this year they looked good for the division playoffs.

By the time I left, Bradshaw had been spoiled almost to death by the nurses. The day had turned lovely, so we decided to walk part of the way back home. Englewood's main street was bustling improbably. You would have thought that an old-fashioned street of small businesses would have crashed by now, but the city had somehow beaten off the big box stores and even the locksmith's shop was busy. We paused for lunch at a diner famous for the way the waitresses yelled old fashioned food jargon to the cook, who owned the place. Apparently I ordered "Two cluck and grunt with shingles!" I took a few photos. You never knew.

Replete with eggs, bacon and toast, we got on the light rail at Oxford Avenue.

We were walking up Colfax from the University of Colorado Auraria stop when my phone buzzed. It was Marshall.

"Omar's dead," he said, without preamble.

CHAPTER 28

" *WHAT?"*

I heard the zippo click, his desk chair creak, and a long exhalation. "Omar's dead," he repeated.

"How?"

"Don't know yet. Just got a call from those two sheriff's bozos out in Rio Blanco. Apparently he didn't show up for his shift. Didn't answer his phone. They did a wellness check on the house. No answer. Anyway, finally, after a lot of highly sophisticated detective work etcetera, they found the back door unlocked, and then they found him. This was about two hours ago."

"He was at home?"

Another long exhale. "You could say so. In his own bed. No signs of violence."

"So ... suicide?"

"Maybe. Maybe not. There's that unlocked door to consider. Also no note." A yawn. "Sorry. I was up half the night on another matter. Anyways, we won't know anything until the coroner out there takes a look at him. One thing, though. Omar had a shitload of drugs in his bathroom cabinet. Ativan, Compazine, Valium, Xanex, Vicodin, etcetera. All prescriptions. He was writing himself some very high-quality highs."

"How could he do that? I mean, pharmacists these days ..."

"Used a false name. Had a fake ID for somebody named Jose Ramirez. So he'd write the prescriptions, and Jose Ramirez would pick them up at different pharmacies. Simple."

"So he did pass as Hispanic."

"Yes he did."

We paused for thought. "So what now?" I asked.

Marshall sighed. I'd noticed he sighed a lot. "Well, it's in Rio Blanco's hands now. I'll just have to wait to see what their Coroner says — homicide, suicide or accident — and go from there. If he determines it's a homicide, I'll probably go out there and talk to folks — his wife, co-workers etcetera."

"Will you want me to come with you?"

"Depends."

"On what?"

"This n that. I'll let you know when I know." He yawned again and I could hear the chair creaking as I assumed he was stretching. "By the way, your contract for crime scene photography came through from HR. You'll need to sign it."

"I ... um ..." Daniel would be incandescent if I signed up for this. He'd made it very clear that he didn't want me working with Marshall at all. But ... I was enjoying the work. It was so completely different from what I'd been doing. I liked serving the community rather than just promoting a bunch of products and tourist destinations. And the photography itself was challenging, required technical expertise, concentration and precision. All of which I liked.

I thought back over all I'd learned in the last month. It was ... exhilarating.

"Um what?" asked Marshall.

"Nothing. Sure. Of course. And thanks."

Marshall chuckled, then began coughing. Once he'd recovered he said, "So you're worried about what Daniel's going to say?"

"Well ... yes."

Marshall didn't comment. "In other news, Pain Jane's been arraigned and remanded, bail denied."

"Great!"

"I'd like you to hop down here and come with me when I interview her. How soon can you get here?"

"An hour?"

"OK, good. See you then." And he was gone.

The day had started bright and warm, but now dark clouds were building in the south-west. As I watched from the train window, golden crepuscular rays shot down from a hole in the clouds. They lit up the Red Rocks amphitheater for just a few moments before moving on to the meadow nearby. Then the clouds closed up, the light vanished, and I saw a curtain of rain sweep the foothills.

We found Pain Jane at the Arapahoe County Detention Center. She was sitting in a small, white-painted interview room in one of three bolted-down chairs at a round table. A uniformed woman guard was sitting in a fourth chair in the corner.

Jane's hands were cuffed, a chain from the cuffs snaked through a staple on the table. She could scratch her nose, but that was about it. She had her feet drawn up and her chin on her knees when we arrived, but when she saw me, she quickly hid her face behind her folded arms. I supposed it was the "if I can't see you, you're not there" principle.

She looked terrible. The blue-black dye had grown out about a half inch showing strawberry blonde roots. Her skin was plaster-white making the meth burns and sores on her face stand out starkly. Without the black eyeliner, her eyes looked small and mud-colored; the whites were yellow and bloodshot. Her lips were chapped raw, the piercings in her nose, eyebrow, ears and mouth looked gray without their many studs and rings. Her tattoos stood out sharply on her arms and her fingers were clubbed and bloody from biting her fingernails. The orange jump suit was not her color and looked about three sizes too big on her tiny, emaciated body.

Marshall sat across from her and signaled to the guard to start recording. I'd had to leave my backpack, camera and phone at the entrance, so I wasn't sure why Marshall had wanted me there. I found out soon enough.

"Please state your full name for the recording," said Marshall.

Jane didn't look up or speak.

"OK. This is Detective Marshall of the Littleton Police interviewing Juanita Maria Obregón on March 30th, 2019, at ..." He looked at the clock, "13:22. Police Photographer Clare Standish, the victim's sister is also present." Jane remained silent. "Why did you shoot Joshua Standish?"

No answer.

"Did someone tell you to shoot Joshua Standish?"

No answer. Marshall let the silence lengthen.

Finally Jane peeked one eye over her crossed arms. She nodded infinitesimally.

"Please answer the question for the recording," said Marshall.

Jane ducked back behind her arms. She shook her head.

"For the record, the prisoner signaled that someone did tell her to shoot Joshua Standish, but she refuses to answer verbally."

"Who told you to shoot Joshua Standish?" No answer. "How did you know where to find Joshua Standish?" No answer. Another long silence.

Then, muffled by her knees and arms, "It was because of *her*."

"Who?" asked Marshall. Jane pointed at me without raising her head.

"For the record, the prisoner indicated Clare Standish. What did she do to you?" Marshall's tone was casual.

Jane shook her head behind her arms and knees and said nothing for perhaps a minute. When she finally looked up I was horrified by the look of hatred on her face. Her chapped lips were pulled back, showing a few blackened teeth separated by empty spaces, like a Halloween mask. Suddenly her feet hit the floor, and she started to stand, pointing at me with one shaking, shackled hand. The guard stood up fast, but Marshall stopped her. "He said *she* was going to turn me in. She was taking pictures of me with that camera she had. He said she was going to give my picture to the police and get me deported! I tried to stop her, but she just ... kept ... on! He told me if I hurt her brother she'd stop."

"Who told you that?" asked Marshall calmly.

"*HE* did. That *guy*. He said she'd stop if her brother was hurt. He told me where he was."

I was completely mystified. What guy? It appeared she didn't know herself, just some guy told her I was trying to get her deported. The logic of the thing didn't make any sense. Her English was perfect, no accent, just a little distorted by her missing teeth. So deported to where? I remembered somebody saying she was DACA. But how would killing Joshua stop me? And what pictures?

Ohhh. The pictures I took on the train the day Dr. Pleasant was killed. That's why she'd been trying to get my cameras and computer. She must have been the one who'd broken into my apartment through the back window. She was so frail she looked like she wouldn't be able to lift a camera, but I'd seen her run down Pennsylvania Street with my big iMac, and I knew she was quick and agile. And strong, too. I had a healing knife wound in my chest to prove it. Meth could give seemingly frail people great strength. Before it killed you, anyway.

Jane sat down suddenly as if exhausted. "She had those pictures of me on the train and the platform," she mumbled. "He said so. He said if I got the pictures he'd destroy them. Then I wouldn't get deported. He gave me some money."

"Who is *He*? What's his name?" asked Marshall. "Tell me who he is, and I'll arrest him."

I thought he was probably lying, but Jane was in no condition to think clearly about anything. She shrugged.

"Just a guy. Kinda tall. Mustache. Beer gut. Always wore shades."

We were back to Martinez or pseudo-Martinez.

"Why did he want the pictures? Why would the pictures get you deported?"

Jane looked at him as if he'd asked if the sky was up. "Because I killed her, asshat. They deport people if they kill somebody. He told me."

"Who did you kill?" Marshall made himself sound bored.

"That lady on the train. The doctor or whatever."

I felt as if a bowling ball had been thrown at my stomach. *She killed Pleasant?* But Marshall kept his face completely blank. I tried to do the same. Probably failed, but Jane wasn't looking. She was back to hiding behind her knees.

"How did you kill her?" Interesting. How, not why.

Jane looked up. "If I tell you, can you make me not be deported?"

Marshall nodded. "I promise," he said.

Could he promise that? Oh, right. He was lying.

Jane returned to her hiding place. "Stabbed her," she mumbled.

"Where did you get the knife?"

Jane shrugged. "Just had it. Maybe somebody gave it to me. How should I know?"

"What kind of knife was it?"

Jane shrugged again. "Big. Like ... like a big knife. *You* know."

"What color was it?"

"I dunno. Silver. Maybe it had like a wooden handle, I dunno. Just a knife." She shrugged.

"Why did you kill her?"

"She had money. I wanted it. It was a lot. Like a hundred dollars." Silence. "I want to go back to my cell now."

Marshall nodded to the guard, who rose and helped Jane up, released the cuffs from the staple and refastened them to a belt she was wearing. Jane shuffled along beside her in her white canvas slip-ons, looking at the floor. She didn't look back.

"Shit," said Marshall. I nodded. We got up and left.

Marshall didn't say anything in the car on our way back to Littleton PD. He was thinking. And smoking.

"Well, I guess that wraps up the Pleasant murder," I said as we got out of the car. The shiny spring day was now clouded over and turning chilly. A light rain had fallen, wetting the pavement but leaving dry semicircles under the trees. I blew a vapor ring with my breath.

Marshall looked at me, his expression unreadable. "What makes you think that?"

"What do you mean? She just confessed!"

Marshall scrubbed his cigar out on the pavement and put the stub in his coat pocket. "She's a meth addict," he said, as if that explained everything. I looked at him and rolled my eyes. "Look," he continued, "one symptom of persistent meth addiction is drug-induced psychosis, which can present as schizophrenia. Schizophrenics can't tell the difference between what's inside and outside their heads. At the very least, Jane is clearly suffering from disordered thinking and delusions, if not full-blown hallucinations. She thinks you are trying to get her deported. She thinks if she confesses to a murder, I can prevent her from being deported. She thinks Pleasant had a hundred dollars, not five thousand. She got the knife totally wrong. There's so much wrong with her story ... The fact that she thinks she committed a murder is beside the point."

"OK, but who else have you got? Omar's dead and ..."

"My guess is that Omar probably did commit suicide. Most of the signs are there, though of course we'll have to wait for the coroner's report. He was deeply depressed. The drugs in his house included several used in doctor-assisted euthanasia. He could have left the back door unlocked to make it easier to find him. The Rio Blanco guys may still find a note. If we're lucky, the note will say he killed himself because he felt guilty for killing Dr. Pleasant, but that's wishful thinking."

"Yeah, and why would he have killed Martinez? If Jane is that irrational, it's more likely that she would have done it." I paused, considering. "I mean, how often do people confess to crimes they didn't commit?"

"More often than you'd think. A lot of the people who have been exonerated by DNA recently were convicted based on false confessions."

I still couldn't imagine it. "So are we still on square one?"

"Not really. There's just things that need to be checked, etcetera. I'm assuming for now that whoever killed Pleasant also killed Martinez. The two murders appear to be connected. And opportunity is more relevant than motive. Omar had the opportunity for Pleasant and doesn't have an alibi for Martinez. Shiela and Kim's alibis are weak, especially for Martinez. They say they don't know where they were when he was killed, but Kim was off duty that evening. Or they could have hired somebody. The only people who certainly didn't kill either of them, were the Demidovs."

"The people whose son died while in her care." I was thoughtful. "And they were the ones with the strongest motive. I get it. By the way, Daniel says the son's death was entirely natural, consistent with his disease."

Marshall nodded. "Yeah, I know. I talked to him about that."

"When?" Marshall waved a hand and didn't answer. I really wanted the murderer to be Jane. "Well, Jane had the opportunity for murdering Dr. Pleasant," I said. "She just said she was on the train that day. So does she have an alibi for Martinez's death?"

Marshall shook his head, hunched his shoulders and jammed his hands in his pockets. "A weak one. She was supposedly down at the homeless camp by the river according to a couple of people. But ... well, they're not any more reliable than she is."

I was disappointed. It would be so much better for everyone if Jane were the murderer. Well, everyone except Jane, that is. But I wasn't sure I cared too much about her welfare. It seemed to me that she was on a fast track to that big Needle Park in the sky anyway. Maybe being in prison would be the best thing for her.

"Look," said Marshall, "I gotta go. There's a couple of things I need to follow up."

"Like what?"

Marshall shrugged. "Another suspect. I don't want to talk about it. Can you get home OK from here?"

"Sure," I said, though I was hurt that he wouldn't share his suspicions with me.

Spring in Denver is always a bad joke. But for the next few days, temperatures soared into the mid 60s and low 70s, and the Denverites, an awful lot of whom seemed to have nothing in particular to do or any place to be, started whizzing around on bicycles, or strolling around in sleeveless dresses and cargo shorts, though personally, I was still in a turtleneck and jacket. They sat around on benches, bought a lot of coffee and hot dogs from Alfred's cart, and spent the late afternoons and evenings drinking beer on the patios of the many brewpubs. The Rockies' Opening Day, on Friday, April 5, was hazy with in-and-out buttery sunshine and a packed Coors stadium at 2:10 p.m. I went over and took a few photos, but the *Denver Post* guys were already there, and I knew I wouldn't be able to get anything salable.

Marshall texted me that the Rio Blanco Coroner had ruled Omar's death a suicide, and that his wife had received a suicide note he'd mailed to her. He hadn't confessed to Pleasant's or Martinez's murders. But other than that, I didn't hear from him for over a week. I tried to call him a few times, but the guy who answered the phone said Marshall was unavailable in various ways — interviewing, out on a location, on the phone — I wondered briefly if he was avoiding me. So Bradshaw and I just mooched around. I had a couple of photo requests that I could fill with my own stock, and I worked on my website. Things seemed to be in a springtime lull. Even Daniel.

He stayed with me, that's true. Came home in the evening, left in the morning, made love to me at night. But there was something going on with him. He seemed distracted and distant. I would have said he was depressed, but that would have been so un-Daniel.

"What's up?" I asked him over smothered tamales one evening.

He looked surprised. "Nothing! What makes you ask?"

"I don't know. You just seem ... distracted ... not yourself. Are you unhappy? Is there something at work bothering you?"

Daniel shrugged and shook his head. "No, I don't think so. Hey! Let's stream that movie .. that one about Mötley Crüe ... *You* know."

I knew he was changing the subject, that's what *I* knew. But he'd brought his giant screen from the Hobbit House, installed it in my main room, and loved to snuggle on the couch and watch movies or Avalanche games. Well, that was more than OK with me, too. But he hadn't answered my question.

So that's how things were until the lazy Sunday afternoon when Marshall finally called.

CHAPTER 29

M arshall's name came up when my phone buzzed on the table.

"Hey," I said.

"Is Daniel there with you?" No hello, as usual. He sounded all business.

I looked over to where Daniel was leaning languidly against the kitchen door jamb. Silver gray slacks, baby blue cashmere v-neck, beloved ... everything. "Yes," I said. "Do you want to talk with him?"

Who is it? Daniel mouthed.

Marshall," I mouthed back.

"No," said Marshall quietly. "Listen to me. You're in grave danger. Give him some excuse and leave your apartment. Do it now."

"But —"

"Just do it. Leave Daniel and everything behind and go. Now. I'm on my way." The line went dead.

"What's up?" Daniel asked. I couldn't read his face, but he seemed ... alarmed? Maybe.

"I don't know," I mused. "He said to leave everything and leave the apartment right away. He said he's on his way here."

Daniel smiled, but it was a smile I'd never seen before. A little mean, a little sad. "Yeah, well, you come with me," he said.

And before I knew what was happening, he'd grabbed my wrist and was dragging me toward the door.

I just had time to stuff my phone in my back pocket. "What about Bradshaw?" I panted. I'd never seen him like this. He was scaring me.

"Marshall said to leave everything. He'll be fine." Daniel was opening my door and pulling me through. He slammed it shut with his heel and dragged me down the corridor toward the back fire door.

"Wait! My camera!" I squeaked. But Daniel didn't stop. He pushed the bar latch to open the door, but the promised fire alarm didn't sound. We were out on the fire escape, and he was pulling me down the metal stairs. Too fast! I was stumbling, slipping on the metal stairs, hips knocking against the railings. "Daniel! Wait!" I panted, but he didn't slow down. I was coatless, and the spring breeze was cold on my neck.

Still holding tightly onto my wrist with one hand — boy! his fingers were strong! — he released the ladder to the ground then, holding my arms, he positioned me facing him and forced me backwards down the ladder ahead of him.

"Daniel! What's going on?" I called up to him. Did he know what Marshall had called me about? Was he protecting me? *Probably*.

He was out of breath. "Go down and get in my car. Hurry up."

Five stories down. I jumped the last few feet to the ground and hurried over to the passenger door of his Ferrari, heard the two unlocking chirps when Daniel pressed the button, and scrambled into the passenger seat. Daniel slid down behind the wheel and started the engine. I could hear sirens far away, or maybe it was a truck backing up. All part of the noise-scape of Denver.

"Seat belt," Daniel ordered, and we sped down the alley fast. Too fast. He careened onto Sixteenth just ahead of the oncoming traffic and squealed around the corner, southbound onto Broadway, a moment too late for the yellow light. The Ferrari was built for speed, but now Daniel slowed to the exact speed that allowed him to make all the green lights.

"Daniel — What's going on? Is this about whatever Marshall was talking about?" He was scaring me, but at the same time I was admiring his profile and his professional-level driving.

"Sort of. Just hold on a few minutes more and I'll tell you," he said. He looked grim, then concentrating silently, he turned down 8th Avenue before negotiating the complicated entrance onto U.S. 6 westbound. The dreaming Rockies were straight ahead, the sun hovering between their peaks and a bank of flat white clouds that reflected an eerie golden light onto the road ahead. He moved expertly across four lanes to the fast lane and stepped hard on the gas, throwing me back into my seat. The Ferrari's speedometer climbed quickly to 90, and the tachometer kissed the red line. A Subaru with a disappointed Hillary Clinton bumper sticker lumbered ahead of us. Daniel passed it on the right, then swerved back into the fast lane. The Sunday westbound traffic was light, only a few cars on the road ahead.

I heard sirens again. Odd. Were they following us? "Daniel — where are we going?" I was clutching my seat with one hand and the door handle with the other.

"Red Rocks," he said.

I was mystified. "Why? I mean, won't the park be closed?"

Daniel pulled around a lumbering landscaper's van with Jalisco plates that had no business in the fast lane before looking over at me. "It's — complicated."

"What is?" The sirens were fainter now. Daniel didn't answer. He was concentrating on driving, and I was very glad he was because we were going *really* fast. Marshall had said to get away from the apartment, and boy were we ever doing that. But why had Daniel dragged me out the back?

"Why did Marshall tell me to get out of the apartment? Do you know?"

"Yes," said Daniel. I waited. Nothing. Then, his eyes still on the road Daniel reached under his seat and pulled out a bluish-looking pistol, an automatic, I thought, not large, and placed it carefully along his left thigh. He sighed, whether with relief or sadness, I couldn't tell. "I have to drive, so you need to just wait."

"OK," I said. The sirens were fading behind us. Maybe the Ferrari was outrunning them? But what was he going to do with that pistol?

Daniel checked the rear-view mirror, then edged the Ferrari up to 95.

We'd reached the interchange with I-70, and I saw the signs for Blackhawk and Central City, and Highway 93 north to Boulder — *Oh, no — full circle. Sort of.* Daniel ran the yellow light to turn right at Red Rocks Parkway, and we wound up the steeply curving road at a speed that made me nauseous. I looked out the back window, but I didn't see anyone following us.

At the Amphitheater, Daniel didn't turn in to any of the empty parking lots but continued the climb up a service road, pulling into the loading zone that served the stage entrance. He pulled the car around to face the spectacular view of Denver, visible between two red sandstone rocks. In the gathering blue dusk, lights were winking on at the speed of the world's turning, sparkling along the street grids like a spider web laced with dew. Downtown stretched upward from the prairie floor, and a full golden moon was just rising out by the Kansas border. In the distance, I could see red and blue lights flashing westbound on Sixth Avenue, and the faint sound of sirens again reached us on the cold breeze.

"Why are we here?" I asked, dread filling my stomach.

Daniel pulled on the hand brake and looked over at me for several seconds before speaking. The pistol still rested on his thigh, his hand on the grip, finger on the trigger. There was no love in his eyes now. They were as hard and blue as the barrel of his gun.

"Because I'm the guy that killed your folks."

In the silence, I stopped breathing.

NO NO NO NO NO! This can't be happening. Not Daniel. Please not Daniel. Please not everyone I love please ...

"And put Joshua in the Blue House. Literally."

I had to breathe. Convulsively my chest expanded and air rushed into my lungs. Tears were pressing on the backs of my eyes. I thought I might throw up. The earth was tilting dangerously.

Daniel sighed again. "You have to understand. I had no choice. I had to run."

I still couldn't speak. I didn't — couldn't — understand. I didn't understand anything at the moment. I could still hear the faint whine of sirens. They seemed to have passed us and be heading toward Golden.

"Tell me why," I said quietly through a sob. My voice was another thing tilting out of control. "*Why* did you run? Tell me. Tell me why you had no choice."

He looked over at me, surprised. "Don't be an idiot! I was only twenty-four in 2005, four years younger than you are now." He settled more comfortably in his seat and seemed to relax slightly. "My folks had died the year before and left me a pile of money, so I bought myself a BFT — a Big Fucking Truck — at a dealership in Jefferson County — you were right about that. It was bad-ass black and *big* — something I'd always wanted. I was heading home on Santa Fe Drive. I lived Downtown at the time. Unlucky for me, I met some friends for a drink or six at a bar in Littleton. I was shit-faced, driving too fast, tried to run the yellow light at Alameda but missed it, and ... well, you know what happened next."

I nodded, speechless. My stomach was roiling, and the pressure of tears was making me light-headed. *Unlucky for him? What about my folks? Joshua? Me?*

"I need you to understand my dilemma, Clare. I saw that my whole life was over. I'd lose everything — my condo, my freedom, everything. I'd go to prison for the rest of my life. So I did what anyone would, I ran away. I had no choice. Do you understand now?"

"I — I can't."

He shrugged, not much caring either way. "Anyway, my truck wasn't too damaged — hitting a Camry won't hurt a BFT!" He was smiling, of all things. "I took off west on Alameda while all the cars were piling up behind your folks, and I drove as fast as I could until I got up on Green Mountain. That crash had knocked me sober! I found a secluded spot, just a dirt lot near some trees. I got out — I was injured but not too bad — broken wrist, cracked knee, cracked ribs, broken nose ..." He pointed to a scar on his nose I'd noticed but never wondered about. "I scraped all the VIN numbers off, took off the plates, siphoned gas from the tank and lit the truck on fire. I was sad to see it go." He stared sadly out at the darkening prairie. "Then I hitched a ride down to St. Anthony's hospital."

"A doc there patched me up. I was like '*Shit*!' when I found out your folks were there too. And horrified about Joshua. I've never forgotten ... any of it. I have nightmares." He closed his eyes, looking as if he were being tortured.

I think I'm supposed to feel sorry for him. What about my nightmares? Unimaginable.

"Well, then time went on and nothing happened to me," he continued. "I bought the Golden place and the Steamboat place and the Blue House. Then one day while I was at the Blue House, Marla — Dr. Pleasant — showed up in my office. She said she knew I was the man who'd killed the Standish family, and that Joshua was at Browning, that nursing home where she was, and that she wanted me to hire her and give Joshua a place at the Blue House. So I did." He shrugged. "Again — no choice."

"My God," I said.

A horrible thought swam into my consciousness. "Did you engineer things so you could meet me?" I asked. What if he'd only wanted to watch me in case I found out who he was? What if the last few happy years had all been a lie? What was he planning to do with me now?

He nodded, thinking back. "Yeah. I saw you coming to visit Joshua all the time. I thought you were hot. So when you got Shiela to introduce us, ... Well, you know, 'keep your enemies close,' or whatever. Imagine how I felt! Knowing I'd killed your parents!"

There was nothing I could say to that. I didn't need to imagine it. I was experiencing it now, myself. I'd fallen in love with the man who killed my parents. The man who'd provided me with 14 years of anguish. I didn't know where to put my breaking heart. My thoughts felt like a flock of pigeons rising before a kicking child.

"Anyway. Marla didn't stop there," he continued. "She just kept up the blackmailing. First it was a promotion to lead physician, then a raise. Then getting rid of Omar. But then she wanted me to ignore those two con artists she brought in to run that scam."

I looked at him, startled. "You actually told me the truth about how the money got into her bag?"

"Yeah, I wanted you to tell Marshall. So yeah. The scam was so simple! And not even illegal! They'd sweet talk the gaga old ladies and convince them they could go home. All they had to do was sign over their houses to these guys, and they'd promise to '*use the equity*'," Daniel made finger quotes, "to fix up ramps and stair climbers ... whatever shit they needed to pass the health and safety requirements. They'd do a half-assed job, or maybe not even finish, and when the old dears died, they'd sell the house, and they'd all walk away with thousands. I made her cut me in, of course." He paused, thinking. "I've never been sure they didn't engineer some of those fatal falls downstairs." He tapped his fingers thoughtfully on the steering wheel.

"But I couldn't let Marla ruin everything. She was already blackmailing me about your folks. Then there was the Demidov kid's parents screaming malpractice, and then a few of the old ladies' heirs were threatening lawsuits."

"Did she kill the Demidov kid?" I snatched at my scattered thoughts.

Daniel looked at me sharply. "No. It was just like I described it to you and Marshall. A natural sudden cardiac death caused by his Brugada Syndrome. Not uncommon, and frankly overdue given how severe his case was. But his parents couldn't accept it. They were threatening all kinds of legal actions. I could see my profits draining away like bathwater."

I nodded. I intimately understood the Demidovs' inability to accept their son's death. If I'd known it was Daniel who'd destroyed my family, there would have been no end to the misery I would have visited on him. I would have ruined him, ruined his life as he'd ruined Joshua's and mine. But now it looked like I wouldn't get the chance.

"Also, she was starting to throw her weight around too much," he continued. "That business with Dr. Hussain — Doc-Omar, as everyone called him. I was very sorry to lose him. He's a fine gerontologist. But she forced me to fire him, I'm not sure why. I shouldn't have let that happen. And now he's dead, too." Daniel shook his head. "So I had to get rid of her. Surely you can see that."

I couldn't. My new friend, the fulminating anger, was starting to replace my shock and grief.

"I knew she went to a Pilates class near the 10th and Osage light rail stop," Daniel continued. "I made a deal with Martin Martinez, who I knew because of his mother being treated at the Blue House. I would disguise myself as him, get on the train at Auraria — right before I knew she would get on at Osage after her class. I knew from experience with my docs where to slip the knife in, so there wouldn't be much external bleeding or time to scream. The red coat was a gift. I didn't want her to be discovered right away, obviously."

"Obviously," I said, sarcastically.

Daniel looked sharply at me but then continued. "Then I got off at the RTD service area where Martinez would get on. I changed my clothes at his locker, then went back to the Blue House to rejoin that stupid conference. Marshall was right that it's not too difficult to slip in and out of these conferences without anyone noticing. Everyone at the conference thought I'd gone for a run. I couldn't believe it when I saw you were on that train! Talk about bad luck! But you didn't recognize me, so that was good."

Jesus! He was smirking!

I couldn't hear the sirens or see the lights anymore. I was on my own. What was he going to do?

"But I fucked up," he continued, absorbed by his own story. "When I left the conference, I dressed like I was going for a run and put my business clothes in a sports bag. But when I changed out of running gear into Martinez's uniform at the Maintenance facility, I realized I'd forgotten to bring black work shoes like those guys wear, so I had to wear my dress shoes. *Then* I forgot the dress shoes in his locker when I changed back into my running gear." Daniel hit his forehead with his hand. "So stupid! So when Martinez found the dress shoes, he started threatening to go to the police. I realized he knew too much. So ..." he shrugged.

I sat there in horror. I was sitting in a red Ferrari with an armed serial killer. A man entirely different from the man I'd been in love with. Where was *my* Daniel? Loving, considerate Daniel. Who was this ... this psychopath who could speak so calmly about killing four people and maiming my brother? Or was it six? Could he have also killed his folks?

I didn't ask. I was scared of the answer and needed to stall him. "Why would Martinez let you impersonate him, and maybe get him arrested for murder?"

"I promised I'd pay him $10,000. I knew his family slightly, and I knew he was under water in debt. And of course, I didn't tell him what I was going to do." He laughed. "But I never did pay him, so that's why the police never found any unexplained money. Just lucky, I guess." He gave me a lopsided smile, more ironic than sad.

"How did you get into the Maintenance facility?" I asked, still stalling. He was clearly enjoying telling me how smart he was. "It was locked up tight when I was there."

"The parking lot is, sure. But not the buildings. I walked through the admin building while nobody was around and out to the building where the drivers and guards hang out. Martinez told me how to get there. I just parked on the street. Easy."

He was staring out over the magnificent view now. The moon was a huge golden ball, the sky rose clear and bright behind it in layers of turquoise and cerulean, the now coral cloud bank reflecting pink down onto the darkening thousand-mile prairie.

If that's going to be the last thing I ever see, it will be OK with me. But then I remembered Joshua. Joshua needed me.

I couldn't hear any cars coming up the winding road. Nothing was moving out there in the dark except the wind. Daniel sat still and stared at the view, the pistol still in his hand along his thigh. "I bribed Pain Jane to scare you and steal your photos of me. When that didn't work, I tried to get you to quit working with Marshall, because I was afraid he'd eventually figure it out. *But you would not quit.*" He looked at me with what I thought was frustration. Or was it anger? "So then I figured if I could get you to marry me, you wouldn't be able to testify against me. When you wouldn't do that, I figured I'd move in and keep an eye on you."

He said it so matter-of-factly that it shocked me to my core. I'd almost married him. I'd been *glad* he was living with me. I'd felt *safer* with him there. What a fool! The world was falling away beneath my feet.

"So are you going to kill *me* now?" I asked finally, looking pointedly at the gun. I didn't much care. My family was dead, my beloved fiancé, to all intents and purposes, was dead. Daniel wouldn't have to use the gun. He could simply throw me off the jagged red rocks that embraced the Amphitheater. I'd courted death from high places so many times it had become a familiar companion. To the police it would look like I'd finally taken that short flight with a sudden stop.

But for all these years, Joshua had tethered me to life. How many times had the thought of him dragged me off the precipice? And now he did it again.

My anger rotted into despair. I wished desperately that none of this had ever happened, that neither of us had ever been born. Perhaps in a different universe, out there between the turquoise and cerulean, it would all have been just a terrible story told by an old woman.

"Kill you? I'd still rather you'd marry me. I'm rich. We could go anywhere. But if you won't ... I guess things have just gotten away from me." He leaned toward me and kissed me on the lips. Out in the trees a nuthatch chuckled, and a robin sang his bitter-sweet goodnight call.

"Get out of the car," he said.

CHAPTER 30

I did as he asked. It was as if I was on autopilot. I couldn't separate this serial killer from my beloved fiancé. My fiancé had asked me to get out of the car, so I did. But then the serial killer came around the car holding the automatic pointed at me. "Over there," he said, waving the gun toward the other side of the parking lot.

My mind jammed like an engine throwing a rod. Daniel walked behind me as I made my way in the semi-darkness toward the stairs leading up into the amphitheater. Its spectacular bowl was surrounded by diagonal slabs of red sandstone, laid down hundreds of millions of years ago for the sole purpose of perfectly amplifying music. The moon began to spill silvery light onto the rows of bench seats, throwing them into ghostly relief. *I wish I had my camera,* I thought, automatically.

Daniel nudged me with the snout of the pistol. "Go up the stairs," he pointed up over my shoulder.

A long staircase climbs uphill beside the rows of benches, a side-aisle that leads from the side of the stage to food, restrooms and beer at the top of the amphitheater. I began to climb, Daniel still behind me with the automatic digging into the small of my back.

"Hold up a sec," I said, about halfway up and out of breath from the climb, more than a thousand feet above Denver. We stopped. I wished I could turn to look out over the spectacular view one last time — One hundred and eighty degrees of moonlit prairie, city lights, stars and the enormous moon. I wanted to say something to Daniel, something that would make him stop doing this. My love for him was fighting with my hatred for the killer, and I wasn't sure which one would win. Or even which one I hoped would win. *What the hell*, I thought, and without caring about the gun at my back, I turned. I was eye to eye with Daniel, standing on the step below me.

He nudged my breastbone with the gun. "Keep going," he said.

I shrugged. "Why should I? I assume you're going to throw me off the rocks. Then you can get rid of Joshua, and I'm sure you can manage to make *that* look like the result of the gunshots. But if you shoot me, everyone will know what you are, and you'll end up in prison where you can't hurt him, so go ahead and shoot me, because I'm not going any farther."

When I thought about all this later, I realized it didn't make much sense, but at the time it seemed crystal clear.

Daniel smiled. He looked like a shark. A shark with a gun. "Yes you are." He stooped and grabbed me around my thighs, hoisting me onto his shoulder. I screamed. He began to climb again, holding my legs tightly against his chest. I'd forgotten how strong he was.

We were almost at the top when a voice from below shouted, "Stop right there and toss down the gun!" I lifted my head to look behind us. Someone — no, several someones — were standing on the stage. One of them was pointing a long rifle our way. Light briefly glinted off what I thought was a scope.

Daniel whirled around, dropping me onto my feet as he did, and held me in front of him, facing the stage, his arm tight around my chest.

"I'm not going to prison," he whispered into my hair. "So I need you to help me get away. When we get to the top, there are some stairs down to the patio, then a walkway out into a parking lot. From there I can get out into the park. I'll let you go once I'm safely away." He paused. "Unless you want to come with me?" I just stared at him, incredulous. "OK, but I need you as a hostage till then. Understand?"

My confusion was now a roaring in my ears. Was he delusional? He was asking me to protect him, as a lover would. But this was the man who had destroyed my family and killed two other people. There was no way I would protect him. How could he not know that? But I nodded. I was between a pistol and a rifle. Not a good place to start an argument.

He pushed me into the deep shadow cast by the southeastern rock wall and together we climbed, backwards, the rest of the stairs. In order to get down the back side, we ultimately had to climb up to the corner of the concession area where the stairs led down. Daniel held me in front of him as he stepped backwards carefully, feeling for the edge of each stair. He was panting into my hair, out of breath from dragging me up all those stairs at 7,000 feet above sea level.

I wasn't being much help. OK, I was being as little help as possible.

"Throw down the gun and let Clare go! You can't escape, and things will go easier for you if you turn yourself in," someone shouted from the stage. It was Marshall. "I have a marksman here with me. He won't miss." Daniel said nothing.

"Are you OK, Clare?" called Marshall from far below. The acoustics of the theater are so good that I could hear the man with the rifle mumble something to him.

Was that Mohammed?? Why was he here?

"Don't answer," hissed Daniel.

I don't know why, maybe it was hearing Marshall's voice, but suddenly my mind cleared. This man was *not* my beloved fiancé. He was a serial killer who was using me as a hostage shield, as careless of my danger, of my very humanity, as he had been of everyone else's. If that was Mohammed, I knew he'd learned his marksmanship in Iraq. I didn't like my odds.

But years ago one of my street companions had taught me some moves in case I ever got caught by the police. They hadn't worked then, but I hoped that what I was about to do would work now. If it didn't, I'd be dead, shot in the front or back, or both.

I'd been to quite a few concerts at Red Rocks. I'd even photographed the Colorado Symphony when they'd recorded Mozart's Requiem here — an experience so profoundly moving it had kept me aloft for days. In my mind's ear I could still hear the chorus singing the heartbreaking Latin refrain "*Dies irae...*" — "Day of wrath, this day, everything will be ashes." So I knew very well the route Daniel was going to take. A walkway led down to some more concessions, stairs, and then, if you could get through a gate, out into the big State Park below. The gate wouldn't be open, but I had no doubt that Daniel could find a way over or through it. From there, he would be able to escape into the foothills, and then ... Well, who knew?

We reached the top of the stairs, and Daniel started backing toward the corner of the taco stand where the stairs down to the walkway began.

I took a deep breath. I dug my heels into the concrete of the floor and pushed hard and fast, my back against Daniel's chest, pushing him backwards at running speed, faster than he was prepared for. If he'd pulled the trigger of the gun he was holding against my back, I would die. But as I'd hoped, he was surprised. Instinctively he reached out behind him with the hand not holding me — his gun hand — to break his fall. His hold around my chest loosened, but I kept pushing him backwards and felt the impact in my whole body as he hit the corner of the taco stand with a sickening thud.

I dove for the concrete as his gun went off.

I heard two shots, one deafeningly close, one a distant *pfut*. Excruciating pain ripped into my left foot and all the way up my leg. But it was nothing compared to the pain in my heart. Because as I sat up, I saw Daniel slumped against the taco-stand wall with a black hole in his forehead.

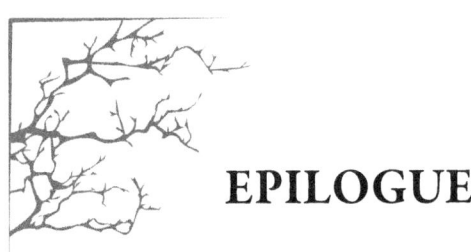

EPILOGUE

M id-June's afternoon sunshine was streaming through my west windows, glancing blindingly off the Capitol's golden dome, when I opened my door to Marshall. Another gorgeous day in Colorado. They would get monotonous by August, but then you'd remember February.

"I need you to come take some pictures of this hellacious mess," he said from the hallway.

I left the door ajar and hobbled on my crutches over to the closet where I kept my now complete stash of crime scene equipment. Backpacked, and with Bradshaw smiling in his packed vest, I rode down in the elevator with Marshall and followed him out to his cruiser. Daniel's red Ferrari was parked in its spot out back, but I couldn't drive it with my cast. Bradshaw hopped into the back "perp" seat, and Marshall pulled smoothly away from the curb.

It had been a crap ten weeks. The gunshot wound in my left foot was healing slowly and painfully. Surgery and physical therapy were taking up a lot of my time. Joshua was now out of his coma and moved onto the surgery ward, but we'd both had a narrow escape. Daniel's escape into an irreversible coma, with Mohammed's bullet in his head, had not been the one he'd been looking for.

Marshall had found us at Red Rocks by tracking my cell phone, which I'd left on. I wish I could say I'd done that on purpose, but it was just a lucky break. I don't think Daniel knew I had it with me, being too busy dragging me out the door when I'd grabbed it.

Then, at the turn-off to Red Rocks, Marshall had sent the Denver cops north toward Golden with sirens blaring, and then he and Mohammed had come quietly and darkly up the road.

"How did you happen to have Mohammed with you?" I asked him later.

He waved his cigar. "I interviewed him after you told me about the break-ins. Just routine, but we got to talking. He trained as a sharpshooter in Iraq, so it was easier to call him than to find one of our own." He sighed with satisfaction. "One of the best collars I ever made," he said. "The only downside was the perp died. Too much paperwork."

To my very great surprise, Daniel had given me power of attorney while we were engaged. I guess he thought I'd have to liquidate some assets to bail him out or pay for his defense someday. So I *was* liquidating his assets — his house, his IRA, his investments, two of his nursing homes and to pay for his care. I'd kept the Blue House for Joshua to go home to.

Shiela and Kim's wedding was simple but beautiful, and I got to photograph it. I put Shiela into the head nurse position and Kim into the lead physician, and they and the Blue House were thriving. I'd kept the Ferrari and had enough money for once in my life. I knew now that most of it was ill-gotten gains, but I tried not to feel guilty.

By this time, shooting crime scenes was becoming routine, and I missed my old life not at all. Douglas County had officially designated me Sheldon Davis's sub, so I'd gimped around with him, learning the county and his expertise. I'd never forgotten his crystal-clear photo of the nearly invisible shoe print in the dust.

But Littleton was always priority one for me. Marshall and I had a bond. We worked together like the parts of a Ferrari's engine, and he often asked me to accompany him on cop business that didn't *necessarily* require a photographer. Marshall wasn't always good at following procedure.

The current hellacious mess was in a Cherry Hills McMansion down a cul-de-sac. The victim was a man whose wife had mysteriously "disappeared" two weeks earlier. He was naked in his hot tub, comprehensively dead of a .357 mm gunshot wound. His safe was open and empty of money, guns and jewelry. His pretty Philopena housekeeper was also nowhere to be found.

Blood and "organic matter" were stuck to the wall behind him, along with a rough circle of pellets, and the water was deep rusty red. The victim, with a large hole in his face, was swollen puce from the hot water. More "organic matter" was floating around and had clogged the water filter, which had then overheated.

But there was also a long black hair in the clapped-out filter and a latent fingerprint on the .357 mm shell casing on the floor. Marshall's smile was a toothy grin around his cigar. If you'd given him a pony for his birthday, he couldn't have been more pleased. Dr. Wallace estimated the time of death between midnight and two a.m.

This one was going to be easy. We decided to go to a local restaurant for dinner to celebrate.

"So you're getting better?" Marshall asked around a mouthful of buffalo filet mignon, the restaurant's specialty. We'd been working together since the "event," but hadn't discussed it.

I nodded. I was having sautéed Montana trout. Bradshaw was enjoying chicken tenders out front.

"It took a while," I said. "But the nightmares have stopped. It helps that I now know who and how my folks got killed. When Daniel told me, I kind of felt my heart sigh with relief. That sounds stupid, I know, but I can't explain it any other way." I was silent for a minute, thinking. "But I miss the Daniel who was my fiancé. It's really hard for me to accept that he and Daniel the psychopath were the same person."

Marshall's cop's eyes regarded me with interest, not sympathy. He nodded. "When you talk to people who knew John Wayne Gacy, they can't believe he's the monster who killed all those boys. 'He was always just the nicest guy!' they say. Psychopaths are adept at reading people and behaving the way they think will make them attractive. That's what Daniel did to you. When they drop the act, you see the reality, and it's like looking into the eyes of a lizard."

I was staring at my eviscerated trout, ashamed to have been so gullible. "Daniel said he asked me to marry him so I couldn't testify against him."

Marshall's face remained immobile. "I know. I started suspecting him around the time he proposed. I made that crack about marriage to Kim and Shiela to try to wake you up. I should have tried harder, but I wasn't sure. I'm sorry about that Clare. He seemed genuinely in love with you, so I didn't think he'd hurt you. He fooled me, too."

I looked up at him, surprised. "How *did* you know it was him?"

Marshall sighed and took out a cigar and held it between his fingers. "It's hard to explain. It started when he began pressuring you to marry him. I checked again with the conference people at the Blue House, and they confirmed that he'd left for a run around the time of Dr. Pleasant's murder, so his alibi wasn't *that* good. *You* found out that Pleasant was working the emergency room at St. Anthony's when your folks and the anonymous guy were there. And she tried to find out who he was. Then she and Joshua coincidentally ended up at the Blue House, so that was another connection to Daniel.

"So I wondered: What if Pleasant had found out Daniel was the driver of the truck? She had that mysterious $5,000 bucks in cash, so I wondered if she was blackmailing him. After all, she'd blackmailed Shiela and Dr. Kim.

But I had to work out how Daniel could have disguised himself as Martinez. It bothered me that Daniel was fair and too tall. But then, I thought about those shades to cover his blue eyes, the hat, the mustache for distraction, some padding, etcetera.

"And there were the dress shoes that Martinez had with him when he was killed, shoes that were too small and expensive for Martinez. That made me think maybe Martinez figured out Daniel killed Pleasant, had blackmailed him, and got killed for it.

"The big break came when I found out from traffic that Daniel had been stopped for reckless driving in a black pickup in 2004. I didn't tell you about that because it wasn't enough to get a warrant. But it made me pull in a favor from the Denver cops to reopen your case, and once we had the partial VIN number on that old truck part, we compared it to the one on the old traffic paperwork and things just fell into place."

"Daniel said he never gave Martinez the money, which is why you never found it. But do you think the money Pleasant had in her gym bag was from Daniel? He said it was from the con artists, but —"

"Yeah, he lied a lot." Marshall shrugged, chewing the last bite of steak. "We won't know unless we catch them. I should probably work on that." He waved at a passing waiter for the check. "Let's go. This cigar won't smoke itself."

We stepped out into the soft, pink and blue June evening. The Rockies shone with the thick snowpack that would bring water to the prairie in July.

"To be fair," he said, lighting up, "Pain Jane was a big help once she got straight enough. She identified Daniel as the guy who 'hired' her to follow, rob and attack you."

"How?" I asked. "When did she see Daniel?"

Marshall waved the cigar. "Obviously she couldn't ID him by sight because of his Martinez disguise, so I got him over to the jail on the pretext of interviewing him again and arranged for Pain Jane to hear him," said Marshall. "She recognized his voice."

So Daniel had sent Pain Jane to rob me of the photos I'd taken of him in his Martinez disguise on the train. It was pure chance that I had kept backing up the pictures up in places he didn't anticipate. But then he'd sent her to attack me and Joshua, to discourage me from working on the case with Marshall. I remembered he always distracted me with sex. That was a very bitter pill to swallow.

I had really believed he loved me. I looked down at the beautiful ring I still wore on my left hand, a central sapphire flanked by diamonds. I sighed. "I guess I ought to liquidate this asset too."

Marshall tapped ash off his cigar. "I think you'd better give it to me." I raised my eyebrows in a question. "It's part of a lot of stolen jewelry from a robbery in South Denver. Daniel got it from the fence. I didn't want to tell you till you were ready."

I looked up in surprise. "Daniel said it was his grandmother's." Marshall shrugged. Wordlessly I took off the ring and handed it to him. And then, inexplicably, I began to cry. I hadn't cried since Joshua was shot. But now the sobs came in gulps. My losses had almost killed me. But Daniel's betrayal made me understand what Hell was. Hell was betrayal: the unbearable grief mixed with volcanic anger, and I thought I was falling, falling past smiling killers, and people screaming, and sweet-faced hypocrites. I couldn't bear it, I couldn't bear it, the pain was searing my guts.

Marshall put his arm around me. "Come on. Let's get you home."

For once he drove sedately north on Broadway to my precious sanctuary overlooking the Capitol's golden dome. I held Bradshaw in my lap and stroked his silky ears. We sat in the car for a while outside my apartment, Marshall silent, but a strong presence.

At last he said, "Duane Mangione — you know, the Douglas County deputy that's running for Sheriff?" I nodded. "Well, Duane and I were talking a couple of years ago about a serial killer he'd arrested in Roxborough. Duane said, 'Remember — one can smile and smile and be a villain.' From something by Shakespeare, he said. I've never forgotten it."

That night I stood at my fifth-floor window looking at the lights of the city, the shining golden dome of the Capitol and the elegant curve of the City and County Building beyond it. Lights like beads of dew on a spider's web ran west on Colfax Avenue to the shining silver mountains. Below me, cars' headlights crawled by looking for nonexistent parking places. People strolled through the yellow pools of streetlights, walking their dogs, or laughing in couples, or talking on cell phones.

Once it might have been a short flight with a sudden stop.

But I turned and went back to my computer. Back to my work.

COMING in 2026

A New Front Range Mystery

SHAMBLES

Join Clare and Detective Marshall for another dangerous mystery when they uncover the secrets behind the murder of a Denver undercover cop and solve the problem of the two con artists running an equity scam on those nice old ladies.

And find out why Marshall is smiling.

ACKNOWLEDGEMENTS

M any thanks to the following for all their help.

As always, my beloved husband, Richard who has stuck with me through thin and thick.

Diane Huntress for her patient explanations of how one would photograph the Aspen World Cup. You can find her work at dianehuntressphoto.com. I have described one of her photos of a racer in Chapter 13. That was hers, not mine.

Matt Miller for his lucid explanation of police venue. Any violations of police procedure are Marshall's, not Matt's.

Littleton Police Department.

Denver Regional Transportation District.

Denver Police Department Traffic and Cold Case Units.

Bryce Cole and the staff at Englewood Camera and my dear father, for teaching me photographic technique and equipment.

Red Rocks Park and Amphitheater for many a fine concert.

And, of course, my editor, Celia Killen at Reedsy for her insight, good sense, close reading, and sensitivity. She should really be writing her own books.

Don't miss out!

Visit the website below and you can sign up to receive emails whenever Kate Grayson publishes a new book. There's no charge and no obligation.

https://books2read.com/r/B-A-MTVEC-QSLWG

Connecting independent readers to independent writers.